Familiar the ca
Ashley's lap

What is it with women? he *thought. I mean, I'm a perfect male specimen. Sleek, handsome, purrfectly irresistible, yet Miss Law and Order, by which I mean Ashley, is staring at that Norwegian lion tamer!*

"Familiar, quit squirming!" The fool cat was distracting Ashley from studying Brak Brunston. The animal trainer was as lean and fit as his cats and probably just as deadly, with chiseled good looks and pale hair neatly gathered at the nape of his neck.

"Brak," Ashley whispered to her brother, "is the foremost authority on training large cats in the world. He uses no force of any kind. He has some kind of *link* with the animals. Like a magic touch...."

Even as she spoke, Brak's eyes met Ashley's. And Brak, she suddenly realized, had a magic touch, all right—with women...with *her.*

Dear Reader,

With his nine lives and wicked sense of adventure, Familiar is everyone's favorite crime-solving cat. And we're delighted to bring you another of his fast-paced, fun-filled mysteries in the FEAR FAMILIAR mystery series.

Caroline Burnes was thrilled to read your letters asking for the eighth Familiar adventure. She has the pleasure of living with the prototype for Familiar—her own black cat E. A. Poe—on her small farm. Caroline says, "Though Poe is less demanding than Familiar, he's just as smart and has his owner thoroughly trained."

If you've missed any of the previous FEAR FAMILIAR mystery books, check the end pages for an opportunity to order them.

Happy reading!

Sincerely,

Debra Matteucci
Senior Editor & Editorial Coordinator
Harlequin Books
300 East 42nd Street
New York, New York 10017

Familiar Heart

Caroline Burnes

Harlequin Books

TORONTO • NEW YORK • LONDON
AMSTERDAM • PARIS • SYDNEY • HAMBURG
STOCKHOLM • ATHENS • TOKYO • MILAN
MADRID • WARSAW • BUDAPEST • AUCKLAND

To Rita Sheffield-Hester—a wonderfully talented cat lover who has the unique ability to recognize talent in others.

ISBN 0-373-22426-5

FAMILIAR HEART

This edition published by arrangement with Harlequin Books S.A.

Printed in U.S.A.

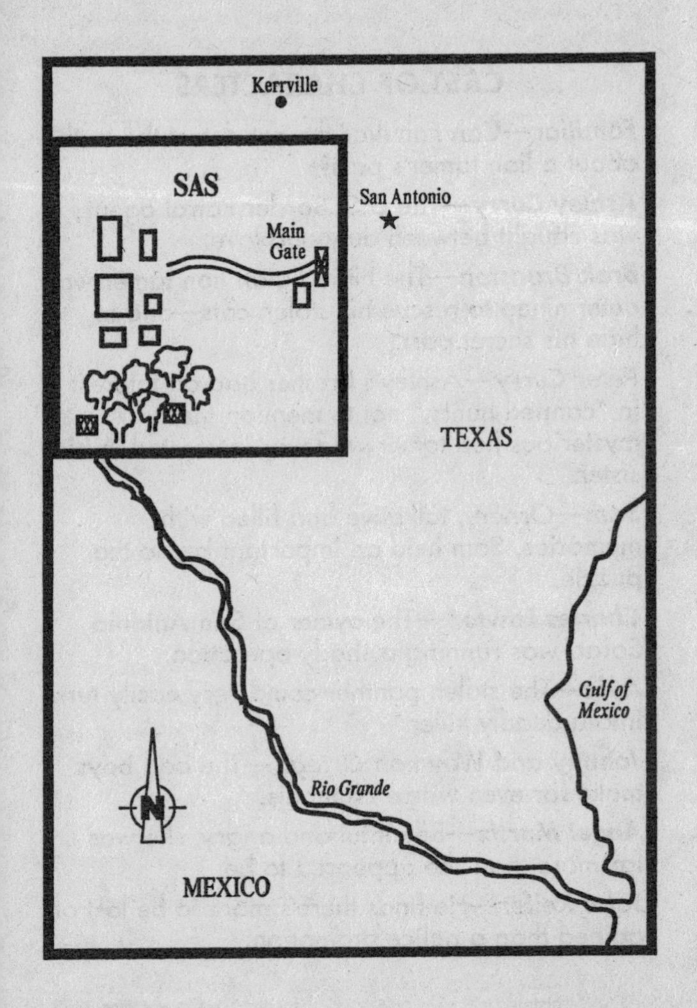
Kerrville
SAS
San Antonio
Main
Gate
TEXAS
Gulf of
Mexico
Rio Grande
N
MEXICO

CAST OF CHARACTERS

Familiar—Can Familiar the cat detect the truth about a lion tamer's past?

Ashley Curry—The U.S. Border Patrol agent was caught between duty and love.

Brak Brunston—The Norwegian lion tamer was determined to rescue his stolen cats—and to hide his secret past.

Peter Curry—Ashley's brother had an interest in "canned hunts," not to mention the mysterious lion tamer who was interested in his sister.

Sam—Ornery, talkative and filled with memories, Sam held an important key to the puzzle.

Charles Lawton—The owner of San Antonio Safari was running a shady operation.

Ayla—The stolen panther could very easily turn into a deadly killer.

Johnny and Waymon Ortega—The bad boys make for even worse criminals.

Angel Martiz—Beautiful and angry, she was far more than she appeared to be.

John Keifer—He finds there's more to be lost or gained than a police promotion.

Chapter One

What is it with women? I mean, I'm a perfect male specimen. Sleek, handsome, purrfectly irresistible, yet Miss Law and Order is looking out from under those bangs at those lions as if she'd never seen a feline. To rephrase a phrase, "I'm not exactly a platter of chopped liver," but that's the way she's treating me! Yesterday, she was all cooing and scratching over me when Peter and I arrived at the San Antonio airport, calling me "famous, fabulous Familiar." Her big brown eyes were about to melt with warm regard for moi. *Now look at her—not even twenty-four hours later, she's almost salivating at those cats. How fickle is the heart of woman! And all because they're at the beck and call of some brawny cat trainer. Hah! If those big pussycats were worth their salt, they wouldn't suck up to that blond bruiser for a few scratches behind the ear. They're giving the animal kingdom a bad name. I don't feel compelled to please anyone for a few scratches.*

Well, except maybe Eleanor. And that two-year-old tyrant Jordan. But the Curry womenfolk, with the exception of pistol-packing Ashley here, aren't in the lovely town of San Antonio. Peter and I flew in sans the ladies to watch this elite, exclusive demonstration of Norwegian talent. And if you ask me, it seems pretty foolish to have huge felines sitting on the stage of the Sam Houston Ballroom of the

San Antonio Towers hotel. If those big cats decide to get rowdy, it's going to be a big mess in this small room. But I'm not responsible for anyone here. Peter is capable of taking care of himself, most of the time. And Ashley has cast me aside for the blonde working the stage.

That makes me a cat of independent means, a solitary man, el lobo, *or more accurately,* el gato, *on the prowl and more than a little rusty at my Spanish. I can only hope that Ashley's new obsession with these big kitties doesn't mean she's going to back out on her promise to whisper sweet nothings in Spanish in my ear. She actually said she'd help Peter polish up his bilingual abilities, since Texas has so many residents with a Spanish heritage. But I need to practice, too. Hmm, I wonder how you say "salmon in cream sauce" in Spanish? As soon as we get out of this fancy, smancy meeting room, I'm going to find one of those wonderful restaurants and practice my menu skills. There seemed to be a very nice restaurant in the lobby. I wonder... No, I'd better stay for the performance.*

What's this? Panthers! And they're coming out to sit at this guy's feet? I don't believe this. In a room of a hundred expensively dressed San Antonians, this guy has four large cats, unrestrained, on a stage not twenty feet from the audience. Is he crazy? I don't know, but those are some lovely creatures. If I'd eaten my Wheaties, I might have grown up to look like those beauties. Oh, yes, the one on the left is my kind of kitty. Long, sleek, and filled with that regal stride. Let me straighten up my posture and make a good impression. I mean, that little honey slinking out on stage does *outweigh me by a few pounds, but she is one sexy babe. I wonder how she feels about shorter men? Eeow! My Clotilde would singe my whiskers for such thoughts.*

Hey! It looks like Blond Bruiser is sending that gorgeous hunk of kitty my way! Do you suppose... Oh, be still, my beating heart. I hope that gleam in her eye is affection and not hunger!

"FAMILIAR, IF YOU'RE going to squirm, you can get off my lap." Ashley Curry picked up the black cat and shifted him to the seat to her right. Beside her, Dr. Peter Curry, her brother, gripped the arms of his seat, his gaze riveted to the small stage, his mouth set in a long line of displeasure.

Ashley gave her brother a concerned look but directed her remarks to the black cat beside her. "I told Peter not to bring you here. That panther could snap you in half with one chomp of her jaws."

Peter used his elbow to gently nudge his sister in the ribs. "Hush, Ashley. I really want to hear how he's going to explain having all of those wild cats in his possession. I wonder what poacher he bought them from."

"Don't jump to any conclusions, big brother." Ashley pushed a strand of sun-gilded hair off the side of her face. As much as she loved Peter, he could sometimes be a pain. He'd promised to behave, but she knew better than to trust him. If he felt an animal was being mistreated or misused, Peter Curry spoke out and to hell with the consequences. She glanced at the cat trainer again, noting the casual grace of his body, the pale hair gathered neatly at the nape of his neck. He was as lean and fit as his cats, and with his chiseled good looks, probably as deadly. "Brak Brunston is the foremost authority on training large cats in the world. His reputation is that he uses no force of any kind. He's supposed to have some kind of link with the animals. Like a magic touch."

"Right. And at night he hangs by his feet and sprouts black wings." Peter lowered his voice. The chairs in the ballroom had been placed close to the stage, and though they were on the next-to-last row, they were still close enough for Peter's voice to travel.

Ashley jabbed an elbow, hard, into her brother's ribs but kept her gaze on the stage where Brak Brunston stood, almost like a sculpted work of art. Very slowly he glanced around the gathering. When his gaze fell on Ashley, she felt as if she'd been touched, just a flutter of fingertips, or lips, brushed over the line of her jaw. She shivered involuntarily and remembered what she'd just told her brother. Brak was supposed to be able to tame wild cats with a touch and a whisper. Undoubtedly a man of his physique had had plenty of opportunity to practice those same skills conquering women.

"Meow!"

Familiar dug his claws into her leg and brought her back to the moment. She stroked the cat and returned her attention to the stage. Brak was flanked on one side by two lions and on the other by two panthers. There was no barrier protecting the audience from the animals. He spoke softly, but loud enough so that everyone in the audience could hear. "Go to the woman in the yellow dress, Ayla."

The biggest of the two panthers bounded off the stage and into the audience, drawing a few mild shrieks from several women.

"She will not harm you," the man on the stage said. "She is as gentle as the average house cat."

"My house cat is here, and if Familiar is the measuring stick we're using, I think we're all in trouble." Peter Curry spoke with a degree of humor, but there was also an edge of aggression in his voice.

Hunting through the audience with a gaze slightly clearer than sky blue, Brak zeroed in on Peter. It was evident in his expression that he'd heard Peter's challenge—and accepted. "You do not believe my training techniques?" He spoke with the trace of an accent, slightly Scandinavian, as he held Peter with his stare.

"I don't believe that wild animals should be used as entertainment." Peter stood so that he could be clearly identified.

"Not even when it is the only choice open to them for survival?" Brak did not back down or get angry. Instead, he came to the edge of the stage. "And tell me, is this entertainment, or the way we'll have to cohabit with wild creatures in the future unless we stop destroying their habitat?" He didn't pause for an answer. "You are the veterinarian Dr. Curry, are you not?"

"I am." All around Peter the small audience had grown quiet.

"Ayla, go to the man." The trainer spoke as if he were conversing with a teenage child.

The big panther padded away from the lady in the front row who wore the yellow dress. The cat chose an indirect route down several aisles to Peter. At Peter's feet, she sat. Only for a fraction of a second did she glance at Familiar, acknowledging the presence of her own kind—in a smaller version.

"Ayla's mother was captured in the wild and sold as a house pet to a woman who had more money than brains. The mother cat, Rayna, grew up and wasn't so very gentle, after all. In order to manage her, the woman starved her nearly to death. And then she hit upon the idea of breeding her. She could sell the cubs and make money. But in transporting Rayna back from the breeder, the woman was careless. Rayna escaped and mauled the woman. The courts intervened. In the meantime, Ayla and her litter mates were born. The authorities decided Rayna was dangerous. They destroyed her. I managed to save the cub Ayla." He paused a few seconds. "It was my care or death."

The entire time Brak spoke, the audience was perfectly still. Ashley found that she could not look away from him. He stood on the stage as if he were carved from some warm, blond wood. Though he never flexed a muscle, his passion and anger were perfectly revealed in his voice. The large cats felt it. Their tails began to flick rhythmically. Beside her, even Familiar's tail had begun to switch in anger.

Peter was completely untouched. "That's a sad story.

That's also what many people say who *choose* to have wild animals as their *captive* show pets."

Instead of showing anger, the trainer smiled. "Give him a kiss, Ayla."

The panther balanced lightly on her hind legs as she gently placed her sheathed claws on Peter's shoulders and licked his jaw. Without being told, she settled back on all fours and waited. Amazed chatter broke out in the seats around Peter.

"It would appear that Ayla forgives you for questioning her life-style, Dr. Curry." He waited until the talk died down. "This is a subject we should discuss in greater depth. If you will meet me after the session." He turned his face a fraction of an inch to show the discussion was closed. "Ayla, come." The big cat moved with silent grace back through the audience and toward the stage.

"Meow!"

All heads in the audience swung back in Peter's direction. The panther was halfway to the stage. Right behind her was a fine, black house cat.

"Familiar!" Peter called the cat's name and grabbed for him, but Familiar was quicker. He dodged and then darted after the panther. "Meow!"

Laughter broke out in the audience.

Going to her brother's rescue, Ashley eased into the aisle and went after Familiar. "When I get you, cat, I'm going to have you shipped back to Washington," she vowed as she made a grab for him.

"MORE CHAMPAGNE?" The waiter hovered beside Ashley with the bottle tipped toward her glass.

Ashley glanced at the corner of the room where Peter and Brak were still going at it as they had been for the past twenty minutes. Peter was not nearly ready to go home. "Sure," she said, smiling her thanks. She sipped the cold, bubbly wine and sighed. She'd stayed out of sight but close enough to intervene, if necessary, during the first ten minutes of the conversation between Peter and Brak. When it became apparent they were like two bulls with locked horns—stalemated—she slipped away to get some champagne and mingle with the guests.

The champagne reception for Brak was being sponsored by the city zoo, and it was a "do." She recognized many of the city's famous socialites—and watched with humor as they aimed themselves like arrows at Brak, only to find themselves deflected by his total absorption in the conversation with Peter. She knew many of the rich and famous in San Antonio society, and she played a game with herself, identifying as many faces as she could. Susanna Shaffer, heir to the cattle industry, stood beside Sally Remington. Both young women were entranced by Brak.

Standing against the wall watching the women as they made an abortive foray at Brak, Ashley developed a fine appreciation for Brak's ability at self-preservation. He smiled, bowed, complimented, and then returned to talking to Peter.

Ashley moved toward the sumptuous buffet table, listening in on the snippets of conversation that she passed. In her job, eavesdropping had become a habit. Here, the entire conversation, at least from the female perspective, was centered on the tall Norwegian and his cats.

Brak was in San Antonio conducting a seminar for the zoo employees, then he was going to do an exhibit with his animals as part of a fund-raiser. Ashley knew her brother objected to using animals in circuses and other arenas of entertainment, where they were often horribly abused. But Brak's cats appeared to be in great shape. Physically, and emotionally, as far as she could tell. But the very idea that they'd been flown to the United States from Norway for a performance had set Peter's teeth on edge. And she knew her older brother well enough to know that he wasn't going to give up on convincing the cat trainer of his point of view.

She slipped a hand out and grabbed a daintily cut cucumber sandwich from a passing tray. Well, the food was light and delicious, and the champagne was free-flowing. There were a million worse places she could be. A brief mental image of a rickety, squalid hut where fifteen humans lived in abject poverty flashed into her mind with the pain of a stiletto. Yeah, there were plenty of worse places to be, and she'd seen some of them. She fought back the image and focused on the thousand-dollar dresses the crème de la crème of San Antonio society had chosen for the early evening cocktail party. It was a stunning array of styles and tastes, all perfect for the elegant event.

Among the fashionably stockinged legs of the women she saw a black blur. The champagne glass almost slipped from her hand. It wasn't possible. After Familiar's humiliating, lovelorn display toward Ayla, Peter had assured Ashley that the cat was safely latched in a carrying kennel. Hotel security had even agreed to watch him.

"Damn." She spat the word as she started forward, her gaze riveted to the floor—and a waving black tail. "Damn that cat, and damn Peter for bringing him. No wonder Eleanor wouldn't let him stay home. She couldn't possibly keep up with Familiar and a two-year-old. She stumbled into two women, nearly knocking them down.

"Excuse me," she said, pushing past. She was just in time to see Familiar clawing at the swinging door that led back to the kitchen, where waiters were busy preparing the hors d'oeuvres. Great. They'd be thrilled to see a cat.

"Familiar!" She called his name in a hard whisper. "Familiar, you little beast. I'm going to put you in a stainless steel kennel when I get my hands on you, and you can spend the entire trip locked up." She reached for him just as he zipped through the swinging door.

Silently cursing her high heels, Ashley lunged and came

up with empty air. She was struggling to regain her balance when she felt a strong hand on her upper arm pulling her back to her feet.

"Thanks," she said. "That darn cat..." She stopped as she stared into the blue gaze of Brak Brunston. "Thanks, Mr. Brunston." She looked to the corner where only seconds before he'd been talking with her brother. He could move as fast as his cats.

"It would seem that your house cat has a mind of his own."

"And the appetite of a glutton, and the misguided notion that he's the Don Juan of felines. Peter and Eleanor have ruined that cat. He was demanding shrimp this morning for breakfast. Can you imagine such a thing?" She felt slightly foolish and smiled to show it. "I must sound like a fool. You can make six-hundred-pound cats behave perfectly, and we have the house cat from hell. Now, that's something you should talk to Peter about."

Brak's eyes danced with blue light. "Tell me, Ms. Curry, did you give it to him?"

"Pardon?" She couldn't follow his conversation.

"The shrimp? Did you give the cat shrimp?"

"There was simply no other way to get a moment's peace."

His laughter drew attention. His touch on her arm tightened. "Then, we should rescue the kitchen help. I doubt they've been trained to deal with a determined cat in search of delicacies."

Before she could respond, he shouldered a wedge through the crowd and pushed through the swinging door with her in tow. On the other side of the door, he stopped and began to systematically survey the room. Although the kitchen was bustling, it became clear after a moment that Familiar wasn't there.

"Your cat is a tricky one, isn't he?"

"You don't know the half of it." Ashley was determined

not to relate any Familiar adventures to the imposing man who continued to hold her arm in his grip. His fingers were amazingly gentle. She had the impression that he was well aware of her flesh, that he never touched anything accidentally. "Familiar is a born troublemaker."

"He took a...liking to Ayla." Brak's concerned expression was chased away by a smile. "A serious liking. I think he might have gone in pursuit of my cats."

"Indeed." Ashley remembered Familiar's blatant display of longing as he'd pursued the panther back to her perch. Before Ashley or Peter could catch him, Familiar had leaped onto the stage and taken a seat right beside Ayla, casting a golden look her way. A look that showed he was absolutely smitten by the magnificent panther. "It's a good thing Ayla wasn't hungry."

Brak's laughter stopped the kitchen staff in their tracks. They stared at him a moment, then couldn't resist smiling as they returned to their work.

"That black rascal has undoubtedly gone courting." He offered the suggestion with one arched eyebrow. "He did not seem like a cat who would forget his purpose. We must go after him."

"The cats are here? In the hotel?" For some reason, Ashley had assumed that the large animals would be kept in the zoo.

"They have special shipping cages, and they'll be taken to the zoo later today and remain there for the rest of my stay. But I don't allow the cats to be moved unless I'm with them, and I was requested to remain here for the gala." He lifted one shoulder. "The city offered to take the cats on to the zoo, but so many people are afraid of large cats. They mistreat them out of fear."

"Yes, I can see how that could happen." Ashley wondered if Peter had found Brak to be as concerned for his charges as she did. "Let's check it out. If we don't look,

Peter will be all over the place hunting for Familiar, and I have a feeling that's one headache you can do without."

"You and Peter are married?"

Ashley's chuckle was rich and slow. "Not on your life. He's my older brother."

"You don't resemble each other." Brak's brow furrowed. "I am sorry, that was a rude thing to say. It's just that you are so blond, with such expressive, dark eyes. He is more..."

"Peter favors Mother, and I take after our dad." Ashley felt a flush begin to creep up her neck. She turned away. She wasn't some callow teenager ready to blush and fluster at compliments from a guy. But Brak Brunston had an unsettling effect on her. "Let's find that cat." She led the way to the only door she saw.

As soon as they were in the corridor, Brak took the lead. "The cats are down here. Very content, I might add. The zoo personnel here in San Antonio had food ready, very professional."

"How long will you be here?" Ashley asked, hoping for a casual tone.

"A week, ten days at most."

"Did you have any trouble getting the cats cleared for entry into the States?"

"None." Brak gave her a quizzical look.

"I'm a...I work for the government. Sort of importing and exporting." She bit her lip lightly.

His eyebrows rose again. "You are a law officer?"

"U.S. Border Patrol." She spoke with pride, but her voice lowered as she finished. "Better known around here as either the devil or the lazy louts. I'm afraid it's a job that never really pleases anyone. According to our many critics, we either do too much or not enough."

Brak nodded as he pushed open a door for her. "Yes, the land of plenty beckons so many. So many who risk everything to come to find a future."

Something in his tone touched her heart. It was almost as if he understood the desperation of the illegals who had become a part of her everyday life. "I only wish it could work out for more of them," she said softly.

His touch on her back surprised her. There seemed to be a hint of encouragement in it, or perhaps comfort. "Then, perhaps it's a good thing that you're one of these law enforcement agents."

Before she could ask what he meant, he ushered her through the door. She found herself in a large room obviously used to unload and store supplies. Heavy metal doors were open wide enough for two eighteen-wheelers to enter, but the room was virtually empty, except for the seven spacious cages. The only trouble was that all of the cages were empty, too.

In the center of the room was Familiar.

"Where are the cats?" Brak asked. His words seemed to echo in the empty room.

"Maybe someone took them on to the zoo." Even as she spoke, Ashley knew better. She saw something on the cement floor and hurried over to it.

An empty syringe lay on the concrete, a drop of pink fluid glistening at the end.

As Brak stooped to pick it up, she grabbed his shoulder. "Don't touch it. Evidence."

When Brak stood up, his face was a mask. Instead of anger, there was deadly control. "Someone has stolen my cats."

There was no point denying it. Ashley nodded. "It would seem so." The trail of evidence, though scant, was clear. The cats had been darted with a sedative and transported out. "Who in the world would steal large, predatory cats?"

Brak's features tightened. "The only answer to that question is bad. Bad for Ayla and the others." His blue eyes iced. "Worse for the people who have taken them when I catch them."

Ashley had seen her brother in a situation where he was determined to win. Peter was an undeniable force. But she'd never sensed a man more committed to keeping his word than Brak Brunston, and that word involved pain and suffering for whomever he caught with his animals.

"This is a matter for the law. The U.S. law, Brak. We'll find your cats."

He nodded, his movement abrupt. "Good. I will hunt, too."

Ashley knew it would do no good to argue. She used a tissue from her purse to pick up the syringe. "Then, let's get busy and get some officers in here and start looking."

"Meow!" Familiar's cry startled Ashley. She swung around to hunt for the feline. She'd almost forgotten about him.

"Come on, Familiar," she said. "Now isn't the time to grandstand."

"Meow."

She started toward him, but she held her purse in one hand and the syringe in the other.

"I'll get him." Brak reached for the feline and stopped short. "Look, he's showing us something."

Ashley squatted, risking the seam of her blue sequined dress. Familiar sat right beside a neat pattern of yellow clay.

"It's from a shoe," Ashley said. She stood up abruptly. "Wait here, Brak. I'll call in the police, but don't let anyone touch that dirt. We can get an imprint from it and later use it as evidence. Even the type of soil could help us pinpoint a specific part of the city."

"I'll guard the print," Brak said. He reached for Familiar, but the cat darted out of his grasp.

"Familiar!" Ashley was in no mood for the cat's antics. To her dismay he rushed behind a tall stack of crates that she'd failed to notice at the rear of the room. The boxes were labeled as cleaning supplies and were stacked in narrow, twenty-foot-high aisles. "Dang that cat." She went after him. All she needed was a four-legged nuisance mucking around in the evidence. "Familiar!"

As soon as she turned the corner, she stopped. A trail of blood disappeared behind the crates.

Chapter Two

Ashley swallowed the copper taste in her mouth that she recognized as fear. The skin along her back and arms prickled. The blood could be feline or human, she couldn't tell. If it was one of the cats, a wounded animal was dangerous. She stepped slowly into the aisle.

The likely scenario was that one of the cats had resisted, had tried to put up a fight. They'd appeared to be so docile and well trained, but perhaps only for Brak. Behind the boxes, she was likely to find a body—cat or robber. She reached instinctively for her gun, realizing as her fingers brushed the sequins of her gown that she was off duty.

"What is it?" Brak called.

"I'll be there in a moment." If it was the cat, she wanted to spare Brak until he could be prepared. Skin crawling with apprehension, she entered the narrow alley. She followed the blood, and Familiar, until she came to a hidden door. A bloody palm print was on the knob. More evidence. DNA testing would determine if it was feline or human blood.

There was no way she could turn the knob without ruining the print, so she backed out. Familiar had slipped around her and was waiting beside Brak.

"What?" Brak's eyebrows rose in question.

"There's some blood," she answered truthfully. "Not enough to indicate a fatality."

"To a human or to one of my cats?" Brak's voice was carefully controlled.

"I couldn't tell. We'll get it tested and then..."

Brak's blue eyes were as icy as a Nordic winter. "If a single hair on one of my cats is injured, I can promise a bloodbath in this city."

Ashley stared into his eyes, unable to look away. In the tawny gold eyes of the panthers she'd seen the potential for wildness. In Brak's gaze there was no element save that of savagery.

"This is a job for the law, Brak. I can promise you that we'll do everything possible to save your animals and to apprehend the people who took them." She saw that her words had no impact on him. It didn't take much imagination to see him with a sword or ax, ready for battle. Eager for battle.

"These cats are like...they *are* my family. Imagine what it would be like for you if your children were taken, leaving only blood on the floor."

Ashley had never had a child, but she'd seen plenty of illegals risking everything they had for their children to have a better life—even if it meant giving them up. "San Antonio has an excellent police department. I'm sure the state will offer some assistance, and I'm certain the proper federal agencies will be brought in. I can promise you that everything humanly possible will be done." She had to convince him not to go off on some vigilante tear.

"Your offer is generous. I believe you'll do everything *humanly* possible." He picked up Familiar and handed him to her. "Call the law officials. I'll wait here."

Ashley started to say something more, but there seemed nothing adequate to say. She took Familiar, who'd become as docile as a newborn kitten, and hurried to the nearest phone.

PETER PACED the dimensions of the room as Ashley leaned wearily against one of the empty cages. Familiar had curled inside the cage and immediately gone to sleep. If Ashley had to guess, she would say the cage belonged to Ayla. Familiar had been more than taken with the panther.

"This defies probability," Peter said.

Ashley looked up at him. "Can we please go home, like everyone else?" She wanted to get out of her dress and heels and call the lab to get the test results on the blood. The theft of the cats didn't exactly fall under her jurisdiction, but she knew plenty of the officers working for the lab. Someone would give her the facts.

"Think about it, Ashley. This guy arrives in town yesterday. He does his little demonstration today, and then his cats are stolen."

Ashley heard the undertone in his voice. "Spit it out, Peter. What are you getting at?"

"Isn't it a little too convenient that his cats are stolen right after he gives a show to the cream of San Antonio society?"

"I'd say it was more like bad luck than convenience. He sincerely seems to care for his cats." Ashley knew she sounded defensive, but if Peter had seen that savage look Brak had worn, he might believe the trainer cared for his charges.

"Think about it. A syringe left conveniently on the floor so the first assumption is that the animals have been sedated. That sets up the chain of thought for abduction. I wouldn't be surprised if we don't get a huge ransom note tonight. Something with all the letters clipped out of a newspaper and mailed from, say, Norway. I mean, the man didn't even stay around here long enough to get the initial police reports. He simply vanished."

"Peter." Ashley was sincerely shocked. Brak had left the area while the police officers were still searching for more evidence, but she'd simply assumed he'd been so upset that he'd needed some time to compose himself. "Are you saying that this entire thing is some kind of press stunt?"

"I'm saying that the thought crossed my mind."

"Because you don't like people who *use* animals."

"Because people who use animals are capable of doing anything if it furthers their reputation or feeds their egos."

Ashley stepped back so she could fully examine her brother. "Brak didn't strike me as that kind of man. He seemed to genuinely care for those cats." She swallowed. He'd seemed to care a great deal for them.

"He's an entertainer. An actor. If he weren't good, he wouldn't be in business." Peter paced the room again. "Actually, Mr. Brunston isn't my concern now. I want to see those cats alive and healthy. Perhaps we can find some alternative life for them, other than caged in a zoo."

Ashley grasped her brother's sleeve. "Are you considering trying to hold them in this country if we find them?"

Peter smiled. "I can only hope there's someplace safe for them. Someplace where they aren't carted from pillar to post and put through their paces for the entertainment of children or socialites."

Ashley dropped her hand. Looking into Peter's eyes, she saw a determination almost as savage as the look she'd seen on Brak's face. "It seems no matter who has these cats, someone is going to get hurt," she said softly. "For my sake, and Eleanor's, I hope you have sense enough to stay out of this, Peter. Brak has wisely turned this over to the law. I urge you to do the same."

"Maybe you aren't aware of the destination these cats may be headed for." He waited. "Do you know what I'm really doing in Texas?"

Ashley knew enough to figure that Peter had not left his busy schedule of testifying before Congress on the use of animals in medical experiments to come for a "vacation" to hear a speaker on wild cats. "Just tell me and don't play twenty questions," she said.

"Canned hunts."

"Oh," she said, floundering, "I should have known." And she should have. Even a moron could have put two and two together. One of the television networks had just done a big exposé on the rich men who paid as much as twenty thousand dollars to "bag" a leopard or tiger or lion. Except the animals were generally declawed, too old to run, or confined in a cage when they were shot. But the big "hunter" got to take home a trophy head and lie about how he'd made his kill.

"There's an operation not too far from here, the SAS, San Antonio Safari. If this entire thing isn't some publicity stunt on Brak's part, then there's a good chance someone snatched those cats for a canned hunt."

Ashley did the math. Seven cats at twenty grand each was a total of one hundred and forty thousand dollars. Not bad for a day's work.

Peter recited the ugly facts. "They'll kill them fast. They don't want the overhead of keeping them up, and they want the trophy heads to look as good as possible."

"Those cats are virtually domesticated." Ashley felt the bile rise in her throat.

Peter's voice was grim. "All the better. The hunter can get up close and maybe it won't take seven or eight shots to finish the animal off."

Ayla and the others were so beautiful, so magnificent. But Ashley knew human nature well enough to realize that some people could only view the beauty of the big cat if it was mounted on the wall or used as a carpet. "Do you know where these hunts are supposed to take place?"

"I do. And I'm going in undercover."

The sickness turned to icy fear. "Peter, you can't. Those people are totally ruthless. They're..."

"Murderers? How well I know."

"Does Eleanor know about this?"

"No, and you aren't going to tell her."

"Peter..." Ashley couldn't allow her brother to put himself at such risk.

"Forget it. The deal is made. I've paid for my "hunt" and I'm going in as a safari man. Now I'll request a panther." His jaw was clenched. "I can only hope that it's Ayla. Then we'll have something to go on."

"Peter, please don't do this. Let one of the local officers go in your place."

"Local law enforcement would try to move in with sirens wailing. I can be more discreet. I have a small video camera. I'll record what I can before I start the hunt. I've also said I'm a doctor, trying to get medicinal powders, ground animal teeth and the like. If all goes as planned, it shouldn't be that dangerous."

"If all goes as planned..." She took a breath. "At least let me go in as backup, as your adoring wife."

Peter hesitated. "You can be my backup, but I need you outside. I'll wear a wire, and you'll run the tape recording equipment. You can also be prepared to call in the cops if anything goes wrong."

"You need someone inside. Someone to watch your back, and a woman is the perfect ploy."

"Not this time, sis." He put his arm around her shoulders. "Now, let's get back to the house. I have to make sure the equipment van has arrived and the wires are working. I've done this kind of thing before."

"So it seems." She walked beside her brother, casting one long look back at the empty cages. "Come on, Familiar," she called to the cat, who was waking and stretching.

As soon as the door closed behind Peter and Ashley, the small side door where the bloody print had been discovered opened the rest of the way. Brak Brunston, eyes burning, stepped into the room. His shoulder-length blond hair hung straight, released from the clasp he'd worn earlier. He walked to the center of the room.

Surveying the cages, he went over every piece of evidence the police had gathered. The bloody print was obviously the best clue, but it was the blood that concerned Brak more than anything.

The door opened, and Brak turned away from the empty cages only to be confronted by a San Antonio police officer. "The chief sent me back over here to personally tell you that preliminary DNA testing shows the blood to be human. Chief Alonzo said you'd want to know right away."

Brak felt his muscles flex from the rigid control he'd held over them. "Yes, thank you. At least we can assume that one of the cats wasn't injured."

"They're trying to run a match on the print, but so far, nothing." The officer looked at the cages. "Who would want to take those animals? It just doesn't make sense."

"What do you know about those..." Brak hesitated, the phrasing unfamiliar even though he knew fluent English. "They call them canned hunts?" He'd heard every word spoken between Ashley and Peter. He'd intended to step out and announce his presence, but then he'd begun to listen, to realize what Peter was saying about his suspicions about him, and more important, the possible fate of his cats.

"Not much. It appeals to rich creeps who're nothing but cowards. I hear some big movie star was nabbed while doing it. One of those guys who pretends to be so tough on television." The officer shook his head. "What cowards."

"If there was such a place, how would I go about finding it?" He spoke softly, but there was no ignoring the deadly intent in his question.

The young officer was green, but he wasn't stupid. "You just leave that to the police, Mr. Brunston. They'll look into all the angles. And from what I can tell, Ms. Curry made sure there's full cooperation with the federal boys.

Whoever took your cats doesn't have a prayer of escaping."

"Thank you." Brak's mask was back in place. "I believe I'll go up to my suite. I'll be there if you get any word."

"I'm to stay here and make sure no one unauthorized even blinks in this direction. If anything turns up, I'm sure you'll be notified immediately."

"Thanks, Officer—" Brak read his name tag "—Keifer."

He left the cages with a heavy heart. He'd heard the secrets shared by the Currys, but he had his own secrets.

From the day he'd first acquired Ayla and the other cats, they had never known a moment of mistreatment or fear. Now their care was out of his hands. They were at the mercy of their captors, and he knew very well how cruel that could be. Especially if the cats felt threatened or fought back.

To all appearances, the cats were docile and well mannered. Only Brak knew the truth.

They were completely wild.

Totally uncivilized.

He had kept them that way, deliberately.

SINCE I'VE HAD A LITTLE nap, my brain is working a lot better. I would recommend a snooze to Peter and Ashley, but I can tell by the set of their jaws that they wouldn't consider a little lie-down. Amazing how much they look alike when they're both jutting out those Curry chins. All determination. Sheer will. I'm afraid Ayla and the other cats are going to need all the determination in the world, and I intend to chip in my full ten pounds' worth.

Several aspects of this case trouble me. For instance, the syringe was left lying in the middle of the floor. Like Peter pointed out, the clear implication is that the animals had been sedated and taken.

There's a shoe print and *a bloody handprint.*

Now, either the cat kidnappers think they'll never get caught, or they're terribly sloppy.

Or this is a publicity stunt, as Peter said.

The problem is, I really bought into it that Blond Bruiser cared about those felines. And they were certainly devoted to him. That Ayla was totally absorbed with him. I mean, I got the sense that she might have been interested in me in her free time, but while she was on the clock for ole Brak, she didn't have a molecule of regard to spare me.

Of course, Ayla and those other cats don't have the sophistication of someone like me, so they might fall victim to a con artist. And, under the right circumstances, even the smartest cat can be tricked. So I'm keeping all options open. But mostly right now I'd like to see the refrigerator door open. Ashley and Peter got some snack food at the soirée, but I got nothing and my stomach's beginning to stick to my backbone. A mild exaggeration, perhaps, but a light snack of lobster with drawn butter would be just the ticket right now.

ASHLEY WAITED UNTIL she'd pulled into the driveway of her home before she broached the subject of the canned hunts again. "Peter, we could get someone else to run the equipment in the van. I'd like to go in with you."

"I can work this scam better if I'm alone. If I were worrying about your safety, I'd be more inclined to mess up."

There was truth in what he said, but Ashley knew there was also an underlying reason, one he wouldn't admit. The danger. "I'm a trained law officer. You know I'm a better shot than you are, and I do have the authority of the law with me."

"How much authority do you have in a case like this?"

The question hit right on target. "Probably none," she

answered honestly. "But if push came to shove, would the operators of the hunt know that?"

"I don't want to put it to the test."

"You'd rather put yourself in a position to get killed."

Peter put his hand on the handle of her car door. Instead of getting out, he leaned back in his seat and turned to her. "It's what I do, Ashley. What I've done for a long time now. Every day when you go down to the border, you could get into trouble. There are drug smugglers and people who trade in human cargo. Those are desperate people, and they could hurt you. It's a fact about you that I accept. You have to do the same for me."

Ashley nodded. Peter was right. Her job was often routine, sometimes tedious, but there was always the chance that one truck she pulled over, or one illegal she detained, might be the one who had more to lose than she thought.

As Peter got out of the car, he waited for her in the driveway. "How are things on the job? Any better?"

"Some." She followed the tiles to the front door of the pale stucco house. She'd bought it only the year before, and she loved every square inch of it.

"Remember, there's nothing wrong in caring about what happens to animals, or people."

"I know." She dropped her keys on the table at the front entrance and headed to the kitchen. "It's just that I let my heart get in the way of doing my job." She put on a pot of coffee. "I don't regret what I did, and even my supervisor said it turned out to be the right decision in the end. It was just that I bent the rules." Her full lips twisted in a wry smile. "Law officers are not supposed to bend the rules. You know that."

Peter laughed at his sister's unrepentant expression. "I know my little sister. You aren't planning on smuggling another illegal family into Texas, are you?"

"Not this week." She put two mugs on the counter and finally acknowledged Familiar as he clawed at the refrigerator door. "This cat eats twenty-four hours a day. He's more expensive than a child."

"Now, Ashley, he's a growing boy." Peter opened the refrigerator. He held out a dish of shelled shrimp in one hand and a bowl of deboned chicken in the other. "What'll it be?"

"Meow." Familiar rubbed against the shrimp.

As Ashley poured the coffee, Peter prepared Familiar's food.

"Does he get champagne and caviar when he's in the mood to celebrate?"

"Only when Socks provides it. Since Familiar solved that mystery in the White House, he generally gets an invitation to their A-list parties."

Ashley laughed out loud. "I can't believe you still insist that Familiar is a sleuth." Ashley's chuckle was abandoned as she jumped straight up, yowling. She bent down to examine the runs in her stockings and the four pinpricks of blood where Familiar's claws had snagged her.

"Familiar doesn't like to be made light of, and for future reference, he prefers the term 'private investigator,' not sleuth."

"Familiar is going to prefer a red kennel or a blue one if he doesn't straighten out and accept the fact that this is my home, and I am not his servant."

Peter got up and went to kiss his sister on the forehead. "You two will get along famously while I'm gone. I know I can count on you to make sure my cat is properly cared for and stays out of trouble. And no kitty abuse. Think how it would look in the newspapers if I had to bust my own sister for animal cruelty."

"You'd better warn him not to be cruel to me." Ashley rubbed her leg and watched as Familiar daintily ate his shrimp. "When are you going, Peter?"

"The van should be here in the morning. Do you think you'll be able to man the recording equipment for me? I've made special arrangements—a preview of the animals on Friday and the actual hunt on Saturday. My plan is shoot some footage and familiarize myself with the compound on Friday, then to bust them Saturday when the other hunters are present. They'll want to do a background check on me, make sure I'm not one of those evil animal activist types."

Though she smiled at his irony, she felt a lump of worry knot in her stomach. "No problem. I'm on vacation for the rest of the week. I'd planned on showing you the sights of San Antonio."

"I'd like nothing better. But after I put these killers out of business. Then we can celebrate and play tourist."

Ashley pushed the coffee toward her brother. She could only hope that Peter's scheme was as foolproof as he seemed to believe it to be. From the little she knew about the men who smuggled animals in for canned hunts, they belonged to the worst breed of criminals around.

It was a good thing Brak didn't know about such hunts. If he ever got wind of what might be happening... She shivered at the thought.

Chapter Three

Brak held the door of his hotel room open, tactfully edging the young woman through it as he smiled and thanked her.

"Those are magnificent cats, Mr. Brunston. I'm sure our excellent police officers will recover them for you, completely unharmed, of course." The tall, slender brunette placed her hand on his forearm. "If you'd like someone to keep you company while you wait...? I know how trying these things can be. Perhaps I could offer myself as some small diversion?" She smiled into his eyes, the diamonds on her earlobes catching the light from the chandelier in the hallway.

"Your offer is too kind." Brak looked away from the diamonds and maneuvered her another inch into the hallway. Sally Remington reminded him of a past that he'd sooner forget. "I would prefer to be alone. I'm not good company when I'm worried, and I'll be honest and tell you that those animals mean everything to me."

"I've called my father. He has a lot of influence in the city, and he's spoken to Chief Alonzo. I assure you that everything possible is being done. My father is a very thorough man." Sally lowered her thick black lashes. "And I told him how very important this is to me."

"I'm sure he is, and I thank you for your interest in my cats' welfare." Brak lifted her hand from his arm and kissed the knuckles lightly. "I will always remember your graciousness and kindness, Miss Remington."

"Please, call me Sally." She lifted the hand to his face. "San Antonio could do with a few men like you. I hope once your cats are recovered you won't be in a hurry to leave."

"Once my animals are safe..." He shrugged.

"Well, if you're certain you don't want some company...?"

"Thank you again, but I need some time alone." He stepped back inside the room and softly—but quickly—closed the door. After a few seconds, he heard her light footfalls on the thick carpet as she finally left.

He latched the door and went to his suitcase. In a flash he was out of the tailored tux and into lean denims and a cool cotton shirt. He went to the telephone, lifted the receiver, then replaced it. There was nothing his family could do to help him now. Nothing. His brother had warned him about leaving Norway, but he hadn't listened.

He found the telephone book, looked up a car rental agency, made the call and booked a fast sports car. Finally, he looked in the white pages for Ashley Curry. He found an E. A. Curry and took down the address. Depressing the switch hook, he dialed the front desk and asked that they notify his room as soon as the rental car was delivered.

Then he paced.

He'd done his best to avoid the press, remembering the accusations Peter had voiced. If he didn't know the truth, he might suspect that the entire thing was a publicity stunt. But it wasn't. He'd never let anyone else touch his cats. The bond he shared with them was too precious, too precarious. The large cats trusted him. And absolutely no one else. Once the animals realized their captors meant them harm—and it wouldn't take long for them to pick up on that—they would be vicious.

They might tear into the men who'd stolen them, or the law officers who tried to help them.

And Brak knew the law well enough to know that if the cats harmed a human, even in self-defense, they would be destroyed. His cats were in a position where they had no one on their side—except him.

There was also the little problem of his past—a time bomb ticking away, waiting for some smart police officer to find it. When that happened, Brak himself would no longer be able to help the cats.

Therefore, he had to act fast. And without remorse. He thought of the slender brunette he'd just shut out of his room. He might have used Sally Remington very effectively. She had social position and family pull with the police. He also got the distinct impression that whatever Sally wanted, Sally usually got. It would be a simple matter to make her want him, at least for long enough to get his cats back. But there was another woman, a brown-eyed blonde who had a level head and wore a badge. There was something sincere about Ashley Curry, something decent and honest...and sexy. He had been drawn to her. Even before he knew who she was, he'd spotted her in the audience and wondered about her.

He hated to use her. But he would. For the cats. And because Brak knew that if anyone could find Ayla and the others before it was too late, it would be Ashley's brother, Peter.

He picked up the phone and dialed the number he'd found in the directory. At the sound of her soft, lazy voice, he felt as if a long, thin fingernail had touched the base of his spine and started a slow, tantalizing dance across his skin.

"Hello?" Ashley's law enforcement officer's intuition snapped to alert when no one answered. "Who is this?"

The wariness in her voice brought Brak back to the situation at hand. "Ms. Curry, this is Brak Brunston."

As if she couldn't recognize that voice anywhere. Her heart beat fast until she realized he was probably calling to see if she'd gotten any more information on the investigation. "So far there's been no match on the print." That was the only real information she could give him. She glanced out the front window where Peter was talking with a man who'd driven up in a dark blue van. The sound equipment, no doubt. The reality of her brother's plans chilled her.

"I was wondering if you might like to have dinner with me tonight? I'm waiting to hear from the police." He hesitated. "It's difficult for me."

The invitation was unexpected, and the pleasure it brought caught Ashley completely off guard. She thought through what Peter had said. He would be home all evening, and there were things she wanted to talk to him about, but she could manage a few hours away. She wanted a few hours with Brak. The man was compelling. "I'd like that," she answered.

"Would your brother care to join us?"

Ashley saw the potential for a tense evening, but it might also prove useful to Peter to learn as much as possible about the cats. If he did find them, anything he learned from Brak could be helpful in handling them safely. As her mind breezed through the thoughts, she realized that, like it or not, she'd thrown in with Peter's crazy plan. "Peter's outside, but I'll ask him when he gets in."

"Then I'll pick you up at nine, if that's agreeable."

"Sounds fine." Ashley replaced the telephone and walked to the window. It was going to prove to be an interesting evening. In more ways than one.

To her surprise, Peter was more than agreeable to the invitation. He was eager. While she showered and changed into something casual, she listened to him whistling. He was positively gleeful, and that worried her.

As they sipped a glass of red wine while waiting for

Brak, Peter studied his sister. He took in the slightly flushed appearance of her cheeks, a natural touch of color that spoke of her apparent anticipation.

"Listen, sis, I don't know what this guy is up to, but I don't want him dragging you into something you'll regret."

"Are we speaking romantically here, or careerwise?" For years Ashley had listened to Peter's harping. Either she wasn't dating enough or she wasn't dating the right guy or she wasn't getting enough sleep because she was dating. It was an endless cycle of brotherly bullying.

Peter hesitated. "Both." He sighed. "I told Brak that I was a spokesperson for Friends of Animals. He was very familiar with our work. This call, tonight—perhaps I've given him some motivation, and, well..."

"It might be that Brak wants a chance to get to you and he's using me?" Ashley had considered the possibility but not for long. Even though she kept her voice cool, perfectly controlled, the idea that Peter had thought of it was disconcerting. She didn't want this to be about the cats. She was honest enough to admit that the fact that Brak had called her was thrilling. She could remember the feel of his hand on her arm, the gentle pressure, the way he made her conscious of his touch.

"If he's a con man, then he's capable of anything. I just don't want to see you hurt." Peter could tell by the way her gaze dropped to the tile patio that he'd upset her. "Look, maybe the guy just wants to go to dinner with you and he was nice enough to ask me along. All I'm saying is, don't wear your heart on your sleeve."

"Is that what I'm doing?" Ashley lifted an eyebrow at her brother. "Am I throwing myself at him?"

Peter leaned back in his chair. He'd overstepped himself and he knew it. His sister was overly sensitive about her private affairs, and she resented his implication that she might be foolish enough to care for this man. He knew enough to back off. "Hey, just a brotherly warning. You know how I am where you're concerned."

"Yes, overbearing and more protective than Dad ever dared to be." Her smile was tentative. "I'll keep what you said in mind, but let me point out that Brak could have had any of the women in the room, and some of them have *mucho* political pull. There were some heavyweight families at the gathering."

"Point made." Peter propped his feet on another chair and sipped the wine. "I wish I had several days to simply relax and talk with you. It's been too long. I feel we've grown apart."

"You have Eleanor and now Jordan." She looked down at the black cat winding in and out of her legs. As if he sensed that someone in the house was eating and drinking, Familiar had awakened and made an appearance. "And Familiar. He's more than a handful." She scratched the top of his head. "I guess we've both become too busy."

"Ashley, I know this is painful, but are you still trying to adopt Maria?"

Ashley played with Familiar, his silken hair gliding under her hand. "I'm still trying. It doesn't look good. There's so much red tape, and the fact that I'm single. It doesn't look hopeful. At least not going through legal channels. I should have kept her, Peter. I should have just taken her, enrolled her in kindergarten and never told a soul she wasn't my own daughter. There are ways to get birth certificates, and I, of all people, could have done it."

Peter reached over and took his sister's hand. "The law isn't always fair or just. But surely you'll get her, eventually."

"If she isn't maimed or killed or sold into prostitution before she's old enough to make it to first grade." Ashley felt the old anger rise in her chest, and she swallowed a large gulp of wine. She couldn't afford to let her emotions get out of control. Not ever again. The price the last time had been too high.

Though they were in the backyard, they heard the car pull into the drive. Ashley stood, smoothing the linen dress she'd chosen for the warm October evening. In San Antonio, the sun shone bright and hot for most of the year. There was no such thing as a fall wardrobe. She walked to the house. "I'll bring him out here for some wine for a few moments before we leave."

"Great." Peter already had the bottle in his hand and was filling the third glass.

Ashley opened the door as Brak's finger rang the bell. At her first glance of him, her heart did a double beat. His hair, thick and straight, hung to the shoulders of a raw silk jacket that was the perfect weight for Texas in October. He turned from staring at the van and smiled down into her eyes.

"Thanks for agreeing to see me."

She pushed open the screen door and invited him in. Making direct eye contact with Brak was dangerous. She had the most bizarre feeling that he could tap into her emotions—and the very sight of him had sent her into a tizzy that she preferred to keep to herself. "Thanks for asking. Peter's looking forward to it, too."

"Your brother likes debate. He likes the thrust and parry of talk. And he has a passion for what he believes." He took her elbow as they walked through the house. "Passion is good. To feel is to be alive."

"He does have passion...for animals," Ashley agreed, trying to ignore the flush that crept over her body as she led Brak to the back patio.

"Perhaps I can make him appreciate my passion for my cats."

Ashley turned at the pensive tone Brak used. "Perhaps you can," she said, ushering him out to the patio, which was vibrant with red and white geraniums, cactus roses, and the colorful mums that seemed to blaze with the dazzling sun colors of red, rust, orange and yellow.

Brak took the glass of wine from Peter while exchanging his greetings. "It's kind of you to share your sister with me," he said.

"My sister is a remarkable woman." There was an edge of warning in Peter's casual tone. "We're a very close family. Very close."

Ashley stepped forward and lightly slapped Peter's arm. "Good Lord, Peter, you sound like Don Corleone. Next thing you'll be telling Brak to ask a favor of you before he dances with me. I'll be lucky if I don't find him 'swimming with the fishes' tomorrow."

Peter had the grace to laugh, and Brak joined him. When the laughter died down, Brak reached for Ashley's hand, scooping it from the table and holding it lightly in his own. "I do have a favor to ask of your brother. A big one."

Ashley's nerves pulsed once, hard, then settled into a steady strum of anxiety. They hadn't even made it to the restaurant and Brak and Peter were squaring off.

"I know you have sources, people who know where they take large cats for hunting. I have to find Ayla, and I'm afraid she and the others have gone to a place like this." He never blinked as he stared into Peter's eyes. "I want to go there and get my animals before they're hurt."

Peter had gone perfectly still. "Even if I knew of such a place, I couldn't tell you. Trust me, Brak, there's nothing you can do except wait for the police to handle this. Tell him, Ashley."

Ashley leaned toward Brak. Peter had neatly tossed the problem into her lap. She waited until Brak's crystal gaze was focused on her, then she concentrated on the matter at hand, shutting out her attraction to him. "You can't do anything, Brak. Even if there were such places and the cats were there, you couldn't get them. As a *visitor,* you can't even carry a gun. You have to let the law take care of this."

"These hunting places exist. They have been filmed and put on television, and still they are in business. No one stops this from happening. It isn't against the law to kill a helpless animal." Brak looked at Peter. "They aren't protected, and you know it."

"There are laws against theft." Ashley wrapped her fingers around his hand, squeezing. "You're right, it isn't against the law to kill a lion or panther in Texas. But it is against the law to steal, and that opens the door to law enforcement to get those people. Besides, there's no indication your cats were taken for a hunt." She squeezed his hand again and released it, looking to Peter for support.

"Why else would someone steal the big cats?"

Brak's question hung in the air. Peter reached for his wine, unable to lie. Ashley swallowed, then stood. "I think we should start for the restaurant. Didn't you say you have reservations?"

Brak didn't remember saying a word about reservations, but he knew Ashley was desperate to change the subject. "I'm going to find these hunters, and I'm going to get my animals back, safely. I was hoping for some help." He saw the first hint of compassion in Peter's eyes, but the veterinarian lifted his sister's jacket from the back of her chair and held it for her.

"Pity the man who gets in my way," Brak added as he offered his arm to Ashley.

Peter exchanged a warning glance with Ashley. They both acknowledged the hard edge of danger that made Brak's accent sound even more deadly.

The restaurant was nearby, and Ashley filled the car with chatter, serving as tour guide to both men. As they walked into Caso Blanco, Ashley felt the eyes of several women turn to her with envy. She could not walk beside Brak without an awareness of his magnetism. His fingers on her elbow were feather-light, but it was impossible to ignore his touch. No matter how casual, the brush of Brak's body against hers ignited a reaction, even if she was determined to make sure he didn't realize how he affected her.

They ordered drinks and a platter of cheese quesadillas. As the appetizers arrived, Brak placed both hands on the edge of the table. "I'm sorry I can't let this go. I know it makes it hard for both of you. Peter, are you here to investigate the canned hunts?"

The wine in Ashley's mouth almost went down the wrong way. She composed herself as she watched her brother's face.

"If I were, I wouldn't talk about it." Peter was perfectly cool.

"I want to go with you."

"There's no evidence that your cats are in any way involved with the hunters."

"You don't believe that." Brak dared him to deny it.

A tense silence fell over the table. Ashley replaced her glass before she spoke. "Brak, if Peter were investigating, the one thing he wouldn't need would be a big, tall Norwegian who would draw undue attention to himself. You walk into a room and people stare. In case you've forgotten, your photo was taken numerous times today. You'll be all over the newspapers and television. You're not exactly the ideal man for undercover work."

Brak nodded slowly. "I see you're right. But there must be something I can do." He furrowed his brow. "Those cats are not a way of making a living. They are my family. I think of them, and I know they're afraid now. I sense their growing panic. They can smell the danger around them, and they're helpless. Caged, defenseless."

"They're caged and defenseless when they're with you," Peter pointed out.

"The difference is, they aren't afraid. They know I'll take care of them."

Peter listened to the trainer, his eyes narrowing. "I don't

know that I believe you can meet the emotional needs of a wild creature.''

''The only thing I can tell you is that the bond between me and the cats is a rare thing. I don't exploit them, except to teach the world that all creatures must learn respect and to coexist.''

''But once they're caged, they aren't wild anymore, and they aren't the creatures they were intended to be.''

''On that point, we agree.'' Brak relaxed slightly. ''But where are they to go? Their habitat is being destroyed. They'll be hunted and killed as predators. I can't change the world, Peter. Neither can you. I can only hope to convince you that I care about those animals, and not about being famous.''

Watching Brak's face as he talked, Ashley felt a deep sorrow. Peter had warned her that Brak might be acting—pretending a regard for the cats because they were his meal ticket. She didn't believe that. She didn't know if it was intuition or foolishness, but her heart told her that Brak Brunston spoke the truth. If he hadn't convinced Peter, he'd convinced her.

''I've said everything I can say,'' Brak finally said. ''I can't make you believe me. But if you change your mind, I'm staying at the hotel. If you find my cats, please call me. I'll do whatever you ask to help them.''

Peter's voice was unusually gentle. ''Then, stay in the hotel and wait.'' He sighed. ''I can't promise you anything except that if I should find something about Ayla and the others, I will call you. You have my word.''

Ashley put one hand on her brother's arm and one on Brak's. ''We should order. There's always a chance some new evidence has turned up.''

Brak nodded sharply. ''Yes, the minute the police find anything, I want to be ready to go to work.''

SO, THE HUMANOIDS HAVE gone off to stuff their faces and left me with the cold cutlets. I took a look at them earlier, and I'm wondering if Peter is trying to slip some soy product over on me. He realizes that my feline nature requires a certain diet, but he isn't above a few vegetarian ploys. He's even threatened to make me catch my own dinner. Imagine that. Me with rodent breath! Not in this lifetime.

But since they've been so nice as to leave me to my own devices, I think I'll inspect the little van that's parked down the street. A nice, conservative navy color. Blackout windows. And one vent cracked enough for a lean, slithery kitty. All of that expensive equipment can't take this Texas heat. Well, I just need to suck in my sexy little tummy, and there I go, right into the passenger seat.

This looks like something out of a Spielberg movie. There's enough technology in here to whip up a brontosaurus. And several nifty little hiding places for moi. *I know the Curry duo thinks they're going to ditch little ole me at home, but* nada. *This wagon train won't be leaving without me.*

I've been thinking about BB, that's short for Blond Bruiser. He came in the door with a trace of another woman's perfume clinging to him. It's not that I don't approve of playing the field. I've done my share of catting about, before I gave my heart to Clotilde, let me hasten to add. But I don't actually care for this type of behavior when Miss Law and Order is in the lineup of babes. Ashley's had enough heartache lately, what with that little girl over the border who she's been trying to adopt. Ashley doesn't need a Norwegian nomad coming into her life and breaking her heart. And even a blind man could see she has a yen for him. I'll just have to keep my eyes and nasal passages open.

Time to get back in the house. It is a little hot for a cat in a black suit. Ah, the wonders of air-conditioning. And there goes the telephone. I wonder who could be calling. When the answering machine picks up, I'll know.

"Agent Curry, this is Officer Keifer down at headquarters. I need to speak with you as soon as possible. Something's come up regarding that guy with the cats." There was a silence. "Ah, I'd better not say anything now, just give me a call at the PD. And don't let him into your home. He's not everything he pretends to be."

Chapter Four

Ashley stood at the edge of the porch where the velvet night was framed by the lace of bougainvillea. Brak had escorted her to the front door, and now he stepped back, a broad-shouldered silhouette against the starry night. Peter took his cue, bade Brak good evening and went inside. The door closed softly behind him.

"Thank you for a lovely dinner, Brak." Ashley felt suddenly shy, and more than a little callow. She'd dated all kinds of men, from daredevil cops to conservative bankers, but none had ever made her so conscious of everything around her. The October air seemed crisper, the sound of crickets louder, the faint trace of the heady four-o'clocks sweeter.

"You made an unbearable night pass swiftly." He found her hand in the darkness and brought it to his lips. "You've given me hope that Ayla and the others will be returned."

The brush of his lips against her knuckles was so intimate that the air rushed from her lungs in a soft sigh.

It was all the invitation Brak needed to draw her into his arms. He held her lightly, letting her determine the level of intimacy.

Of their own volition, her hands lifted to touch his hair. It was as cool and thick and silky as it looked. Blond ice. She felt his hands move so that they captured her shoulderblades, exerting just enough pressure to mold her against him.

"Am I being too presumptuous?" Brak asked, his breath teasing her cheek.

"Probably." This *was* moving faster than Ashley wanted to go, but her attraction was undeniable. The mere idea of a kiss made her weak. She relished the sweetness of desire. This was definitely playing with fire, and she suddenly understood the compulsion of the pyromaniac.

He tightened his hold on her. "Shall I kiss you?"

The question held a dangerous edge that honed the excitement for her. One kiss would do no real harm. "That would be the smart thing to do." She felt his reaction to the whisper of her words against his neck and smiled to herself. "Are you feeling wise tonight?"

"I've felt many things tonight." He brushed a finger along her jaw and lifted her sun-gilded blond hair so that the night breeze chilled her neck. The cold air was followed by his warm breath as he nuzzled the flesh he'd just exposed. Very slowly he drew far enough away so that he could talk to her. "At this moment, it is not my intellectual capabilities that are engaged. I want to kiss you."

Ashley lifted her face. Just when her eyes closed and she gave herself to the anticipation of pleasure, the front door opened behind her. Peter cleared his throat, demanding her attention. Reluctantly she opened her eyes as Brak gently released her, one hand on her waist as he steadied her until she found her balance without his body for support.

"Ashley, you need to come in now."

There was something of the disapproving parent in Peter's voice, and Ashley felt the quick heat of anger. And no small degree of guilt. She realized that she felt like a teenager who'd been caught necking by her father.

"What is it, Peter?" She turned to face him, using her professional law enforcement voice to keep the irritation out of her question.

"Come inside," Peter said, his voice equally polite.

"Can't this wait?" she asked.

"No, it cannot," he answered, pushing the screen door out toward her. "I need you now. I'm sure Brak will excuse you. This is, ah, something of an emergency."

Ashley felt the jolt in her chest. "Is it Maria?" All pretense at composure was gone and raw fear echoed in her voice. "Has she been hurt? Did her stepfather hurt her?"

Peter flipped on the porch light. "No, Ashley, it's not Maria." He sighed. "Please come inside so I can explain. Good night, Brak," he added, lest there be any chance that the animal tamer might come inside, too. Peter swung the screen door wider.

"I'm sorry, Brak," Ashley said, fear giving way to puzzlement at Peter's brusque and borderline rude behavior. "Thanks again for dinner."

"Thank you. If I can be of service to you in any way, please call me at the hotel." He gave a half bow before he walked across the lawn and headed toward a black convertible parked at the curb.

Ashley watched him go and tried to sort through her emotions and gain control. By the time she got to the kitchen, she'd composed herself enough to confront Peter. "What's the emergency?"

He pointed toward the answering machine. "I didn't mean to pry, but I thought maybe Eleanor had called. There's a message for you." He saw the panic in her brown eyes. "It isn't Maria. It's about Brak."

Ashley went to the machine and hit the replay button. There were two calls from friends, and finally the voice of a man who sounded vaguely familiar. When Officer Keifer identified himself, she frowned. At his words of warning about Brak, she looked up at Peter.

As soon as the message was complete, Ashley picked up the phone and dialed the San Antonio police department. "Whatever this is about, I'll get to the bottom of it," she promised Peter. She couldn't help the sliver of defensiveness in her tone.

Peter busied himself putting the wineglasses and cups into the dishwasher and giving Familiar the mesquite-broiled *maui maui* that Ashley had not finished in the restaurant.

It seemed forever to Ashley before someone found Officer Keifer asleep in the facilities provided for officers working round-the-clock duty. It was a groggy voice that finally spoke into the phone.

"What's with the cryptic message about Brak Brunston?" she asked, trying to soften her tone.

"Very peculiar," Keifer answered, not awake enough to hear the dangerous undertones in Ashley's voice. "It has to be him, it has to be. We just haven't lined up the evidence yet."

"Keifer, if you value your beating heart, you'd better tell me what you're talking about or I'll drive down to headquarters and rip that muscle out of your chest."

At last her frustration penetrated his sleep and all playfulness left the young officer. "We believe Brak Brunston is actually a man who went by the name of Nils Lofthammer." He hesitated. "Lofthammer was a professional jewel thief. One of the finest cat burglars in the world."

"You think Brak is a jewel thief." Ashley couldn't assimilate the information. It was too unbelievable.

"When we started running the info on the stolen cats, we got a strange call from the NYPD. It was one of those fluky things where Brunston's photo got sent out when we were doing a nationwide search on people who might have an interest in stealing large cats." Keifer was obviously proud of his detective work.

"Anyway, I got this call from a detective in New York City who recognized Brunston as the guy who supposedly pulled off a jewelry heist from some socialite in Manhattan. He got away with close to a quarter of a million in diamonds and emeralds and pearls. He was never caught.'' He waited for Ashley's response.

"Brunston is an animal tamer. He lives in Norway. I don't think he's ever set foot in the United States..." She left the sentence unfinished. She'd *assumed* this was his first visit to the States. He'd never said or implied any such thing. "The identification was made from a faxed photo?"

"The detective was pretty certain. It seems this Lofthammer was pretty smooth with the ladies. He dated several and settled on the richest one. He learned the layout of her apartment and then made plans to meet her at her place in Martha's Vineyard. She went out there, but he never showed. She came home to find the family jewels were long gone. End of story."

Ashley looked up to find Peter staring at her, cat dish in his hand. She looked away. "How can they be certain it was this Lofthammer?"

"Well," Keifer hedged, "he was never charged, but he's wanted for questioning. One of the pieces was fenced in Paris. The fence was also dealing in stolen paintings. When he got popped on the art theft, he had the necklace, and he identified the guy who'd sold it to him as Nils Lofthammer. Simple as that."

"And this Lofthammer never put in an appearance in the U.S. again, right?"

"Until now." Keifer yawned. "This is gonna get me a promotion, don't you think? I mean, I've been working hard, and this is a breakthrough in a case that has international repercussions."

"I don't like the idea of charging a man on a photo ID, and a fax photo at that." Ashley was grasping at straws.

"He'll get a lineup." Keifer sounded hurt. "I want a promotion, but I don't want to railroad the guy."

"Sorry," Ashley muttered. Keifer was not the kind of cop who bulldozed others down just to get ahead. He was enthusiastic about a case he considered "international" in scope.

"Well, I wanted you to know about this. You took a special interest in the case, and I didn't want some of the guys springing it on you." Keifer cleared his throat. "I know you're a couple of years older than me, but if you'd ever like to go out for some drinks, or maybe dancing..."

"That's sweet of you," Ashley answered, reminding herself that Keifer was young and inexperienced. "I'm sort of involved with someone right now, and I don't feel comfortable going out with two men at the same time. But I am flattered."

"Well, if you break up..."

"I'll let you know. And thanks for the information, John," she said. "It was very nice of you to think to tell me."

"Later," he said as he replaced the receiver.

Ashley looked up to find Peter giving her a puzzled look. "Who are you involved with?" he asked.

"No one, but I thought that was a kinder rejection than 'you're too young' or 'you're not my type' or 'you don't interest me.'"

Peter nodded. "I see your point. Keifer has a crush on you. I sensed it at the hotel."

"He's a nice kid."

"*Kid* being the operative word."

"You've got it." Ashley stretched and yawned. "I think I'll hit the sack."

Peter stepped from the kitchen to block the entrance to the hallway. "Not until you spill the beans on that phone message. What's Brak Brunston up to? Jewelry theft, from what I could hear. Big cities. Cat burglary, which is too appropriate, I might note. What other nasty detail did I miss?"

"It seems your radar ears took in every little innuendo, even the side of the conversation you couldn't hear."

Peter grinned. "Don't look so sour. It was sort of obvious. But I want the details." He pointed toward the living room sofa. "Let's sit and talk."

Ashley looked longingly down the hallway toward her bedroom door. She really wanted to go to her room and sink into the solitude of her clean sheets. She needed time to think through what John Keifer had told her. Was her gut reaction to the accusations sheer hardheadedness, lust or the sixth sense that made a law officer truly good at her work? Brak Brunston had not struck her as a thief.

Groaning, she allowed Peter to propel her toward the sofa. After she was seated she looked into her brother's eyes. "I'm telling you this because there's a chance you might run into his cats, and if you do, you'll eventually run into him." Grabbing a pillow so that she could fold it on her lap and lean into it, she told him everything the young police officer had related to her about Nils Lofthammer.

NILS LOFTHAMMER. Now, that's an alias if ever I heard one. Why didn't he just call himself Thor and be done with it? I'd better saunter over to the sofa so that I can hook a claw in Peter if he fails to show the proper sensitivity. It's clear to me that Ashley has more invested in this cat tamer than a casual interest. If he is a thief, I hope it isn't her heart that's in danger of being purloined.

ASHLEY PACED THE CONFINES of her bedroom, the thick carpet absorbing the sound of her footsteps as she glided through the shadows and the slant of moonlight that fell through the open window. The night was perfect, chill enough for delicious sleeping, but the sandman had failed to visit.

Several times she stopped at the telephone beside her bed, but it would do no good to call the San Antonio police. Whatever tests were being conducted, the reports would not be filed until morning. To call would show an unprofessional interest in the case—a case that was far out of her territory. The fact that she was extremely attracted to Brak Brunston did not qualify her as an interested party. By all law enforcement standards, she should close the book on the stolen cats and Brak Brunston and take what remained of her vacation and put it to some other use. Something like trying to keep her brother from getting killed.

She went to the telephone book in the drawer of her bedside table and flipped to the yellow pages under the listing for firearms. If Peter wouldn't tell her the location of the canned hunt, then she'd find it for herself. She might be stuck in a van running sound equipment, but she'd be able to drive to his assistance if he needed her.

Sitting in the glow of the bedside lamp, she found a pen and a tablet and composed a list of sporting stores that also sold firearms. By the time dawn bathed the room with a hazy gray light, she'd jotted down ten places. Exhausted, she finally fell into a troubled sleep where panthers slithered along the hallways of her home.

BRAK SLIPPED THE STRAP of the leather carry-all over his shoulder and eased along the corridor of the hotel. He'd awakened at dawn, an intuition warning him to get up and get out of the room. He heard the elevators and stopped at door 611. Even as he slipped the lock he prayed the door was unchained and the room unoccupied. Working the plastic tool that could open the new coded doors, he felt the lock give just in time.

As he slipped into the room, the elevator doors opened and two uniformed police officers and a reluctant hotel employee came down the hallway. While the hotel manager tried to halt the procession, the policemen's expressions remained blank. Their forward momentum spoke volumes about their intentions.

Brak knew the score. Somehow, they'd discovered his

alias. The past that he'd tried so hard to bury had been resurrected.

And it couldn't have happened at a worse time.

He hardly dared to breathe as he waited in the hotel room, his eyes adjusting to the darkness. Just his luck that the first items he saw were dresses hanging in the closet beside the door. The room was occupied, and by a female. He could not afford to awaken her.

He cracked the door and watched the officers go to his room and rap on the door. When it didn't open, the hotel employee used the master key, and all three went into the room. In a moment they came back out, looking up and down the corridor as if they could pick up his scent.

"You said he hadn't checked out," an officer said accusingly to the hotel manager.

"There's no record that he left." The man shrugged. "Whatever Mr. Brunston has done, I'm sure we can handle this without further disturbing the guests of the hotel."

"What about a room-to-room search?" the second officer asked.

"Over my dead body." The manager jerked to attention. "I have allowed you access to the room of a guest, but you cannot disturb the entire hotel."

"We can, and we will," the first officer threatened.

"Then, you'll have to produce a warrant." The manager had finally grown angry. "Until I see a document signed by a judge, there will be no further searches in the San Antonio Towers."

Brak felt a flash of relief as he eased the door closed. He was safe. For the moment. Somehow he had to get out of the hotel without being detected. He had to find out how much the San Antonio police had pieced together. Before it was too late for Ayla and the others.

As soon as the hallway was clear, he eased out of the room. The sleeping occupant, or occupants, had never been aware of his presence. With his leather bag slung on his shoulder, he stepped into the hallway with no hint of secretiveness. He walked directly toward the bank of elevators, then turned left as he took the one reserved for service. Bypassing the mezzanine and lobby, he went directly to the parking garage, where a sharp red sports car caught his eye. He was tempted, but he passed up the Porsche for a sedate Towncar. It wasn't exactly his style, but it was big, fast and totally inconspicuous in San Antonio. In a few seconds he had matched the wires by the steering wheel and had the motor going. Once he was through with the car, he would leave it in a safe place.

The cashier at the gate only gave him a wave as he exited, and he realized that along with his other crimes, he'd apparently taken a vehicle belonging to a member of the hotel staff. There had been no alternative. Now that the cops were onto him, the rental car would be the first thing they'd stake out.

Turning into the sun, Brak saw the city that had tamed a river begin to glow in the golden pink hues of dawn. The beauty was lost on him; his thoughts were centered on the cats he had to recover while avoiding being picked up by the law. The whole messy problem of getting his cats out of the country he pushed to the back of his mind.

An hour later, he filled the gas tank at a service station. He'd driven around the city, but he was no closer to finding a plan than he'd been at daybreak. Since he was an outlaw, he couldn't even find out what the police had discovered about the missing cats.

If they were still looking for them at all. Now that he was considered a criminal, they might have decided the cats weren't worth the chase.

Ashley's face came into his mind for the hundredth time. Reluctantly, he turned the car toward her house. She'd probably been notified that he was wanted for questioning. As a member of a federal law enforcement agency, she would be obligated to apprehend him and turn him over to the city police. It was her job. Her duty. The one thing that had struck him about Ashley—aside from the softness of her skin and the scent of April rain in her hair—was her strong sense of duty. She was the type of woman who did what was right, no matter the personal cost.

But somehow he *could* convince her that it was right for her to help him. He had sensed that she had a unique compassion, a willingness to empathize that was rare. How far would she be willing to take it?

He pulled the car over to the curb several blocks from her house. The yards in her neighborhood were big and filled with trees and shrubs. It was an older neighborhood with Spanish architecture. Cottonwood trees grew close to the road, and he waited in the morning shade until he saw Peter leave the house. Peter stopped in the yard and handed Ashley the morning paper before he got in his car and drove away.

For a long moment Ashley stood on the sidewalk staring after her brother's disappearing car. She was wrapped in a white terry-cloth robe. A towel swirled around her head indicated that she'd already showered. She held the newspaper tucked close to her body, and she seemed to linger, barefoot, on the sidewalk. At last, shoulders slumping, she started toward the house.

Sensing his moment had arrived, Brak shot from the car and caught up with her just as she was pulling open the screen door. He caught her with one arm around her waist and the other hand over her mouth.

"Don't scream," he urged.

He had to bite his tongue to stifle the cry that rose in his throat as he felt her teeth lock on the flesh of his palm. She twisted out of his grip and advanced, hands held in a martial arts attack mode that looked menacing. Before he could speak, her hand descended in a blur that resulted in a painful burning sensation in the tendons on the side of his neck.

He twisted instinctively and shot toward her, tumbling

her backward into the screen. Together they rolled through the flimsy wire and fell into the foyer. Before she could launch another attack, Brak straddled her, pinning her shoulders to the floor with both hands.

"Don't scream," he warned. "If you scream I'll have to tie you and gag you."

Ashley pulled in oxygen and prepared to shriek with every ounce of strength she had.

"Do it and I will be forced to take appropriate measures."

She saw his determination in blue eyes unclouded by doubt or hesitation. "What do you want?"

"To talk. To explain something."

"Explain that you're an international thief? How hard could that be? You could have put it on a postcard and mailed it to me and saved us both a lot of trouble."

A smile teased the left corner of his mouth. "You have a flair for sarcasm, but this isn't the time. In case you've forgotten, my animals are in danger."

Ashley tried to wriggle free, only to discover that with each movement she just managed to wedge herself more firmly under him. His well-muscled haunches were already pressing much too closely against her ribs. Awareness of each inch of his body made her go completely rigid. "Get off me," she spat out.

"What have you heard about me?" He saw there was no point beating around the bush. Ashley had been told about him, which meant there would be news coverage in a matter of hours. He was probably on the morning television even as he straddled her.

"You're a thief. An international jewel thief who also happens to use large cats to promote his image as an animal tamer. Is this some other scam to get into people's pockets?" She found her position less than dignified, but she tucked her chin and glared at him. "Peter was right about you. He said you would try to use me. Well you can forget it, Brunston. I won't do a thing to help you, and as soon as you let me up I'm calling the police."

Brak felt a moment of desperation, and he pressed her more firmly into the floor. He leaned down so that his mouth was only a quarter of an inch from hers. "I regret your choice of words. I suppose that means I won't be letting you up anytime soon."

Chapter Five

"I gave up being a thief."

Ashley couldn't avoid looking at Brak's handsome face. He was still sitting on top of her. In the blueness of his eyes, she saw pools of emotion and what appeared to be sincere emotion. But he had tricked her once. "Just because you've stopped being a criminal doesn't mean you don't have to pay for the crimes you committed. Most murders are acts of emotion, passion, if you will. Those people would probably never kill again, but they still have to pay. Our society doesn't have room for killers or thieves."

"It's very complicated."

Ashley swallowed. "The law isn't always fair. If you're innocent..."

"There isn't time for this." He released her shoulders and moved away from her. "If you believe that with all your heart, call the police. I need your help, but I can't force you."

Ashley found herself unrestrained. Slowly she sat up, drawing the robe over her legs where it had been pushed aside by the pressure of his body. "What do you want?"

"Your help."

"That's not possible." She refused to meet his gaze. In turning away from him she spotted the golden eyes of Familiar as he sat on the back of the sofa. Some help he'd been. She would refuse to listen to another single story of how he'd solved mysteries and saved lives. The least he could have done was jump on Brak's back!

"I know I'm asking a lot, but there's no one else I can turn to. It isn't just me, Ashley. What will happen to Ayla if I'm arrested?"

That was exactly the question Peter had asked her the night before. One she had no good answer for. If the cats were recovered, they would undoubtedly be placed in a zoo. Or destroyed. "You should have thought of that before."

"Those animals will suffer for my past. Is that fair?"

His voice affected her. She looked into his eyes, matching his will with her own. "You crossed the line, Brak. My entire career has been about protecting that line, about making sure that laws are upheld. It's been damn hard, and if I won't forget the law for an innocent child, I surely won't forget it for a grown man who had other choices."

Brak sighed softly. "How can you be so certain there were other choices? You know nothing about the circumstance of my past. You don't know what I did or didn't do. You only know what I've been accused of. I promise you that I never hurt anyone."

"Oh, no, I'm sure that woman was tickled pink to have her jewels stolen. It probably gave her a real sense of accomplishment. Not to mention the fact that you deceived her in the worst way, pretending that you cared for her. That's despicable." The last words were loaded with anger.

"Is it the deception or the theft you find more objectionable?"

"You know, I'm not certain." She pushed off the floor, gaining her feet in a smooth motion. "My advice to you is to stay right here. I'm calling the San Antonio police. If you give yourself up, Peter and I will help you as much as we can in finding the cats and making sure they're well provided for."

Brak rose, too, a movement so quick that Ashley wanted to draw back from him.

"If you think I'll sit here and turn myself in, you're very mistaken. If you won't help me, I won't allow you to detain me." He played his trump card. "But if you'll help me find the cats and get them safely shipped back to my brother in Oslo, I promise that I'll turn myself in."

"Like I'd believe that." Ashley's hands moved up to tug the belt of the robe tighter. She was totally covered, yet she felt a vulnerability that made her uncomfortable. In all of her days in law enforcement, she'd never made an arrest in a bathrobe, without a gun, in the den of her own home.

The brush of his fingers along her elbow was electric, and she looked up to find that he'd closed the distance between them in the blink of an eye. "Whatever else you may think I've done, I have never lied to you. I *will* give myself up. Once the cats are safe with my brother, Erik will care for them. I will surrender myself to your *justice* system then."

Ashley wanted to move away from his touch, to put the entire room between them. She was too aware of him, and when he was so close, she found that she wanted to believe him. "I'm not in a position to make deals with you," she said. "My duty is clear. If there's a deal to be made, it'll have to come from someone higher up the chain of command."

"Ashley, I know little of your love for the child you call Maria. I listened to you talk about your job during dinner, and I heard your fear for the child's safety in your voice last night when you thought she was in danger. It was enough. By following the chain of command, as you call it, you have put her future in jeopardy. Perhaps you can live with such a thing, but I cannot. Those cats are my responsibility. They rely on me to protect them. Neither you nor your system of justice will prevent me from seeing that they are safe and happy and in a place where they can live to old age and die without fear of harm." His fingers closed ever so softly around her arm. "Whatever it takes to accomplish that, I will do it." He halted the sudden anger he saw in her eyes with a gentle shake of his head. "I'm not threatening you. Not at all. And I have a proposal to make."

"What?" She knew in her heart that even to listen to him was foolhardy. He had the persuasive powers of a snake charmer. Against all of her training, she believed him, and she knew that was exactly the power he'd used to rob another woman of her heart and jewels. This time it was her career, and her future, that was on the line.

"My family has money and influence in Norway. If you'll help me with the cats, I'll help you with Maria."

Ashley held up a hand. "If you have money, why were you stealing jewels? And what could you possibly do to help Maria?"

Brak turned, giving her his profile. "The past is not mine to reveal, but I can tell you the jewelry had nothing to do with money. As for the child, I'll send her to my brother and his wife. They have two sons, and they love them totally. Anna cannot have another child, and they long for a daughter. Maria would have the finest schools, the best education, loving parents." He leaned closer to her so that his words were an intense whisper. "If you cannot bend your rules enough to save this child, let me. If you can get her to me, I can get the documents and tickets to send her to a life of love and safety."

Ashley felt as if her bones had turned brittle. One step and she might break. "I can't believe you'd bargain for your own safety with the life of a child."

Brak shook his head. "Not my safety. The safety of something I love. The cats. You have my word that I'll suffer the consequences of my past actions. I ask only that you allow me to make sure my cats are safe. As well as the child that you obviously love."

Ashley wanted to block his words from her mind, but they had already traveled straight to her heart. She thought of Maria, standing outside the hovel of her home, her mother inside in a stupor of drugs and liquor. She saw Maria's stepfather, a man who waited only for the passage of months before he could claim the money he would be offered for his stepdaughter's flesh. The legal process was in place, justice was grinding toward giving Ashley legal guardianship of Maria, but justice was so slow. So terribly slow. And once Maria had been sold and abused, there would be no undoing such acts.

"Can you really get papers on her?"

"With ease."

"How do I know you even have a brother and a sister-in-law?"

"For someone with your law enforcement connections, it should be simple enough to check out." Brak saw the torment in her eyes and he knew that he'd done a cruel thing. If she did her duty, she would be leaving a child to dangle in a fate worse than death. If she saved Maria, she would have to distort the rules of duty.

"Let me check out your relatives."

"Until then, I can remain here?" He looked around.

"Peter!" Ashley had forgotten that her brother would be returning sometime during the day. He'd gone out to rent a plane and do a flyover of the "hunt" area. "He'll be back soon."

"You have another place?"

Ashley thought. There were several places, but she'd have to do some checking first. "You can stay here for now. I have some things to take care of. Checking out your background story, for one." She nodded to the phone. "Don't use it, Brak. I don't want any calls traced back here, should this all blow up in my face. And I'm not saying I'll help you," she warned.

"By all means, protect yourself." He didn't smile.

"Whether you believe it or not, whatever crimes you think I've committed, I was doing what was right. Consider all of your options. If you decide you can't help me, I'll disappear without a trace."

"Right." Ashley cut him off. "I have to get dressed, and I have to run some errands." She looked at him. "There's coffee made and raisin bread for toast."

At last Brak offered a feeble smile. "Texas hospitality?"

"I don't know," Ashley honestly answered. "Maybe I'm just as big a sucker as the woman you robbed." She hurried down the hall to her bedroom, unwilling to analyze her offer of food any further. If he was going to be in her home, there was no reason for him to be hungry.

She was fully dressed when she strapped her gun under her arm and covered it with a light jacket. She was off duty, and she didn't think she'd need a gun to operate one of the San Antonio police department's computers, but she didn't want to leave the gun in the house with Brak. He wasn't accused of killing, or even shooting at anyone. Yet when he said he'd do whatever was necessary to save his cats, she believed him. That was the trouble. When he said he had a reason for his past actions, she believed that, too.

Brak was at the kitchen table reading the newspaper. She stopped in the doorway.

"Your press has made me a hero," he said, holding up the front page. "Tomorrow I'll be an arch villain."

"In the eyes of the public, fame is fame." Ashley found herself drawn toward the table. It was as if Brak's blue eyes compelled her to him. "You'll be headlines for several days, and then something else will happen."

"I regret that they used my picture."

Ashley examined the shot of Brak standing on stage with the black panther, Ayla, beside him. It looked like something from a movie set. She made a cup of coffee for herself, putting in the cream and sugar she was constantly trying to give up. "Why did you become an animal tamer?

That's about as high profile as a man who looks like you could get.''

Brak folded the paper. ''I didn't choose this profession. It chose me. I told you the truth when I said I wound up with Ayla. She was the first, and there was a link between us. Once I had Ayla, people called to tell me about the other cats. Before I knew it, I had them all.''

''And they respond to you without training?'' Skepticism dripped.

''There is training, but not like you think. They have to be taught that they can hurt me. They swat one another in play, and such a blow would kill a man. They have to learn that we are more fragile than they are. But what they must also learn is to trust. Once an animal gives you her trust, it is up to you never to destroy it. In that way, the cats are very much like children.''

Though she tried to harden her heart, Ashley couldn't help the rush of emotion that Brak evoked. If he was only pretending to care about animals, he knew all the right words. ''I'll be back in three hours.''

''I'll be here,'' Brak promised.

Ashley half hoped he was lying as she walked out the door and into another perfect Texas day.

THE GUN SHOPS had not been as forthcoming with information as she'd hoped. Ashley tucked her notes into her purse and turned on the car engine, headed for the last place on her list. She'd prioritized the shops by size and location, rationalizing that the larger shops would carry more weapons and therefore be more likely to know about all aspects of hunting. Legal and illegal. What she'd discovered was that the men were hesitant to discuss guns of any type with a woman. Even a knowledgeable woman. It was as if they didn't believe women hunted for sport.

The last shop, Guerrilla Guns, was painted to simulate the mottled brown and white that had become proper fatigue coloring during the Desert Storm war. Litter blew across the parking lot, and she grimaced at the iron bars on the windows and the air of menace that seemed to come from the building. More than likely the place would be manned by a couple of bubbas who would give her the cold shoulder or a come-on. She was tempted to blow the place off, but she went inside, assuming her most predatory attitude.

The man behind the counter had a prominent forehead with eyebrows that grew together in a straight, thick line.

"Can I help you, little lady?" he asked.

"Maybe." She assessed him. "I'm looking for something special."

"In the way of a firearm?"

She nodded. "And in the excitement of the hunt."

He laughed. "What's the problem, you got some rabid squirrels tearing up your yard?"

Ashley chuckled along with him. "What I'm looking for won't be found in a yard, or even in the deep, dark woods." She placed her hands on the counter and leaned forward. "I'm interested in something with an automatic feed that powers a bullet that can stop, say, a lion or tiger. Or a big, bad bear." She looked up at him from beneath her eyelashes.

"A little lady like yourself shouldn't be having...bear trouble."

"The only trouble I'm having is finding a place to go hunting. You see, my boyfriend and I have a bet going. He's off in Alaska now, going after—" she looked around the store and leaned closer "—grizzlies. He wouldn't let me go because he didn't want a woman tagging along." She pouted. "So I made him a little wager. I put up five grand and said I'd bag something more impressive than he would."

"Five grand." The man eyed her with interest.

"Money isn't really a problem. The trouble is time. I

don't have two weeks to book a flight to Kenya and track something through the jungles. A friend of Rich's, that's my boyfriend, told me that I might not have to go so far from home, if I had the cash."

"How much cash are you willing to spend?"

Ashley felt her pulse jump. "Well, how about ten thousand?"

"That's a start." The man looked around the store. "I mean, if there were any animals of that nature to be had. I've *heard* that a female lioness isn't that hard to bag."

"Those are the yellow ones without the hair around their necks, right?" Ashley wrinkled her nose. "I'd rather have one of those sleek black ones. They look a lot more dangerous. If I'm going to pull the wool over Rich's eyes, I'd rather do it in style."

"Panthers are harder to come by, saying there's any out there at all."

"I'm a girl who gets what she wants." Ashley shrugged. "There are other places to check."

"Like where?" His lips were a hard, thin line.

She gave him a sideways glance and smiled. "I think that's gonna be my little secret. Somehow I see you getting together with your competition and jacking up the price. I get what I want, but I don't pay more than I have to." She smiled wider. "I'm not a fool, mister. Not by a long shot."

"You want to look at the guns?"

"Why buy a gun if I don't have something to kill with it? I'm sure that whoever helps me can provide me with every little thing I need. Guns, ammunition, transportation, taxidermist. Maybe even some good company. The whole road show."

The man drew his lips into his mouth in a quick motion. His gaze moved over her, and then his expression went blank. "Suit yourself."

Ashley felt the crush of disappointment, but she'd played her hand as best she could. Maybe she'd overplayed it with her obvious come-on. "Thanks, anyway." She left the counter and walked to the door, making sure her hips swung in a sultry rhythm. It was the last thing he'd see of her, and she wanted to keep up the pretense. Just in case...

"Hey!" he called out.

She turned at the door. "Yes?"

"Is there someplace I can get in touch with you if I hear of anything?"

"Rich wouldn't care for it if he checked the messages and heard another man's voice. I mean, grizzlies aren't nearly as mean as Rich is when he's jealous." She made her voice fluttery. "I'll be back by here." When he didn't object, she pressed harder. "Tomorrow."

"A panther will cost at least twenty. And you have to do it the way you're told. There are rules."

"Oh, I'm good at following directions when I'm on the road to getting my way."

"Cash up front."

"I don't do business any other way. Cash. But only fifty percent up front. The other fifty when I have my trophy." She walked out the door and into high noon. It was only at the car that she allowed her hand to move along the small of her back, drying the sweat that had gathered there.

BRAK FINISHED THE SECOND pot of coffee and paced the floor. He knew he should eat something, at least to absorb the quantities of caffeine he'd consumed. He'd had the foresight to take the screen door he and Ashley had demolished off its hinges and move it around to the back of the house, but he'd done little else except worry. Pace and worry. He didn't want food. He wanted his cats safely on their way to Oslo.

He'd made a bargain with the devil: his freedom for the cats' safety. The only consolation was that the devil had seemed, just for a moment, to be touched by his arguments. And a beautiful devil she was, too. Beautiful, smart, intelligent. A woman of substance. He stopped pacing and listened intently. There was the sound of a vehicle stopping in front of the house.

Easing to the front window, Brak pulled back a wooden blind and looked out. A police car had stopped; the uniformed officer sat gazing at a map pressed over the steering wheel.

For a split second, Brak considered that Ashley had betrayed him, that she'd gone to the police and turned him in. The thought faded as quickly as it had come. The officer seemed confused, hesitant. Not a man who knew a wanted man was lurking nearby. He was young, too. And alone. Brak knew enough about law enforcement procedures to know that officers weren't sent to pick up suspects alone. They worked in teams.

The officer folded the map, got out of the car and started up the front steps. Brak dropped the shade back into place and stepped away from the window.

"Meow."

He looked down at the black cat who had materialized by his foot.

"Familiar," he whispered. "Where have you been?"

"Meow." The cat sauntered toward the back door.

"Now isn't the time to become demanding," Brak murmured. He waved the cat away.

"Meow!" Familiar's cry was louder.

From outside the front door came a surprised, "Kitty, kitty, kitty!"

"Wonderful," Brak moaned.

"Meow!" Familiar slammed into the back door with a force that startled Brak. He remembered what Ashley had said about giving him shrimp or there would be no peace in the house. Moving quietly, he hurried to the back door and opened it. Rubbing along the edge, Familiar disappeared outside.

"When Ashley gets back, we're going to have a talk

about your domination complex,'' Brak whispered to Familiar. ''For a ten-pound feline, you sure think the world dances to your tune.''

Familiar stopped, turning only his head so that his golden gaze focused on Brak. He flicked his tail once, then again.

''Meow,'' he said, sauntering across the patio and through the flowers.

The front doorbell rang, and Brak made certain he latched the back door. The only thing to do was hide out. It occurred to him that the officer might be bringing news of the cats, and that thought was like a slap. He could do nothing. Not even ask a question.

The doorbell rang again. Brak took a seat on the hallway floor, safe from prying eyes at any window. It was all he could do, and he cursed his helplessness.

The sound of a second car pulling in the drive perked his hopes. Taking precautions so that no one outside could see his movement, he eased back to the front window. When he peeled the blinds back, he saw Peter Curry standing in the front yard talking with the police officer. The window was firmly closed, and Brak was nearly mad with frustration as he watched their mouths open and shut and couldn't hear a word of the conversation.

He didn't need to hear the invitation as Peter pointed to the front door and the two men began to walk toward it.

Before Brak could scramble away from the window, an ear-splitting shriek came from the street. The hairs on his arm stood on end at the sound, and he watched as the policeman and Peter ran toward the roadside.

''Familiar!''

He heard Peter's cry as the veterinarian rushed into the road and picked up a writhing black cat.

Brak was stunned. Familiar had been in the backyard, perfectly fine, only moments before. To his knowledge no car had traveled in front of the house, other than Peter's. The cat surely had not been struck by a car.

Familiar gave another loud scream and then went limp in Peter's arms. The veterinarian wasted no time rushing across the lawn toward the front door.

Peter was still ten yards away when a red Saturn squealed to a halt in front of the house.

"Peter! What's wrong?" Ashley sprang from the car as if she'd been pressure loaded. "What's wrong with Familiar?" She cast a worried glance at the house, then focused on the cat. "Was he hit?"

"I don't know," Peter admitted, already walking to the house. "I need to examine him."

"What's John doing here?" she asked, glancing at the young officer who waited on the sidewalk.

"He has news about the cats. Let's get Familiar inside and he can tell you."

Ashley almost froze, but she kept her body moving forward. "You take Familiar inside. I'll talk to John out here."

"Ashley, I may need your help...." Before Peter could finish, Familiar jumped from his arms and landed softly on the ground. He looked up at Peter, golden eyes clear and perfectly calm.

"Meow," he said.

Peter stared at him in disbelief.

"I've never seen anything like that," John Keifer said, awe in his voice. "I thought for sure that cat was dying. Now look at him. He acts like he's fit as a fiddle."

"Meow." Familiar stood and began to weave figure eights around Peter's legs.

"Something isn't right here." Peter glared down at the cat, then at Ashley. "What's going on?"

"I just got home," Ashley pointed out, but a dark suspicion was blooming in her mind. Familiar had been faking his injury. He had deliberately staged an "attack" to prevent Peter from letting John in the house where Brak was hiding.

"Ashley?" Peter's voice held certainty now that something was amiss.

"I don't have a clue," Ashley maintained. She glanced down at Familiar. "But I think I owe your cat an apology. John, could you help me with the computers at the PD? Peter, you'll be fascinated by this technology." Before Peter could protest, she grabbed his arm and squeezed it hard enough to let him know she meant business. "Familiar, want to come?" she asked.

"Meow." Familiar looked back at the front window, one golden eye winking at the blind where Brak peered out.

Chapter Six

Peter balked at the edge of the sidewalk. "I have some things I really *must* take care of," he said, escaping his sister's grip.

She saw the tension laced in the fine wrinkles around his eyes. Peter was angry, and concerned. She didn't need to be a rocket scientist to figure that he'd discovered something bad about Brak's cats. Brak! Her heart pounded at the thought of him. "I need you to come with me," she said to Peter.

"I can't." He was immovable. "I have to make some calls. Now."

She nodded. Peter would not deny her unless it was really urgent, and nothing would sway him from his path. It was up to her to deal with John Keifer, who waited patiently by his car.

"John, I need to talk with my brother. Can I meet you down at headquarters?"

"I just got off."

"I really need your help with the computer system." She turned a pleading look in his direction. "It's important, and I can't use the system by myself. I really need you."

"Sure." He stood a little taller. "Why don't we ride over together? On the way back we could have dinner."

Ashley tried not to smile. It was only noon. "Why don't

I meet you there after I talk with Peter? I know you're worn out, but it would mean a lot to me.''

''I'll be there.'' He held out his hand. ''It's a pleasure to meet you, Peter. I hope your stay in San Antonio settles down and becomes more enjoyable.''

Peter shook his hand. ''Watch out for my little sister,'' he said, giving Ashley a speculative look. ''She looks like an angel, but she has her devilish ways.''

John laughed. ''That must be why I like her so much.''

Ashley glared at Peter as they headed toward the house. ''You don't need to egg him on,'' she whispered.

''No, you were doing a fine job of manipulating the young man. Why didn't you just tie him in a knot while you were at it?''

''Oh, shut up.'' She waited at the door, watching as the policeman drove off. ''First of all, he isn't a child. He's twenty-eight or nine. Second, I had to get rid of him. He couldn't come in the house.'' She rolled her eyes. ''Even Familiar was aware of that.''

Peter skipped all the subterfuge. ''Why couldn't he come in the house?''

''Peter—'' she put her hand on his arm ''—Brak's in there.''

''I'm certain I didn't hear you correctly.''

''You know you did. He had nowhere else to go.''

''A man who is wanted for questioning as a possible international jewel thief is in this house?''

''A man who had no place else to turn is in the house.'' She pressed her lips tight. ''Besides, I don't think my jewelry collection is in any danger.''

''Just when I begin to believe you've finally grown up a little...''

''That's enough!'' She brought her hand down in a sharp motion. ''That's more than enough. You're getting ready to infiltrate a compound where men have high-powered rifles and commit atrocities to make a profit. You're lying to these men and trying to capture them on film so that you can bust their chops. And you call me immature because I'm trying to help someone accused of burglary. Well, in case you haven't studied the implications, burglary is a lot less violent. I'd say if we put these facts on a scale of balance, I'd be on the winning side in the area of better choices."

Peter looked into his sister's face and then broke out into soft laughter.

"What are you laughing at?" Her hackles were still up, and she didn't appreciate the idea of being the source of Peter's amusement.

"At you. At me." He laughed again. "At us."

Ashley couldn't help the smile that touched the left corner of her mouth. It was pretty pathetic. They were both fighting about degrees of insane behavior. In truth, neither of them looked too smart.

"We're both doing our best to break the law and make the outcome turn in our favor." Peter's laughter had diminished to an ironic chuckle. "I guess I don't have any room to point the finger."

Drawing a deep breath, Ashley pushed open the door. "Whatever else you may think, you have to believe Brak cares about those cats." He'd convinced her of that. At least. "If he didn't, he'd be packed up and figuring a way back to Norway."

"You may be correct," Peter said softly as he followed her inside, glancing once at the hinges where the screen door had once hung but asking no questions.

Ashley started to turn around, but she stopped herself. That was the first hint of concession she'd heard in Peter's tone, the first chink in his armor. She had no idea what she was going to do about Brak, but whatever it was, it was her decision to make, not Peter's. She wanted that clearly understood.

Peter bent down and scooped Familiar into his arms. "So, you were playing possum out there in the yard."

"Meow." Familiar put a paw on Peter's chin and stared into his eyes.

"What's wrong?"

"Meow." Familiar twisted out of his hands and jumped to the floor.

"What's wrong with him?" Peter asked, concern in his voice. "Maybe he *is* sick."

"He was fine earlier." Ashley gave the cat an assessing look. "Could it be that he's tired of lobster and shrimp and *maui maui?* Perhaps he'd like some...chicken liver pâté!"

"Me-e-eow." Familiar headed for the kitchen.

"Nothing a light snack of rich and fatty food won't cure," Ashley said. "I'll make some toast for all of us. I, for one, am starved, and some pâté and cheese sounds as good as it's going to get around here. Unless you want salsa and chips."

Peter glanced around the den and kitchen. "Where's Brak?"

"Here."

At the sound of the soft voice, Peter whirled around to find the large blond cat tamer standing at his back. "How do you do that?" he asked, startled and a tiny bit annoyed.

"I learned it from watching the cats." Brak was not at all distressed by Peter's annoyance. "I've learned many things from the cats. Things I could show you before you try to go into that hunting compound."

Peter turned on Ashley. She shrugged her shoulders, hiding the shiver that went down her spine at Brak's tone. Whatever he said, whatever he did, he evoked a reaction in her. "I didn't tell him." She cast a sidelong glance at Brak, who appeared totally unruffled by his near scrape with a policeman and Peter. She had to admire his composure.

"I can help you, Peter. If you'll let me, I can be a valuable partner," Brak said. "I know my cats, and I know those men have taken them." His blue eyes held Peter's. "Whatever else you think about me, know that I would die for those animals."

"Well, I hope it doesn't come down to that." Peter looked away, unwilling to show the tall Norwegian that he sympathized with his plight. There had been something in his gaze that confirmed what Ashley had said all along—Brak cared for his cats. Peter's skepticism faltered. Unless it was all an act.

Ashley finished cutting the crusty bread and slipped it into the oven to toast. In a few moments she had the counter stacked with cheeses, crackers and an assortment of things from the refrigerator.

"Smorgasbord," Brak said, nodding approvingly.

"Cleaning the refrigerator," Ashley replied, putting a bottle of red wine out with two glasses. "You guys help yourselves. I have to meet John, and I don't want to keep him waiting any longer." She felt a twinge of guilt at asking him to wait for her at the PD after he'd clocked out of his shift. "Can you two behave until I get back?"

"Meow."

She looked down at Familiar. "Forgive me. Can you three behave?"

"I have no alternative," Brak said, cutting a wedge of cheese to go with the bread.

"I have a lot of questions," Peter said.

"I'll take that as a verbal agreement." Ashley picked up several crisps of bread, a couple of slices of cheese and an apple from the bowl in the center of the counter. "Later, boys."

"Meow." Familiar sat with his tail curled around him as if he were the most obedient of all felines.

Driving to the police department, Ashley was amazed that she'd escaped her home without having to answer a million questions. Peter's attention had obviously been taken with Brak. And Brak didn't know enough to ask what she was up to.

She pulled into the lot and went to the busy offices where detectives sat at their desks taking information over the phone, interviewing perps or victims, or eating a late lunch. She knew several of the detectives and gave them friendly waves before she found John Keifer tucked at a scarred desk in the corner. He had not reached detective level—yet. His work on Brak was sure to earn him the promotion he craved.

"Ashley." He stood up, nervously shifting from foot to foot.

"Thanks for coming back up here, John." She glanced at his desk, which was devoid of the computer terminals that some of the detectives used. "Is there a terminal we can use for a moment? I need some help looking up some facts."

"On Nils Lofthammer?"

"None other." She tried not to show surprise that he'd anticipated her interest.

"I was a little curious myself, so I got one of the research assistants to find what she could on the international system." He pulled a file folder from his desk. Instead of handing it over, he held it against his chest. "You're welcome to share the information, but why are you so interested?"

Ashley smiled as she fumbled for a reason. "I guess part of it is just personal curiosity. I'm amazed that a man with an international reputation as a thief strolled into San Antonio and started performing in front of an audience with TV cameras rolling. It just seems that he would worry that someone might identify him as the man wanted for questioning in the burglaries."

John nodded. "He's bold. Is there another reason?"

Ashley wasn't certain how to take his question. It was slightly unnerving if John was probing into her personal life. "There's Peter," she said. "He's worried about the cats. As you know, he's very active in the struggle for animal rights."

"I see." John finally extended the file toward her.

"Is there somewhere I can sit?" She looked around for an empty space but could see none.

"Use my desk. I've got some things to clean out of my locker. I'll be back in about fifteen minutes. Ah, about dinner, after I drove away, I realized it was too early to go out to dinner." He turned red up to his ears. "Maybe we could get some coffee or an ice cream?"

Ashley smiled up at him as she settled into his chair. "Ice cream sounds lovely. I haven't had a cone in a long time. I might even splurge and go for a chocolate milkshake."

"I'll be back in about twenty minutes," he said, leaving her to pore over the file.

As she flipped the manila folder open, Brak's picture caught her off guard. She felt a sudden twinge that was undefined, just a quick catch of something deep inside as she looked at the chiseled features. In the photo he wore a black turtleneck and his hair was loosely gathered at the nape of his neck. He looked directly into the camera, as if he dared the photographer to do his worst.

The data sheet was next, a rundown of his birth in Oslo, Norway, to Dreke and Marlay Brunston. She noted that Erik was his older brother's name and mentally gave him a point for telling the truth on that score. There had been another brother, but he'd been killed in an accident. There was an account of his schooling, which wasn't easily translatable into the American parallel, but his grades were consistently high and his focus of study seemed to be... psychology. That was both interesting and disconcerting.

She continued reading about his life. No marriages. No children. He was thirty-three. She came at last to his identification as the man police suspected of stealing nearly a quarter million dollars in jewels—including one emerald-and-diamond necklace—from Cleo Lane Farmington, world-class socialite.

A photo of the necklace in question showed an unusually large emerald cut in a heart shape and dangling from a gold necklace dripping with smaller diamonds and emeralds. It was more like a bejeweled collar than a necklace, she thought. Perfect for the right strapless gown. And the proper complexion.

She didn't particularly want to imagine the woman who'd been confident enough to wear such a necklace. Cleo Lane Farmington was not only wealthy, she was undoubtedly pretty.

She turned the page and discovered another photo of the necklace in a Paris shop. It was nestled in among other valuables in the interior of a safe, and she knew it was the shop where the fence had identified Nils Lofthammer as the thief.

The black words on the white page were hard to accept as anything other than fact. Disappointment was a bitter taste in her mouth. She'd actually hoped that the facts had been misinterpreted. That somehow Brak wasn't guilty. But he hadn't even bothered to deny the theft. He hadn't explained it or denied it. She pondered that for a moment before she turned the page.

She wanted to check his MO. According to the report, he'd gained Cleo Farmington's confidence, studied her home, then robbed her. It appeared that Brak was a pretty smooth operator.

She closed the file and tapped her fingernails on it.

"Finished?"

She looked up into John's expectant face.

"I am. And that was exactly the information I was looking for." She patted the file with a flourish. "Now I'm starved. I left Peter and...Familiar to forage for themselves, but I'd love that chocolate milkshake and maybe even a burger—on the condition that I treat."

"I know just the place." John pulled back her chair.

"Hey, Keifer!"

They both turned at the sound of the voice that belonged to a ruddy-faced policeman who came toward them. "Len, this is Ashley Curry," John said. "Ashley, this is my friend Len Lovett. And no, he isn't related to the singer."

"I would never have thought such a thing," Ashley said of the plump, blond young man who took her hand with a firm grip.

"I got some new facts on those cats." He frowned at Ashley. "I read the report. Weren't you on the scene?"

"I was, and I'm very interested."

"She's a fed," John said.

"Oh." Len adopted a more professional manner immediately. "The drug in the syringe was a very strong anesthesia used specifically for cats. From what the state veterinarian said, cats have a peculiar nervous system and require special handling. Whoever took the cats knew at least that much."

Ashley waited, knowing that each tidbit of information would both torment and help Brak.

"The blood was human, type A, which rules out the cat's owner. We didn't think it was his, but you never know." He leaned closer. "There're no matching prints on file for the bloody print on the knob, so that means our catnappers are either very good or very new at thieving."

"And..." Ashley could sense there was an "and" coming.

"And we have a line on a delivery truck that pulled into the back of the room shortly before the animals disappeared. It was a truck delivering sparkling water, only there's no such company that we can find with that name that sells water."

Ashley's grin split her face. "Good work. What's the company?"

Len looked at John. "I'm sorry, but I don't feel right about sharing that information. Our guys are working on it."

"I'm Border Patrol, not FBI. It's not like I'm trying to snatch the case away from you." Ashley saw her words had stung Len and she was immediately sorry. He'd been far more generous in sharing information than some local officers would have been, and she understood how sensitive city police officers were about the superior attitude that some federal officers displayed. "Sorry, it's just that it's sort of personal to me now."

"She's an animal lover," John explained, coming to her rescue.

"Well, it was Crystal Creek Containers. They don't have a listing in the local phone book, and they aren't on the inventory sheet of the hotel. So..."

"That is really good work. And fast." She held out her hand again and shook his in congratulations. "Any leads on Crystal Creek?"

"So far, nothing, but we haven't really begun to shake this city down," Len promised. "Of course, we believe the truck was painted to look like a delivery truck and that it went into the hotel empty so that the cats could be stolen."

"What about surrounding areas? Maybe there is such a company, but it isn't local. The catnappers might have stolen a truck," Ashley pointed out.

"We'll begin by canvassing the city, then move outward."

"I might be able to help," Ashley offered without hesitation. "In the outlying areas, I mean. Crystal Creek could be a company from across the border."

"It could be from anywhere," Len agreed. "We could use all the help we can get."

"No one knows the outlying areas better than Border Patrol." That much was true.

"Let's grab that lunch," John said, taking her elbow.

"Lead on," Ashley said, determined to be as gracious as she could since he'd been so helpful.

BRAK MADE NO EFFORT to initiate the conversation with Peter. He matched Ashley's brother mouthful for mouthful as they worked their way through the things Ashley had put out on the counter. Peter stopped only long enough to give Familiar a morsel of cheese or a daub of pâté.

"More wine?" Peter asked, holding up the bottle.

"Please." Brak watched the ruby red liquid splash into his glass.

"What are you going to do?" Peter asked. "You can't hide here. Ashley's job would be in jeopardy."

"I'm going after my cats. When I find them, I'll make arrangements to have them shipped home. Then I promised your sister I would turn myself in."

Peter was startled. "You intend to do that?"

"I intend to turn myself in." Brak's blue gaze matched Peter's. "I have no intention of remaining in custody, but I will do as I promised your sister. Don't think that I'm such a fool that I don't recognize what she's risking. For a stranger."

Peter's grin was reluctant. "So, you intend to honor your word. And after that, you're free to do whatever you need to do to regain your freedom. Somehow, I'm sure Ashley won't be surprised."

"Little surprises your sister." Brak put his wineglass down untouched. "Or you. I want to help you find the hunters."

"I think we've been over this ground before." But Peter felt a slight desire to have the big blonde on his side. Brak was not subtle; he stuck out like a sore thumb. But he could move more quickly and silently than any human being he'd ever met. And he was likely more ruthless. The idea of him in the sound van protecting Ashley gave Peter a sense of relief. "I'll tell you what," he said, "you can help protect Ashley. You have my word, if your cats are there, I'll do everything I can to save them."

Brak nodded.

"Now, I have to make a few arrangements. I'll be back in half an hour or so."

Brak stood. "I'll take care of the kitchen."

"See if you can teach Familiar a trick or two." Peter's grin was a challenge. "I've worked with a lot of animals before, and I say Familiar is untrainable."

Brak eyed the cat. "I think perhaps the trouble is that Familiar is smarter than you."

Peter's laughter was loud and long. "I believe you may have something there, Brak. Make yourself comfortable. I'll be back."

"Peter?"

Brak's question stopped Peter in the hallway. "What?"

"How long before they kill the cats? The truth."

"I've done a little research on this group. They're busier on the weekends. Folks fly down on Friday and do the hunt on Saturday. Go home on Sunday."

"Have you made contact with them yet?"

Peter started to tell a fib, but he decided against it. "I'm going to make the call now. I've set myself up as a rich doctor who wants a panther, possibly a buffalo."

Brak snorted. "Don't tell me they kill buffalo, too. That's like shooting large cows."

"I know."

"Have they bought into your cover?"

"They were checking it. I did all the legwork before I came, and there shouldn't be any glitches. As far as they know, I'm Dr. Peter Curtain, board-certified orthopedic surgeon with a new home in Washington, D.C., that needs a few bits of masculine decor. Recently divorced. On the lookout for a new, more exciting life-style.''

Brak's jaw tightened. ''When will you go in?''

''Early Friday morning for a special preview of the cats. I said I wanted to check the animals in case I found something I wanted more than the panther. The actual hunt is Saturday.''

''And they said that they'd just stocked two new panthers. Two lovely black panthers. Young and sleek. Healthy.''

Peter felt real pity for Brak. ''That's what they said.'' He decided to tell the whole truth. ''And he said there were three other guys waiting for a panther if I didn't want one.''

Brak was across the room almost before Peter could move. ''We have to go now. We can't risk the fact that someone won't shoot them before you get in.''

Peter put his hand on Brak's shoulder. ''Easy, there. I told them I'd throw in an extra three grand over the top price if I got my pick first. We have to use caution, Brak, or they will kill all of them. And you have to make certain my headstrong sister stays out of trouble. She's risking a lot for you, and I'm counting on you to protect her.'' Peter saw with a sense of relief that Brak's features softened at the mention of Ashley.

''Her safety comes first. Always.'' He met Peter's gaze and his eyes turned flinty. ''Once the cats and Ashley are safe, I want a little time alone with these men.''

Peter squeezed Brak's shoulder. ''Don't think that thought hasn't crossed my mind, but our goal is to get them arrested.''

''The police can have what's left,'' Brak vowed.

Chapter Seven

Okay, okay, humanoids, there's a lot of pheromones running rampant here in San Antonio, and not a lot of brain-cell activity. Since a good P.I., that's private investigator to those of you who haven't read a lot of Sam Spade, is seldom seen and never heard, I've been cozying down here on the sofa, pretending to snooze and listening to the deal-making. As ole Will Shakespeare once put it, "Something's rotten in Denmark."

As much as I fear for the beautiful Ayla, I wonder if Peter isn't making a bargain with the devil. Brak concerns me. Not the jewel business. There's certainly more to that than meets the eye, and my gut instincts tell me Brak's involvement isn't about jewels or greed. So what would motivate a hunk of manly man to use his body to con women out of their sparklies? This is a question that deserves an answer. From a catly point of view, revenge is the answer that comes to mind. And a man willing to ruin his life for revenge is not exactly the kind of man I want to see playing on Peter's team.

There's also an underlying tension in the man. Peter is the kind of guy who will apprehend the hunters. Brak, judging from his voice and demeanor, might take it further, as in too far. I won't quibble about whether these cretins deserve to die or not—but I don't want my human caught in the middle of a firefight. Peter's hide is certainly not as lovely or luxurious as mine, but I'm quite fond of his. Not to mention that Eleanor thinks the sun rises and sets on him. And even though I get involved in other adventures, taking care of Eleanor is always my primary job.

I've been keeping a rather low profile here in the living room, kneading Ashley's plush sofa cushion with my razor-sharp claws as I listen to the pact Blond Bruiser and Dr. Dolittle have cooked up. As a fine Irish lad once said to me, it's all in the details. The way this hunt is coming down is that Brak will be in the van with Ashley. That's somewhat reassuring, since I'll be there, too. I'll have my paws full making sure BB stays in that van. I don't want to imagine him on the loose in the compound. He doesn't need a gun or a knife. Looking at him, I believe he can kill with his bare hands. There's something savage about him. Savage and proud. Like the cats he's trying to save.

Aside from Brak, there's another piece of news that bothers me. Peter casually drops the tidbit that other hunters are waiting in line to kill the big cats. If Peter isn't successful in shutting this business down immediately, all the king's horses and all the king's men won't be able to save Ayla. Once Peter gets inside, his goal is to catch all of the culprits on videotape. That's all well and good, but videotaping a kill won't save the animal in question. He'll have to use some type of force to close up the place until he can call in the proper authorities.

And this is where the wicket really gets sticky. Peter has his reputation, and more, on the line, and Ashley has her career. Once Peter steps onto that compound, it's his life that's at stake. With all of this hanging in the balance, Peter and Ashley have decided to join forces with a wanted man, albeit wanted only for questioning.

I shake my aching but extremely handsome cat head. It's an amazing thing about those Currys. They lead with their hearts and let the rest follow. If things go wrong—and I shall use all of my feline wiles to make sure that doesn't happen—they'll be caught aiding and abetting a man wanted for questioning in a jewel heist. Probably not a major problem for Peter, but for Ashley, it could be a real mess. At the very least, she would lose her job. Even worse, a legal complication could jeopardize her chances of adopting Maria. Sure, it's fine for Brak to make fancy promises about helping Maria, but if he's in jail, he might not be able to make them come true.

So, you see, I'm not just being paranoid—which is superior to being humanoid, I might add. This is not the best setup I've seen. It's not that the Currys are dumb, it's just that they tend to...well, act on instinct. It's my duty as the smartest member of the clan to keep them out of as much trouble as possible. It's all in a day's work for Familiar, the cat for all seasons.

Oops! Here's Ashley pulling into the drive. I'd better yield the sofa or she'll be squawking like a wet hen. I can see that before I leave here I need to make certain she adopts a frisky little kitten and learns to loosen up over the hair-food-litter situation. While I'm up and about, I'll make a little foray into the kitchen. The pâté was delicious, but I think I need something with a little crunch. Fried clams. Now, that sounds like heaven. I wonder how I'm going to get Peter to call in an order for me. Sometimes, he's pretty obtuse when it comes to picking up on my desires. He needs just a little more training, I suppose. You know what they say, humans grow old but they never really grow up! It's just a cross a cat has to bear.

"FAMILIAR!" PETER caught the phone book just as the cat shoved it off the counter and to the floor.

The front door closed behind her and Ashley headed straight for the kitchen, where she found her brother and Brak bending over the phone book as quick black paws shuffled the yellow pages.

"Is this a new game?" she asked, trying not to smile. "Cat hockey with the phone book for a puck?"

"Familiar is obsessed with the yellow pages," Peter said, standing.

"He wants something," Brak agreed. "Look." He bent closer to the ad Familiar had pinned with his claws. "Seafood Delight."

"Forget it, you feline food funnel," Ashley said. "We're not ordering food for you when you've got a regular gourmet deli in the refrigerator."

"Meow." Familiar sat neatly on the page, curled his tail around his body and looked up at her. "Meow."

"Not even asking nicely is going to work." Ashley glanced at her brother and then at Brak. The whole time she'd been gone, she'd worried about how Peter would react to Brak. For the half hour she'd sat with John at Dizzy's Deluxe Burger, she'd been too keyed-up to eat. Now it seemed her concerns had been unwarranted. "Did the two of you come to some arrangement?"

"Brak will accompany you in the van," Peter said. "I'll feel safer about you, and you can make sure he doesn't get into trouble." His tone was stern. "No arguing or you're both out."

Brak nodded as he cast his blue gaze on Ashley. "I'll do whatever I need to do—to keep you and the cats safe."

Ashley swallowed and forced herself to confront the facts. "And then you'll turn yourself in." She had a sudden vision of Brak being led away in handcuffs. She swallowed again because her throat felt as if it were closing.

"I'll do what's right." Brak held her gaze, long and steady. When Ashley looked away, he picked up the phone book and began to read the ad aloud. When he got to fried clams, Familiar gave a loud cry. "He wants the clams," he said matter-of-factly.

"Forget it," Ashley said, still unsettled by the exchange between her and Brak. She shook her head, trying to set a tone of ease to disguise her own disquiet. "I can't believe the two of you, taking food orders from a cat."

"Not just any cat." Brak scooped up the black feline in his arms. "From Familiar. A very special cat."

The sound of Familiar's purr filled the room.

Peter arched his eyebrows at his sister. "You can't fight him, sis. Eleanor and I learned the hard way. Shall I order for all of us? A shrimp po'boy would be wonderful."

"I'm not believing this." Ashley frowned. "Go ahead and order whatever you want. I need a word with Brak." He met her gaze, and she felt as if she'd received a small electric shock. She motioned him out the kitchen door and onto the patio. Around them the evening was lush, a perfect blend of the first hint of autumn and the lingering warmth of summer sun.

For a moment they didn't speak, and the silence stretched between them. She felt him looking at her, and she kept her gaze on the intricate tile pattern, watching the progress of an ant as it inched over the sun-baked terra cotta.

"There's so much at stake here," she said. "My brother's life..." Her heart was beating too fast. In a few short days her life had been turned upside down. Brak's appearance had awakened longings and desires—feelings she knew she would suffer from when he left. Glancing at him, so controlled and handsome, she had the crazy compulsion to ask him to leave, to order him out of her life before she had to damage both of them. At the same time, she wanted to feel his touch, to bask in the sensation of the simple contact of his hand against her skin. She fumbled on. "Peter is my only close relative...."

"I know." Brak offered no assurances, no explanations.

"Everything you said checked out." She walked to the wrought-iron table and tightened her hand on the back of a chair. The metal was cool, calming.

"I haven't lied to you." He did not move toward her.

"Peter has agreed that you'll help." She stated the obvious. "How did you convince him?"

"With the truth. I'll do whatever it takes to rescue the animals. I'll risk everything—except your safety."

Ashley was framed in the dusky light that made the setting of the patio seem both modern and ancient. It was a warm, golden light that turned molten in her hair and gave her pale skin a honeyed tone.

She lifted her head, and the sunlight seemed to shimmer down on her. "I've been through this with Peter. I'm better qualified than either of you." She turned to confront him and found him staring at her, an unreadable expression on his face. "What?"

"Your heart is so generous. You understand the shades of gray that exist between right and wrong." He crossed the distance between them in two easy strides, his hand softly caressing her shoulder. "It's remarkable, but you trust."

The fact that he spoke the truth made Ashley turn away from him. His touch had sent shivers through her, and she needed a few seconds to draw a deep breath, to blink his image out of her eyes. Brak Brunston was a very dangerous man. He spoke in a voice that her heart listened to. His touch was both primitive and somehow reassuring. He managed to bypass her intellect and speak directly to her emotions. Against all reason and sanity, she did trust him. God help her.

"I've agreed to help you with the cats," she said, fighting hard to keep her voice level. "You've agreed to help me protect my brother. Let's leave it at that for now."

ONCE THE REMAINS of the meal had been cleared away, Peter unrolled several large scrolls that contained aerial photographs of the compound. Though he was perfectly willing to go over the enormous compound, Peter refused to reveal the location of the San Antonio Safari. His plan was that Ashley and Brak would be in the van in a safe location some distance away—listening. Only listening.

"If anything goes wrong, I can take care of myself better if I don't have to worry about you," he'd said. "If I'm alone, I can do whatever is necessary. If I think you might be there, I'd have to modify my reaction to consider saving you." When Ashley opened her mouth to argue, Peter held up a hand. "One word and you'll be left behind." With that he'd rolled up the photographs and headed to the guest room.

As she watched her brother's lanky body disappear down the hallway, Ashley couldn't shake his warning from her mind. Peter had told her that she operated on gut instinct, and this time her instinct was giving her a big nudge—one that spoke of trouble. One man, even Peter, would not be able to handle half a dozen desperate men.

Brak's thumb tentatively touched between her eyebrows, and he began stroking the frown that marred her face. "Your brother is stubborn," he said. "And if you don't relax, you're going to have a headache."

"I know. You're right about both things. Except the headache is already in residence."

Brak's thumb moved across the pain, dulling it, and finally numbing it.

"I sense it's a characteristic you share, this stubbornness."

"Probably." She sighed and closed her eyes. It didn't matter that her head warned her against relaxing with Brak. Her defenses were going mushy at the soothing touch of his hand. "Where did you learn to do this?"

"Massage is an age-old technique. It's one of my favorite tools in working with the cats."

"Really?" She opened her brown eyes to find that his blue ones were very close.

"All living creatures respond to a confident touch." He settled his other hand on her spine, between her shoulders, inviting her to let him support her. "Animals hate a tentative touch. They don't want to sense nervousness. When you pet Ayla or the other cats, always touch so that you feel the muscle beneath the skin. Touch them as if you wanted to know them."

"The same way you're touching me?"

"Well, perhaps not exactly the same." His serious face lightened into a smile. "There are some variables. Touch is primarily a form of comfort, but it can also bring intense pleasure."

Ashley felt the heat rise to her cheeks. Brak was not a flirtatious man, but he was direct.

"Ashley?"

She realized that she'd dropped her gaze to the kitchen table. When she looked up at him, the blue of his eyes was startling. She'd seen those eyes grow cold with anger, but now she saw something warm and enticing.

"Yes?"

"I need to ask a favor."

"Okay." Staring into his eyes, she had no hesitation.

"Once the cats are safe and on their way home, will you give me a day or two before I turn myself in?"

The first emotion that struck her was regret. She did not want to be the agent of his imprisonment. The idea of Brak in a jail cell was repugnant. There was a wildness about him, a savage pride that matched the big cats she'd first seen him with. A wildness that drew her with an attraction she could not resist, and finally had no desire to fight. And ultimately, she would be the one to turn him over to the authorities.

He continued, "If I'm asking too much, I'll understand."

"No," she said. "A day or so won't make a difference." Unless he was captured before he had a chance to turn himself in. She couldn't banish the sadness from her voice. "Let's just see about getting those cats, and my brother, out of there safe and sound."

Brak's smile was also tinged with sadness. "Then if I can have a day or so, I have another favor to ask."

"Okay?" She waited.

"Will you reserve that time for me? Trust me for that long?"

His request took her by surprise. Despite herself she felt her stomach knot with anticipation. A few days with him...

His hands, which had stilled in their massage, moved to frame her face. "If I can think about that time, make plans and imagine, it will help me get through this."

Ashley wanted to offer him more than he'd asked. She wanted to say that once the cats were safe she'd turn her back and count to a hundred, giving him a head start on escaping. But she knew too well the boundaries of duty. If she gave Brak his freedom, she would also give up her self-respect. Instead of saying what she wanted, she nodded slowly. "I'd like that more than you know."

Brak slipped his hands through her hair, down her back, and finally pulled her into his arms. He kissed her lightly, giving them both a chance to adjust to the idea.

To her surprise, Ashley found that she deepened the kiss. Whatever her reservations about Brak, none of them involved her desire for him. Her arms wound around his neck, her fingers catching in the thick blond hair. She felt as if she'd been swimming in strong, deep currents and at last something solid had happened by in the flow of water, something she could hang on to.

PETER PUSHED ASIDE the aerial photographs and stood. He'd marked off the boundaries of San Antonio Safari in the shots, but what he really needed was some detail. The aerials had been taken before the hunting compound existed. While topography was important, he needed details—maps of buildings and fences. His plan had to be perfect. Letter perfect. As much as he denied it to Ashley, he knew he was going into dangerous territory. He would be alone, a fact that gave him freedom to maneuver, but also put him at a great disadvantage.

He paced across the room and returned to the desk, picking up the telephone and dialing rapidly.

"Sky King Photography," a perky young female answered. "Penny speaking."

Peter couldn't help the smile. "Penny, I need a plane and a good pilot who can take some photos near Kerrville."

"That would be aerials," she said, the sound of shuffling pages blending with her voice. "What about ten tomorrow? We have a plane available for two hours. If it's going to take longer than that, we'll have to schedule for Friday."

"Two hours will be sufficient. Can I have the prints by tomorrow evening?"

"Color or black and white?"

"Doesn't matter to me, whatever's easiest."

"So this isn't a permanent record you're making."

Peter was startled by her astute observation. "No, it's just to...settle a bet."

"I won't ask," she said, her voice filled with good nature. "Okay, Mr...."

"Dr. Curtain. Dr. Peter Curtain."

"Ten tomorrow morning, and be on time. Do you need directions?"

Peter took down the instructions and thanked her before he hung up. He was still smiling. Penny was a young woman with potential. She wouldn't be a receptionist at a photo studio for long.

Before he packed away his phone, he dialed Washington. At the sound of Eleanor's voice and Jordan babbling away in the background, he was struck by a wave of homesickness.

"Peter," Eleanor said, "when are you coming home? There's a certain young lady here who's been asking for Da."

"I should be headed back by Sunday night. Monday at the latest."

Eleanor hesitated. "Is something wrong?"

"Of course not."

She didn't respond immediately. "Is it something with Ashley?"

And because he couldn't lie to Eleanor, Peter chuckled softly. "It's complicated. I think my sister has taken an arrow to the heart."

"Really?" Eleanor's voice bubbled with excitement. "Do tell."

"Suffice it to say that Ashley is following the Curry tradition of complicated affairs of the heart."

"Give up a name, at least," Eleanor pleaded.

"How about a description? Tall and blond."

Several seconds ticked away. "Not the animal tamer you were going to hear?"

"Bingo."

"Peter! I read where his panthers and lions were stolen." Eleanor rushed on before he could respond. "I don't like the feeling I'm getting. Tell me he's not involved in whatever you're doing in San Antonio."

Peter had kept the details of his assignment as sketchy as possible. Eleanor tended to worry obsessively. With an active toddler to care for, she didn't need to lose sleep wondering if he was okay.

"We're going to recover the cats, and then we'll see about Brak. He's also wanted for questioning in a jewelry heist from a couple of years back."

"This is not sounding good." Eleanor had adopted a stern tone. "How can you stand right there and allow your sister to get involved with..."

"Eleanor, you've met Ashley. I'm not allowing anything."

"Well, I suppose that's accurate. Still..."

"I just called to make sure the guys got that telephone line put in. The patch is essential."

"Dr. Peter Curtain, I know." Eleanor sighed. "I know you're doing something dangerous, Peter. It would be easier if I knew more."

"I love you, Eleanor. And Jordan, too."

"I love you, Peter. And keep an eye on your sister."

"I'd need a dozen eyes and several sets of handcuffs and manacles to keep her out of trouble."

"Do the best you can, sweetheart. And hurry home."

Peter replaced the phone and turned to face the unblinking gaze of Familiar. The cat was giving him a look that was positively accusatorial.

"I'm doing my best to spare her worry," he said.

Familiar left the room without even a meow.

Chapter Eight

"Are you sure the quilt will be enough?" Ashley transferred the sheets, pillows and quilt into Brak's arms.

She was careful not to let his hand graze hers. So careful that he couldn't help but notice and draw his own implications.

"I'm hot-natured," he said, his lips curving upward as he gently teased her. "I could demonstrate with another kiss," he whispered. Ashley was like a kitten. She came to him so tentatively. So unsure of him, and of herself. Yet as soon as she allowed him to touch her, she gave in to her feelings. She was in tune with that deeper level of consciousness that made up intuition and the rare ability to understand oneself. For reasons she didn't completely understand—yet—she was drawn to him. And though she fought against it, shé could not stop herself. It was remarkable to experience. She wanted to trust him, and he needed her to. He reached out to touch her face, to feel the smooth texture of her skin and determine one more time that she was real and not some woman he'd conjured in his mind.

Ashley took an involuntary step backward. "No," she whispered shakily. "There're too many things to think about. Too many things that could go wrong."

"Too many things to control?" He couldn't help teasing her. She was so alive, so open.

"Exactly. Control. Of my actions and emotions. Now, let me help you make up the bed," she offered, avoiding his amused gaze by bending to pull the cushions off the sofa. His hand on her back stilled her.

"I can make my own bed," he said. "You don't have to wait on me. I'm not helpless."

She stood up and faced him. "You are many things, Brak, and helpless certainly isn't one of them."

"You are not a helpless woman, either. You...take charge."

Ashley straightened her shoulders. "Some men have trouble with that fact."

Brak's laughter was instant. "I can imagine." He laughed again. "It's a difficult thing, for some men, to come face-to-face with a woman as smart or smarter than they are, and one who doesn't attempt to hide it." It was something about her he was growing to appreciate more and more. She put up no pretenses. Ashley Curry was a woman you could take, or if you were a fool, leave. But you took her as she was.

Ashley shook her head. "You were teasing me again. Sorry, it's sort of a touchy area."

He reached out and trailed his fingers along her cheek. "That's exactly what I'd like to do. Touch you."

She took one step away from him. "I'd better get some sleep. We have some things to do tomorrow."

Brak leaned forward and lightly kissed her forehead. "Until the morning," he whispered.

"Good night," she answered. Turning quickly, she hurried to her bedroom and closed the door.

AH, THE GENTLE SNORTING of humanoids in the throes of slumber. I pose an observation to you. Humans and canines snore. Cats do not. Felines purr, cuddle and, in a few rare instances, shed. But we do not snore. So think about it.

Who would you rather share your bed with, a cat or a snorer? I rest my case.

Of course, if you're Familiar, private "eye," you don't get to sleep. You see, I discovered something earlier this evening when Peter was doing his best to patch over the potholes of his latest adventure to Eleanor. A tiny white card fluttered down to the floor from the maps he was examining. Something told me that card could prove to be important later on. Let's see, here it is beside his shoe.

It says Sky King Photography. Hmmm. Dr. Dolittle is having his photo taken? Not possible. Maybe an ID card or passport or something. Anyhow, I'll just tuck this little card away. Now, I suppose a few hours of shut-eye would put me in a better mood. I'm not overly happy about the good veterinarian telling half truths to Eleanor. It seems to me most of the trouble in the world could be avoided if humanoids learned not to speak with a forked tongue.

Come on, sandman, I've got a busy day tomorrow. Hey, Peter, quit hogging all the pillows. Hey! Hey! Quit pushing.

"I HAVE AN APPOINTMENT with a gun club," Peter said. He lifted his juice glass and drained it. "I'm hoping to get some names there. Something I can check out."

"San Antonio Safari, the SAS." Brak said the name with venom.

Peter nodded, having filled Brak in about his dealings with the SAS. "That's what they call themselves, but it's very private, very elite. No phone book listings." Peter saw Ashley's face fall a fraction. "There's no way to trace them, sis."

Ashley gave him a dark look. "I'm going to follow some leads on Crystal Creek Containers. I'm sure it's a bogus company, but maybe there's a warehouse, something that would give us some leads."

Peter nodded. Her idea was a good one. Solid. One that

could lead to trouble for her. "Good thinking, but you should stay..."

"Forget it." Ashley poured more coffee into his cup, then Brak's and her own.

"We need something to do. Something to make us feel as if we're helping," Brak said.

Peter put his coffee cup down. "I need to know that you aren't involved. In any way. I need to be able to act, without worrying what consequences will result. I appreciate your thoughts and help in figuring this out, but I don't want you—either of you—involved."

Brak spoke softly, but with an edge of steel in his voice. "I have to find the cats. As you said, they *might* not be in the compound. In that case, I must follow every lead. I gave you my word I would not interfere with your plan. I never said I would not pursue my own ideas."

Peter tensed, then visibly forced himself to relax. "Stay out of my way," he cautioned, directing the remark to Ashley.

"Right, chief." Ashley rolled her eyes.

"Sarcasm might be one of your problems at work," Peter said.

Ashley's laughter was dark, angry. "It could be," she admitted. "I find that people who take on authoritarian attitudes often lose their sense of humor first."

Brak shook his head. "You are like two children." His observation was tinged with kindness. "Two very bad children. I can imagine how your parents suffered."

"Ashley nearly drove them insane," Peter said quickly, taking the opening to turn the conversation down less treacherous paths. "She was always in trouble. Bad grades, bad company, bad...hair."

Ashley threw her napkin across the table, striking Peter on the shoulder. "Ignore him, Brak, he's the one who got expelled for long hair. He's the one who organized a protest against the use of frogs in the biology labs and nearly shut the entire school system down. I was the straight A student who never even got a tardy slip.''

''As if you never did anything naughty. You just didn't get caught.''

Ashley's grin was Cheshire cat wide. ''Exactly, Dr. Curry. *I* never got *caught.* You always stood up and said, 'Yes, I did it. I did it, and I'm proud that I did.' Which indicates a level of deviousness on my part that you don't have and that you'll need to carry off this plan.''

Brak shrugged his shoulders at Peter. ''I think your sister has a point. A very good one.''

Ashley took the bull by the horns. ''Okay, our plans are set. We'll meet at The Rumble, down on Cabrillo Street. Say, four o'clock?'' Ashley looked at Peter to make certain he'd remember the small restaurant.

Peter nodded as he left the room. ''Good luck, and be careful.''

''You, too.'' Ashley stood to clear the table, but Brak stopped her. ''Go ahead and get ready. I'll take care of the dishes.''

Ashley threw him a smile. ''Everyone is dazzled by your training abilities. Personally, I'd like to meet the woman who trained you.''

Brak grinned. ''My mother would appreciate the compliment.''

Laughing, Ashley bent to scratch Familiar's ears. He was rubbing against her legs, purring a blue streak. ''This bodes badly. Familiar is being too nice. Before we leave, maybe we should get a padlock for the refrigerator. Possibly have the phone disconnected so he can't call in food orders.'' She laughed at her own joke.

Brak's eyebrow arched at her. ''I advise you not to apply your sarcasm to Familiar. Peter may tolerate it, but let me assure you, a cat's dignity is vital. Be careful, Ashley. Be very careful.''

''I never would have thought that a big, brawny guy

could be buffaloed by a kitty." She was still laughing as she left the kitchen and headed to the shower.

"She may be smart, but she's not cautious," Brak said to Familiar. "A point that would serve me well to keep in mind."

ASHLEY PARKED THE CAR in the shade of a cottonwood tree and pulled her sunglasses down the bridge of her nose so that she could peer at Brak.

"You'll stay in the car?" She was having second thoughts at being persuaded to take the big Norwegian to Guerrilla Guns. The deciding factor had been that it was on the south side of the city—near the area where she wanted to start her search for Crystal Creek Containers.

"I will sit here, in this car." Brak's grin belied his serious words.

"Swear it on your mother's life."

A frown wrinkled his forehead. "I will not. My mother's life is not something to be used in a conversation. My word will have to suffice."

Ashley nodded okay. Brak was touchy where his family was involved. She'd mentioned his brother, Erik, just asking what he did for a living. Brak had said "business" and changed the subject. Interesting.

"I'll be back," she said. She pulled the rearview mirror down and checked the deep red lipstick she'd applied. Her brown eyes, made more vivid by the dark shadow, heavy eyeliner and mascara that she'd applied at home startled her. She was a minimal makeup person, but the heavy hand she'd used in making up her face had worked. She looked wealthy, bored and dangerous. She touched both diamond earrings and brushed her hands over the red silk blouse that was carefully unbuttoned just a little too far and tucked tightly into her jeans.

"You look...stunning," Brak assured her.

"Stunningly available."

"That, too. You should certainly get the man's undivided attention."

"Thanks."

She clutched her purse. Inside the leather bag was twelve thousand dollars. It was everything she had in savings and the last of Brak's cash. The thought of losing it made her queasy. It had taken so long to save the six thousand that was her part. Brak had flipped out his money as if it were insignificant.

As if he trusted her to make sure it was safe.

Walking the half block to the store, she forced her mind off the money and concentrated on putting a wiggle in her hips—a hitch in her get-along—as one of her cowboy beaus had called it. She pushed open the door and stepped into the air-conditioned store that smelled of gun oil and new hunting clothes. A big smile decorated her face.

"How are you doing today?" she asked. It was the same man behind the counter, his close-set eyes blinking twice in greedy anticipation.

"You're back."

"I'm back." She walked to the counter and opened her purse. "Half the money up front." She pulled out the stack of cash and placed it on the counter. When he reached for it, she quickly covered the stack with her hand and pulled it back toward her. "Not so fast. What about my big black cat?"

"I, uh, talked with some friends." He glanced furtively around the store. Even though there were no other customers, he still leaned toward her and lowered his voice. "There are two panthers available. There's a doctor got first dibs, but you can have the second one, if you put up the money right now. And it'll be twenty-five big ones."

"Honey, I could get me a Tasmanian devil for twenty-five large," she said, laughing through her pout. "I only brought twelve." She started to stuff the money back in her purse. "And I guess that's not enough. Oh, well, I'll have to go bargain hunting."

The man licked his lips. "Hold on a minute." His gaze darted to the phone and then to her purse. "Maybe I can talk them down to twenty-four."

Ashley's hand brought the money back out of the purse. "Now, that would be a real help to a lady. A very gentlemanly thing to do."

"It'll have to be this Saturday. And you do what I tell you, no questions asked."

"Oh, darlin', that would be fine. I can have that big old black head stuffed and mounted and hanging on the bedroom wall before Rich drags back into town." She laughed. "I hope he gets frostbite on his..." She caught the clerk's eyes and let the laughter bubble in her throat. "Well, you get the picture."

He laughed nervously. "Lady, I'd hate to get on your bad side. Now, you'll have to let me take you in. Alone. You understand?"

For a moment, Ashley panicked. How could she be in the compound and man the sound equipment at the same time? Brak would have to monitor Peter on the sound equipment. It would have to work out. And from what the weasel behind the counter was saying, she was positive it was the same outfit Peter was investigating.

"What's the matter? Getting cold feet?"

"Are you a betting man?" She leaned forward and focused on his lips. She had to buy a little time, think things through. "Want to make a little bet with me?"

"What kind of bet?"

"I'll bet you—" she directed her gaze up to his eyes and held him with her stare "—I'll bet you an evening of fun and adventure that you won't regret helping me. I'm a generous woman, and I know how to pay my debts."

His gaze drifted down to her lips, then settled on the

open collar of her shirt. "I thought you said Rich is a jealous man."

"He's jealous, but he's not too bright." She eased back from the counter. She could manage this. She could surely manage the bubba behind the counter. If all of the hunters were as dumb as he was...piece of cake. At least if she could get into the compound, Peter would have some assistance. Whether he wanted it or not. She focused on the job in front of her. "There are ways for a woman to get what she wants, if that woman is smart, and careful. Now, about this panther. Where do I go and what do I need to take?"

"Come back up here Saturday about 3:00 a.m."

"What are we going to do, hunt in the dark?" she asked. The time would be a drawback. Of course, Peter would already be gone.

"I'll take you to the place." He glanced at her hard. "But you have to come alone, and I'll drive you in. Blindfolded."

"You're making this sound like the CIA might be involved."

"The folks that run this place are mighty particular about who hunts. You got a problem with the rules, then we'd better forget about the entire thing."

"Hold on, just hold on," Ashley soothed him. "I told you the last time, I'm a lady who follows the rules when it leads to what I want. Now, I want to bag this cat. But you have to see things from my point of view. You want me up here in the dead of night, and, honey, this isn't the best part of town. Next I have to agree to go off with a man I don't know wearing a blindfold. You could be some pervert for all I can tell."

The man behind the counter considered. "That's the way it has to be."

"What's your name? Since we're going to have to be spending so much time together, what should I call you?"

"Zeke."

"You got a last name, Zeke, or are you somebody like Cher or Madonna?"

"Zeke Mallette."

"Pleased to make your acquaintance, Zeke. I'm Cherry. Cherry Wells, of Wells Funeral Chapel and Memorial Gardens."

Zeke pointed at her purse. "Names are nice, but money talks louder."

She pulled the cash out of her bag and felt a moment of queasiness as she put it in his hand. It was everything she had. But if she messed this up, the money would be the least of her troubles.

At last the man grinned. "It looks to me like we have to trust each other, Ms. Wells. For all I know, you could be some kind of troublemaker."

"Honey, I know how to make trouble, but not the kind you're talking about. My specialty is...domestic strife."

He laughed aloud. "I'll just bet you can tear up a happy household."

"So I'm to be up here at three o'clock Saturday morning?"

"That's right. Now, I'd like some information." He pulled a pen out of a drawer and a notebook. "My friends are a little particular about who they do business with. So you won't mind if I check out a few facts about you, will you?"

"Not a bit." Ashley smiled. She'd anticipated this and carefully chosen a real person, a person who would corroborate her story.

"Where do you live, Ms. Wells?"

"One-eleven Alamo Plaza."

He looked up. "You *are* slumming, aren't you?"

She shrugged.

"I'll just check out a few things. Bring the rest of the

money Saturday morning. My friends will want their pay beforehand."

"Of course."

"Now, what about a weapon?"

"Oh, I'll use one of Rich's." She shrugged. "Now that I'm going to get my trophy, I'm not all that interested in the gun part. By the way, when will we be finished? I have a hair appointment at five o'clock. There's a charity symphony I have to preside at. Certainly we'll be back here by, say, three in the afternoon?"

"You are some character. I'll make it a point to have you home by three, and that'll include stopping at the taxidermist to get your head taken care of."

"I'll hold you to it, Mr. Mallette," she said. "I like a man who can tell time and keep his word. Now, I've got to dash. See you Saturday."

"Wear something..."

"Comfortable," she finished for him. "I've been to Montana and the Australian outback. I think I can manage a few hours in the Texas backwoods."

She stepped out into the heat and thought for a moment that she was seeing things. Her car was parked under the cottonwood tree down the block, but it looked empty. She hurried away from the gun shop, shifting her gaze from left to right as she searched for Brak. He'd promised to wait in the car. He'd promised... Her hopes plunged, a quick descent that involuntarily tightened all of her muscles. He'd given his word, and now he was gone. A dull sickness settled in.

She looked into the car only to find it was truly empty. Slapping the fender, she let out a curse. "Dammit, Brak, I've got to get to a phone." She looked around but saw no sign of him.

"Ashley!"

She turned and saw him jogging across the street, his arms loaded with boxes and a bag.

"Where have you been? You promised to stay in the car." Relief vied with anger. She was so damn glad to see him, and so mad that he'd needlessly frightened her.

"I saw that pawnshop sign and thought I'd take care of a little business while you were busy."

She eyed his purchases. "What's that?"

He motioned for her to open the trunk. When she did he tumbled the bags down. An automatic pistol slipped free of a bag. He closed the trunk before she could ask any questions, saying, "It never hurts to be ready." He brushed a leaf from the shoulder of her blouse. "I worried you. I'm sorry. I thought I'd be back, and I didn't want to go inside the gun shop and tell you where I was going."

She nodded, at last conceding that he'd taken the best course of action. Now that Brak would be alone in the van, it would be best for him to be armed. Just in case.

"What is it?" He lifted her chin and stared intently into her eyes.

She'd intended to withhold the deal she'd made with Zeke, but she decided to tell him. "I'm in. Saturday morning, early. He took the bait."

Brak's grin was a congratulations. "When?"

"I have to be up here at 3:00 a.m. He'll drive me to the compound."

"You couldn't get him to give you directions?"

She shook her head. "I didn't really try. Obviously, Zeke isn't one of the players. He's just on the fringes. He doesn't make the rules, and there was no point trying to talk him into a change. He just would have pulled out. But I'll be inside, and I'll have a weapon. One that will provide me a lot of protection."

Brak looked beyond her. "I wish it were me."

"Peter's life may depend on you being in that van."

Brak nodded. "I know. I'll be there."

"Brak, we can't let Peter know about this. He would absolutely have a fit."

His hand brushed her hair back from her face. "I wish I could forbid this and somehow take your place."

For Ashley, Brak's touch and the intensity of the moment stopped everything around them. She no longer heard the traffic, no longer saw the first gentle drifting of the cottonwood leaves. There was only Brak, and his clear intention to take the most dangerous part of the job. "You can't do this and neither can Peter. But he can make it a lot more difficult."

Brak's hand closed around the back of her neck, his fingers caressing the tense muscles with such gentle pressure that Ashley almost melted.

"Why are you doing this, Ashley?" he asked.

She thought for a moment, closing her eyes and seeking the truth. "For you. And for myself. For Peter. For the cats. Because I'm trained to do it." Her eyes were still closed, and his kiss was a surprise. It was not the passionate kiss of the night before, but a kiss of gratitude, and one of concern. She opened her eyes to his worried gaze.

"Promise me that you'll be careful. A woman with all of the right answers is very hard to find these days."

Chapter Nine

The small airstrip where Peter was supposed to meet his pilot-photographer was a grass landing field with large metal buildings on either side. He had found the location in the biggest hangar—right beside the cola machine and the candy and cracker display—where he was supposed to wait. As he stood in the shade, he saw the heat devils dancing across the flat expanse of land. If it was this hot in October, it would be an oven in the summer.

The smell of fuel was thick in the air, and as he watched, a small red-and-white Spitfire taxied away from the pump and swung into position for takeoff.

"Dr. Curtain?"

He turned to face the speaker and was surprised that the woman's voice had come from a young girl.

"I've slotted two hours for you," the woman-child said.

"You're the pilot?" The question slipped out before he thought how condescending it sounded.

"You got a problem with that?"

The chip on the girl's shoulder was bigger than she was. "How old are you?" No way was he getting into a plane with a precocious grammar schooler. Not even one who went out of her way to sound as tough and old as Texas shoe leather.

"I'm twenty-one, if you must know."

Peter almost bit his lip. "You don't look..."

"Older than twelve?" She reached into her back pocket and drew out a leather card holder. "Check the license. And there's also a pilot's license in there, too. I'm Penny Wise King. And if you think you have any pertinent remarks to make about my name, consider that I've heard them all. Between my name and my appearance, I've had to grow up tough. So now that you've examined my credentials, get in the plane or get in your car and go home. I don't care which one you choose, just keep in mind that I don't have time to waste."

Peter stared at her in amazement. He'd never heard someone so diminutive talk so big. Not that she was actually so short. She was close to five feet. But she had the appearance of a sweet, loving...on closer inspection, she was older than she appeared. And not nearly as sweet and innocent. "Sky King is your photography business?"

"Along with getting my pilot's license and my driver's license, I managed to wedge in a few hours at the Art Institute of Atlanta. If you want to check out my diploma in photography, we'll have to go into the studio, but it's your air time you're spending. If you want to waste it reading the fine print, I don't mind. Saves a bundle in fuel."

"I didn't mean to imply..."

"Good. Let's go to the plane."

Peter followed her outside the hangar to the twin-engine Cessna that waited at the edge of the small landing strip. The plane was bright yellow and aqua, an admirable paint job. Beside the wheel was a large leather case. "Now, if you want actual photos, you'll have to focus and shoot the cameras. When I do aerials, my partner either flies or shoots. I can't do both, and you specified that no one else could accompany us."

"I can manage a camera."

"Okay, let's go. She's fueled and waiting. Now, you were interested in the area northwest of town, correct?"

"Just a little to the north of Kerrville."

"If you can be a little more specific about what you're hunting?"

"*Hunting* being the operative word. I'm looking for an...animal compound."

She halted. "What kind of animals?"

Peter caught the hint of eagerness in her question. "Animals that shouldn't be there."

She nodded. "I've heard some of my friends who sky dive talk about a place.... It could be what you're looking for. Save you a lot of time and money, if that's it. But, of course, I'd have to know more to be able to tell. Compound can have a lot of meanings. Some good, some bad."

Peter watched her reaction as he spoke. "High fences. Animals in cages. Men with high-powered guns taking trophy heads. That kind of thing."

"Yeah, that could be the place they were talking about. Of course, the pilots fly with a lot more altitude for skydiving, so I don't know what they actually saw." She bit her bottom lip and lifted her eyebrows. "But the good news is that those crazy sky divers fly over that area all the time. That should make it easier for us. At least maybe they won't shoot us down." She motioned him toward the back seat of the plane, settled him in and then explained the cameras and how to change the film. "Use that telephoto lens. We'll go down pretty close, but if you're doing surveillance, we don't want to spook them."

"Right."

"Listen, this ride is half price. I've heard about those canned hunts. I don't approve." She slipped into the pilot's seat and lifted her thumb to signal she was starting the engine.

The roar of the plane drowned out all further chance of conversation.

WATCHING THE LANDSCAPE pass as Ashley drove, Brak saw nothing that was familiar. The vast expanse of flat land was as different from his native country as photos of the moon. America was a vast land. A place of adventure and opportunity. The sheer size of it was astonishing, and food for despair, when he thought about trying to pinpoint the location where his cats might be.

The image of Ayla came to him suddenly. He saw her, pressed against the far wall of her cage. Fear roared through her veins and he felt her lashing out, snarling at some undetermined foe. He tried to focus, to see something of the surroundings, but all he got was a sensation of a small, sturdy cage and overwhelming fear and anger.

The image faded, but Brak was left with rage boiling inside. His hand clenched the door handle and he held his body perfectly still. If he'd connected with Ayla, and he wasn't certain, he could not allow Ashley to sense his emotions. He would only increase her fear.

Glancing at Ashley, he was struck once again by the beauty of her profile. She was intent on driving, her booted foot pressed hard on the accelerator. She glanced at him and smiled quickly, but a sharp curve in the two-lane road required her attention. Brak returned to his own bitter thoughts.

Ayla and the other cats were in danger, and he knew it. Deep in his heart he knew he'd have to get there before Peter or anyone else. Ayla would not wait. He knew her. Knew her agility and strength and power. If those men ever foolishly gave her the tiniest chance to escape, she would be on them. And then, no matter how just her actions were, she would die.

He was so deep in thought he didn't notice when Ashley slowed the car and finally stopped, pulling to the side of the empty road.

"What's wrong?" she asked.

He shook his head, unwilling to meet her gaze. He could

not hide his emotions completely. If he looked into her eyes, she'd see his fury, his fear and his desperation.

"Are you sick?"

"No," he answered.

He heard her seat belt unbuckle. In a moment she was beside him, one palm gently touching his forehead.

"You don't have a fever, but you look positively ill, Brak."

"I'm fine," he insisted. He was more in control. Better. He finally looked at her and tried for a feeble smile. He could see that she was worried about him. "I'm fine. We're doing everything we can."

"And it's not enough." She slid back behind the wheel but didn't start the car. "I know we need to work faster. It's just that we don't have any real leads. This truck thing is the most solid evidence the police have come up with. The print and blood aren't much use unless we have something to match them against." Her shoulders sagged, then straightened. "We'll save them, Brak. We'll do everything we can."

Brak saw a hint of moisture in her eyes, and he felt something deep inside loosen. "I've never tried to talk about this, and I don't know if you can understand what I'm feeling. They're afraid, Ashley. Terrified. They don't understand what's happening to them, but they can sense the danger. For as long as most of them have known, humans are their benefactors." He turned abruptly away and stared out the window. "Peter was right. I've done a very cruel thing. They expected me to protect them. Because of me, they're in this situation."

"Brak, you couldn't have foreseen that something like this would happen. It's unheard of. And for now, they're safe. We have to concentrate on that. They're safe."

"I know that a lot of people would say that they're only animals, but they're suffering. I can sometimes feel what they feel. See bits of what they see. It's how I learned to communicate with them.'' Once again he felt the rage building, and he knew he had to dam the flow of emotion. ''I can't fail them.''

''Maybe I don't know exactly how you feel. I'm not like Peter, I know he believes exactly the same way you do. But it doesn't matter if I understand it intellectually. I understand in my heart, Brak. When I think about Maria, that tiny little girl, and the danger around her every day, I feel so helpless and so frustrated. It makes me want to do something, anything, even something illegal, to offer her a shred of protection.'' She bit her bottom lip. ''I hurt for you, and for your cats. I'll do whatever I can to find them and keep them safe. The only thing I can offer is hope. Hope and all of my efforts to bring the people who took them to justice.''

Brak reached across the seat and pulled her into his arms, holding her tightly as he spoke. Perhaps Ashley would never totally understand his bond with the cats, but she did understand how important it was to him. And she cared. That, in and of itself, was the greatest gift he'd ever been given.

Holding her against him, he felt as if she were a fragile treasure. Yet she was so strong, so solid and real. So capable of giving strength. She was the most magnificent combination of the best qualities found in a person. And eventually, he would have to hurt her.

He squeezed her tightly, then released her. ''We should find that water company. It's going to be a long drive home.''

Ashley's hand shook as she turned the key and put the car in gear. She pushed her hair off her cheek and cast a quick glance at Brak. ''I don't know everything about you and those cats. I don't know enough about your past. What I do know is that you have a powerful effect on me. One that bears watching.''

Before Brak could reply, she pressed the gas pedal and the moment was lost.

Thirty minutes later, Brak held his hand in front of his eyes to block the glare of the sun. Heat shimmered in the distance, giving the ragtag remains of the town before him the sense of being a mirage.

"I think that's the place," Brak said, pointing toward a huge old wooden building with a tin roof that looked as if a third of it had been blown away.

Ashley accommodated him by putting the car in drive and creeping along the abandoned street toward the building.

"Even the pavement got up and left," Ashley said. "Or at least most of it." She nodded toward a hunk of asphalt that had once been paved road. "Talk about a wild-goose chase." She lifted her hair off her neck. Even though the air conditioner in the car was going full blast, the relentless glare of the sun made everything hot.

"It's abandoned," Brak answered. The building was rundown and seedy. Ashley had stopped beside a sign that hung by one rusty chain. The other chain had rusted through.

Ashley pushed her sunglasses up the bridge of her nose. "What's the sign say?"

Brak could barely make out the green logo with white printing. "Crystal Creek Containers."

"This doesn't make a lot of sense. When Officer Keifer questioned some of the staff at the San Antonio Towers, the guy who saw the truck said it wasn't in bad condition. Not anything like this building."

"Where are we?" Brak unfolded the map. For the past three hours they'd been tracing the Crystal Creek lead, and it had proved to be a snaky ride.

Crystal Creek Containers had been a glass manufacturing company some thirty years ago, long before plastic had become the wave of the future. Heading south, they'd left behind the slight roll of the hills that marked the land north of San Antonio. For the past two hours they'd driven through the flat fields of cattle country. Land that stretched forever, in Brak's opinion. At last the small town of Lenton, or what was left of it, had filled the windshield.

"We're just this side of the Mexican border." Ashley took the map from him and studied it. "The Rio Grande is probably only a mile or so from here."

Brak nodded as he studied the building again. He did not speak for fear his disappointment would show in his voice. The lead had always been a longshot, but it was one of the few they had. He felt Ashley's hand on his arm and saw the compassion in her eyes.

"We should check it out. Just to be certain. Maybe there're some records, some clues." She hesitated. "I know how important those cats are to you. I see some of that animal-human bonding between Peter and Familiar."

"Same principle, smaller cat." Brak's smile was wry. "I never talk about this with anyone. Now, along with your other doubts about me, you have to wonder if I am a crazy man who has some kind of delusion about communicating with wild animals."

"You said one thing that really struck home, Brak. It was when you were talking about how the trust of a living creature can make a person honest."

Brak watched the emotions play across Ashley's face. A bond had developed between them, a fragile thing that had been built by his unexpected willingness to share something of his feelings with her. He seldom talked about Ayla and the cats and how he'd come to know them. Most people thought he was crazy when he even hinted at their unique relationship. But Ashley had accepted his link with the cats. He wasn't certain she understood—he wasn't certain that *he* truly understood. But she had accepted his word, and that acceptance was the beginning of something very special between them. As important as the questions she'd asked about the cats was the fact that she'd asked no questions at all about the stolen jewels. For a woman with a background in law enforcement, it was more than a measure of trust.

Ashley started the car and drove toward the door of the old building. "I'll go in and look around." She reached instinctively for her gun as she stopped the car.

"This time I won't stay in the car."

She cast a sidelong glance at him. "You didn't stay in the car the last time."

"This time I'll accompany you," he amended. "No arguments allowed."

"Every driver needs someone to ride shotgun," she answered with a smile. "I doubt there're any desperados here, but there might be a few rattlers or rats. The weather hasn't cooled enough for the reptiles to hibernate, and the flatlands produce some record snakes."

"Thanks for the pep talk," Brak answered. "I wonder if there's more to the town than this." He waved at the ruins of a few buildings that marked what once had been the center of the community.

"I'm afraid this is it. Just another small town that dried up and blew away when the interstate came through."

Together they walked to the door that hung on hinges pulled loose from the wood. Ashley nudged it open with her foot, and they stepped into the gloom, Brak taking the lead.

Dust moats filtered down through a shaft of light that entered through a hole in the roof. For the most part, the building was empty. Stacks of old lumber, metal crates, the debris of what once had been a business, were scattered about.

Ashley jumped when a nest of birds in the rafters scattered at her approach.

Brak steadied her with a hand on her shoulder. His cursory examination showed nothing that indicated a container factory had ever existed. Someone had long ago taken any equipment of value. Judging from the dust in the air, if

Crystal Creek had been a water company, even the spring or creek had dried up and moved away.

"It reminds me of some of the stories I read about ghost towns when I was a boy," Brak said, his voice sounding hollow in the large empty space.

"Empty and a dead-end lead. We've driven for hours to wind up here." Disappointment tinged her voice.

"Sleuthing is often the process of elimination. I read that somewhere, too."

"The Hardy Boys?" Ashley asked.

"What are hardy boys?"

"Books. Mysteries written for young readers. I loved them." Ashley walked into the center of the building. "I guess we can go home." She kicked at an old bottle top.

The sound of a shotgun breech being snapped shut echoed through the old building. Brak and Ashley froze.

"I was hoping you'd be back," a thin, ancient voice called out. "Now, put your hands on your head and turn around."

Slowly, side by side, Ashley and Brak turned to confront what appeared at first to be an apparition. An elderly man with a long beard flowing down his chest stood on what had once been a loading dock. Though he looked old and frail enough to be a ghost, the shiny double-barrel shotgun he aimed at them was very real and very well-cared-for.

"I knew you'd be back," he cackled gleefully. "They always return to the scene of the crime. Learned that from *The Rockford Files.*" He swung the barrel back and forth between them. "Now I have to decide whether to shoot you right away or make you talk first."

"My name is Ashley Curry, and I'm with the U.S. Border Patrol." Ashley stepped slightly forward.

"Hold it right there, missy, or you'll have a hole in that leg."

Brak didn't wait. He reached for her and pulled her back beside him. "Stay put," he ordered under his breath.

"Don't do anything to antagonize him. He doesn't look mentally stable."

"Quit whispering!" the old man ordered. "You think I'm old and you're young. Well, that may be true. But I've got a gun and you..." He stepped forward. "Take that pistol out of your holster and drop it on the ground." He cocked one barrel. "I'm not asking, I'm telling. Do it or I'll shoot you. Last woman I knew carried a gun was a redheaded whore from Laredo. She knocked me in the head and cleaned my pockets."

Ashley slipped the gun from her holster. Holding it carefully by the butt, she slowly bent and eased it to the dirt. "Mister, I'm a federal law officer. You're making a big mistake. We're here investigating a crime."

"Right. I called the local sheriff, and he came out and looked around. That was the end of the investigation. Lawmen are the same all over. They want to park down at the café and talk and eat. He said he'd put out a bulletin on my truck but that it was probably across the river by now and in the hands of some *banditos* hauling illegals over the border. He didn't even try, that's how much good calling the law is."

"We're hunting for a truck," Brak said. "A large truck with the logo for Crystal Creek Containers on the side."

The shotgun lowered an inch, and the squinty eyes stared at Brak. "Where in the hell are you from, boy?"

"Oslo, Norway," Brak answered. "The person driving that truck stole something from me. Something I want back. Something of infinite value."

"Yeah, well get in line. Whoever stole your 'thing of infinite value' also stole my truck."

The barrel of the shotgun lowered another inch and the old man stepped forward. "How do I know you're not with the same bunch of crooks who stole my truck?"

"I can show you my badge," Ashley said.

"Badge, smadge! Any fool can get a piece of tin in the

shape of a star. Hell, they hung one on that lazy fool Amos Grant and named him sheriff."

"I'm a federal agent," Ashley said. "U.S. Border Patrol. We're looking for a truck that was used in a theft in San Antonio two days ago. Several wild animals were stolen from the San Antonio Towers."

"Wild animals. Like bears?"

The old man's interest was piqued, and Brak saw his opportunity. "Not bears. My cats were taken. Animals I've trained and cared for. And when I find the bastards who took them, I'm going to make them pay."

"You talk funny, mister, but I like what you're saying. What we need around here are a few vigilantes. Folks who stand up for right and wrong." The old man lowered the gun until it was pointing at the ground several feet in front of Ashley and Brak. "Now, if you're who you say you are, I want some proof. And don't make a mistake and go for that pistol. I may be old, but I'm a dead shot. I can kill a rattler at a hundred feet with a .22 pistol. Hell, with the scatter pattern on this old thing I couldn't miss you if I tried."

Brak took Ashley's elbow and steered her toward the loading dock where the old man stood. "You can help us, Mr...."

"Folks call me Sam. You can drop the mister. I don't stand on formalities when I talk to folks...or when I shoot them."

"We need your help," Brak said as he continued walking forward. "Ms. Curry and I are working against time to find my lost animals. We believe your truck was used in the theft. And I'll tell you, if we find the cats, we'll find your truck."

"And the men who stole it?"

"More than likely."

"Then, maybe I can help you," Sam said, pulling at the

long beard that hung almost to his waist. "On one condition."

"Which is?" Ashley's voice held grave concern.

"I get to be there when you find them. This time, I want to make certain those young hellions pay for knocking an old man on the head and stealing the only way he has of making a living."

"Oh, brother," Ashley said under her breath. She jumped when she felt Brak's fingers tighten on her arm.

"You look like an excellent addition to our...posse," Brak said. "Let's talk."

Twenty minutes later, Sam sat at an old, dust-covered desk in what had once been the main office. As he talked, he compiled a list of names. It was titled Possible Suspects.

"It could be Johnny O. That's Ortega. He's a little runt, but he's got a bad attitude. Likes to think he's big and bad."

"Why would Ortega steal your truck?" Ashley asked. So far, Sam's list seemed to include every woodchuck on the prairie.

"Ortega's got a brother up San Antonio way. Waymon did some time in Huntsville. Cattle rustling that turned out to be running illegals over the border. Except he didn't always deliver the people to the destination he promised. About half the time he delivered them to a grave."

"Waymon Ortega!" Ashley stood up so abruptly that Sam nearly fell out of his chair.

"Sit down if you want to talk to me," he said grumpily. "You likely startled me out of ten years' growth. Sit down!" He waved her back into her chair. "That's the hombre. The other day, Johnny said Waymon had gotten out, and that he was up around San Antone in a new business. A business for rich folks." Sam stroked his beard. "In fact, he said the words *trophy kill*. Now that I think about it, that's exactly what that little runt said.'' He nodded. ''I think he's your guy.''

''Where does Johnny Ortega live?''

''Johnny O. lives anywhere. He's here for a few days, then gone for a month. Most likely he shacks up with some girl who's too young to see him for what he is, a punk.''

For the first time in a while, Brak spoke. ''Is there anyone here who would know about Johnny O.? Anyone who could tell us more?''

Sam shook his head. ''Nope. Johnny didn't have a lot of friends. I only hired him to drive the truck once because my regular guy was out...sick.'' He looked at Brak. ''I had one delivery and I had to have a driver who could unload some boards. Johnny was handy. And a bad choice, I see now.''

Ashley stood and reached for the list. ''Thanks for your help, Sam, but we have to get going. If we hear about your truck...''

Sam's hand was quicker. ''Not so fast, my pretty! You can't have the list unless you take the man who wrote it.''

Ashley shook her head. ''This is business for law enforcement. We appreciate your help, but...''

''You'll never find a soul who'll give you the time of day. Folks around here don't cotton much to the law. If I'm along, I could open a lot of doors.''

''Grab your jacket, Sam,'' Brak said. He gave Ashley a look. ''My cats hang in the balance. We don't have time to dance around with this. Besides, if you go into the compound, Sam can help me in the van. What if we need to send for reinforcements?''

Ashley cut a look at the old man who grinned back at her. ''This isn't going to work. I have a feeling this is a bad mistake.''

''We have no choice,'' Brak answered.

''Okay, cowboys...and girls, let's ride.'' Sam picked up the shotgun, handed Ashley the gun Brak had retrieved from the dirt, then reached into the desk drawer and pulled out a small wooden box. The label Explosives was clearly written on the side.

"What is that?" Ashley asked.

"Just a little insurance," Sam said, nodding rapidly. "Just a little insurance, my girl. Nothing dangerous, I assure you."

"Is that dynamite?" She couldn't believe a man, even a crazy old coot like Sam, would be tossing dynamite around. It was a very delicate explosive.

"Of course it ain't dynamite," Sam said. "You think I'm an idiot?"

"Well..."

"Dynamite could blow us to smithereens." He walked past her. "Dang fool women. Who ever got the idea to give them a badge and let them tote a gun? Thinking I'd carry dynamite. I can't believe such a thing," he grumbled to no one as he walked out the door.

"I'll go get the car," Ashley said.

As soon as she was gone, Brak looked at the old man. "What's in the box?" he asked.

"I used to be a prospector, back in my youth."

"Is that dynamite?" Brak eyed the box warily.

"Hell no, it's *plastique.* When I find those yellow-bellies who knocked me in the head and stole my truck, I'm gonna blow them sky high."

Brak held out his hand for a handshake. "Sam, you and I are going to get along just fine."

Chapter Ten

It didn't seem possible that the day had gotten hotter. Ashley felt the trickle of sweat down her spine. The feeling was almost as annoying as the sound of Sam's voice in the back seat of the car.

"When I was a boy, folks knew how to stand up for what was right. Some punk like Johnny O. wouldn't have dared to try and make a living as a thief. Why, we'd've strung him up from the rafter of the general store and..."

"Where is the sheriff's office?" Ashley couldn't keep the irritation out of her voice. Ever since they'd gotten into the car, Sam had talked nonstop.

"It won't do any good to talk to Amos. Most of the time I think he's in cahoots with Johnny O."

Sam's comment was enough to make her apply the brakes. Her natural inclination was to go to the law officer in charge. But the one thing she didn't need was to talk to a dirty sheriff, especially one who would, in all likelihood, recognize her as a federal agent. She knew Amos Grant, by reputation, at least. She wouldn't go so far as to call him crooked, but the thought had crossed her mind that he might be on the wrong side of the law where illegals were concerned. She kept her hands on the steering wheel, worried that if she let it go she might strangle Sam. "Okay, so forget the sheriff. Where's Johnny's girl?"

"Tina lives about six miles from here, but she won't tell you a thing. I've already been out to talk to her. Besides, if she did talk, she'd only get in trouble for it later. Johnny might cut her tongue out."

Ashley swung around to look in the back seat.

"It's just a figure of speech," Sam assured her.

"Good, because we're going to talk to her, and she's going to talk to us."

Sam threw up his hands. "I shoulda known you'd do exactly the opposite of what I suggested. You are a hard-headed woman. Downright ornery." He turned to Brak. "Women! You can't tell 'em a darn thing. Back when I was in my prime, women knew their place. Creatures of loveliness and comfort, that's what they were. They wouldn't—"

"Which way?" Ashley asked through clenched teeth.

Brak watched Ashley intently. He felt sympathy and a hint of amusement at her apparent frustration. He started to reach over to her, then changed his mind. Instead, he cocked his head at Sam. "I'd give her the directions, if I were you." His lips turned up at the corners even as he fought the smile that threatened to break across his face. "Be careful, Sam, she's got a nasty temper. Just yesterday she pushed me through a screen door."

Ashley started a vehement protest, but she saw the glint of mischief in Brak's blue eyes. He was enjoying her frustration with the old man.

"Head west, Miz Curry. About four miles, then hang a right."

Ashley left behind the remnants of the town. As she drove, she had a sinking feeling that the passenger in the back seat was a big mistake. But there was no way to avoid Sam going with them. She covered her sigh by turning on the radio. When Sam began to comment on her choice of music, she hit the volume button and drowned him out.

"A man can't hear himself think," Sam protested.

"And I can't hear you complain," Ashley replied.

In the passenger side of the car, Brak only smiled, his thoughtful gaze drifting repeatedly to Ashley.

By the time they reached Tina's house, Ashley had lowered the volume of the music, and Sam had leaned back in the seat, lulled into quiet by the drone of the air conditioner. Ashley cast a glance in the mirror and started to ask him if they'd had air-conditioning back when folks stood up for what was right and women knew their place. But the old man looked rather worn, so she dropped it. She couldn't tell for certain, but he looked close to seventy. At least sixty-five. For all of his nuisance value, he had been through a rough week.

"That's it," Sam said, coming out of his lethargy to point to a small yellow house with dark blue trim.

Ashley pulled into the area that served as a driveway, noting that the yard was neatly raked and a few chickens clucked busily under the house.

When Ashley didn't immediately get out of the car, Brak reached across the seat, giving her support with a touch. His fingers were light, gentle, but delivered an amazing ability to soothe. For a split second, Ashley forgot about Tina and Sam. She was aware only of Brak. Of his concern for her and the pressing need to figure out who had taken the big cats that were so important to him.

"I'm thinking of the right approach," Ashley said. "If she's really afraid of being hurt, I don't want to panic her."

"Your thinking time is done." Sam pointed to a pair of dark eyes looking out through the starched curtain on the door. "She knows we're here."

There wasn't time for a plan. Ashley got out of the car, making sure her gun was holstered but easy to reach. Badge in hand, she walked to the front door. She didn't have time to knock before the door was thrown open.

"Is he dead?" The young woman's large brown eyes held fear and acceptance.

"We're looking for Johnny Ortega," Ashley said, showing the badge. She took in the slender form of Tina. She was young and beautiful, and obviously under a lot of stress. "Is he here?"

Defeat registered on the young woman's face. Instead of answering, she shook her head and tears zigzagged crazily down her cheeks. "I've been waiting now for three nights. He should have been back. I knew he was going to get in big trouble when he got involved with that brother of his. They never should have let Waymon out of prison. He's an evil man. Evil to the bone." She made the sign of the cross over her chest.

"Is your name Tina?" Ashley asked the question, though she knew the answer.

"*Sí,* Tina Cervantes." As she spoke, she stood a little taller and lifted her chin. "Cervantes is an old name. An honorable one."

"Johnny Ortega lives here with you?"

"Johnny has cost me my family. My citizenship." She looked Ashley in the eye, refusing to lower her gaze. "My future. Until he left the last time, he lived here. He lives here no longer." She glanced over her shoulder into the interior of the house. "And neither do I. I am going home, if my family will have me back."

Ashley's first impulse was to offer assistance. But there was nothing she could do. Nothing. Whatever mistakes Tina had made and paid for, it was up to her to straighten it all out. At least she had come to her senses.

"Are you certain Johnny is with his brother Waymon?"

Tina considered before she answered. "He left here saying he had to 'take a ride' to his brother's. Then old Crazy Sam comes by and says Johnny was driving for him last week. Now Sam's truck has been stolen and the thief hit him in the head and nearly killed him. Stealing the truck sounds like Johnny. Striking an old man sounds like Waymon. But why would they steal *this* truck? There are trucks in San Antonio to steal. This doesn't make sense." She sighed heavily. "Nothing in my life for the past year makes sense." Once again she straightened her shoulders. "Except going home."

"Tina, do you have any idea where I might find Johnny in San Antonio? An address. A phone number. Anything?"

"He said that I should not try to contact him there. I knew he was up to no good, but I tried not to think about it."

"Did he ever mention animals? Like wild animals?"

Tina shook her head.

Ashley pulled a card from the pocket of her jeans. Standing in the sun, she felt as if the heavy makeup she'd applied earlier in the day was melting off her face. "Keep my card, and if you think of anything that might help, give me a call. Time is critical."

"I'll call if I think of anything. Now I must pack."

Ashley looked around. There wasn't a car. No means of transportation, and certainly no telephone lines running to the house. "Do you need me to send someone out to help you?"

"My father will come. I can walk to the neighbor's and use their telephone."

The certainty in the girl's voice relieved Ashley. "Okay." She started down the steps.

"Wait!"

She turned back to see Tina disappearing into the house. In a moment she came running across the porch, her dark hair flying out behind her. In her hand was a slip of paper. "It's a receipt for gloves. Leather gloves, like a cowboy wears. I thought it was funny, because Johnny never did hard work. Not outdoor work that would require gloves. It fell out of his pocket when I was doing the laundry."

Ashley took the receipt. It was from Harry's Hardware in Kerrville, Texas. Kerrville. About sixty miles northwest of San Antonio. "Thanks, Tina."

"Will it help?"

"A great deal. Good luck to you."

"And to you." Tina stepped forward. "Johnny is not mean. Not really, though he talks and swaggers like a tough man. But Waymon is very mean. Cruel. Be careful of him. Not even your badge can protect you from him."

Ashley saw the worry in the girl's troubled brown eyes. "Thanks. I'll be careful."

She walked back to the car. She wasn't certain how much Sam and Brak had heard, but for once, blessed quiet ruled in the vehicle as she got in, turned on the motor and cranked the air up full blast.

"Well, we're about to pop to know what happened," Sam said as soon as they were back on the dusty road.

"I think the cats are in Kerrville, just as Peter suspected."

"Is that good or bad?" Brak had no idea of the geography.

"A little of both," Ashley said. "At least we've confirmed the search area. Now we'll have to do a lot of legwork and hope we can find folks in that town sympathetic to our cause. Maybe we can find some people to tell us more about the operation and fast."

METHINKS THE HOUSE has been taken over by aliens. There's Cowboy Sam, the cowpoke, in the back of the house, and Blond Bruiser here in the kitchen, eyeing the car keys as if they were about to spring to life. Ashley is in the bathroom scrubbing what must be a pound of goo off her face. I knew when they left this morning they weren't to be trusted.

Big kitty sigh. How can I conduct my investigation and also keep tabs on the humanoids? Every single time Ashley goes out that door, she comes back with another stray. I have a soft spot in my heart for those wonderful folks who bring home a mewling kitten or a hungry tom. But an old cowpoke! One who talks nonstop. I'll bet if Ashley pushed him near a tub of water he'd knock a hole in the wall running away. And good Lord. How can she complain about the few sleek black hairs I've left around on the sofa and beds? That old geezer is nothing but a hair ball. A talking hair ball.

My investigation today has taken me to the bookshelves, which I found embarrassingly bare of true merit. Law enforcement books are so boring. And those history and geography-related tomes. Almost as much fun as reading about dental extractions from the Middle Ages when there were no painkillers.

I had more in mind some psychology, of which I understand Brak is a former student. Maybe some—now, don't laugh—psychic reading. I've been giving this thing between Brak and those cats a lot of study. What I sensed between them had nothing to do with training or discipline or Pavlovian response to a cue. Ayla understood what Brak requested of her. She obliged him without resentment or any other negative response.

How?

Why?

See, in my relationship with the less-developed humanoids, I'm the one who's always in control. What's astounding about Brak is that sometimes he's the one in control. And he doesn't have to try to connect. It comes naturally. How did he discover this connection with Ayla? These are the questions Ashley and Peter are studiously avoiding. It's because they don't believe. They don't believe and they don't think. Or they haven't thought—yet.

I think now is the time for a little exercise. How acute is Brak's link? I need to figure out a way to test it. If I can get his mind off Ashley long enough.

BRAK STOOD AT THE KITCHEN counter, his gaze shifting between the car keys and Familiar's golden gaze. The cat was scoping him out, and in a big-time kind of way. He'd seldom felt such intense scrutiny. From man or beast.

"Later, big boy," Brak said softly to the cat. "I've got to take care of something."

Ashley had put Sam in her bedroom for a "quick nap." The sound of water running came from the hall bathroom, and Brak knew Ashley was busy removing the makeup. He picked up her car keys and went out to the trunk of her car. Checking in both directions to make sure the coast was clear, he lifted out the guns he'd purchased earlier and the small box of *plastique* Sam had contributed. He felt a flash of remorse. Ashley would be furious. More than furious. She'd feel betrayed if she knew she'd just transported *plastique* across half the state of Texas.

Of all the human emotions, betrayal was one of the most devastating. He held the weapons in his hands and hesitated. Finally he turned toward the house. There was no turning back. Everything he loved was at risk. His cats, but more than that, Ashley.

His feelings for Ashley were strong. Unexpectedly strong. For the past several years, he hadn't allowed a woman near the fringes of his life. At the thought, he felt his muscles begin to tense. Once, long ago, he'd allowed his emotions to lead him to near disaster. Something he was still paying for now. If Cleo hadn't tricked him... Heisting Cleo's jewels had been the final act in a role he'd never liked playing. But perhaps it had been Cleo's greed that had opened the door to his bond with the cats. That thought brought him up short. Was it possible that something so good had come of such a cold and calculating woman?

"Hey, big fella!"

Brak heard Sam's harsh voice and wanted to hide behind the open trunk. Hiding would do no good. Sam would come after him. He eased the lid down and snapped it shut. "Yes?"

"I just thought of my rectifier, that's what we used to call explosives back when I was younger, rectifiers. Anyway, I figured it might be smart to get it out of the sun. It's supposed to be stable, but my experience with explosives is better safe than sorry."

"I agree." Brak's own experience with explosives was limited. He only hoped drastic measures wouldn't be necessary. But if that's what it took to free his cats, so be it.

"What about the two of us ditch the lady and go out on our own?" Pete glanced toward the house. "She's a pretty thing, but catchin' crooks is no job for a woman."

Brak leaned his hands down on the trunk of the car. "Sam, it's a long trip to the 1990s from where you're living, but I'm going to help you make the journey. Fast. Before Ashley hears you and decides to send you home in a coffin." Despite his own concerns for Ashley's safety, he was irritated by Sam's lack of faith in her. Ashley was one of the most competent people he'd ever met.

"Why, that sweet thing couldn't put a bullet in a man." Sam waved a hand in front of his face. "She just about loaded Johnny's girlfriend in the car with us and brought her home, too. Her heart's as big as Texas, and this is a mighty big state."

Brak's desire to argue that issue died quickly. Ashley was extremely compassionate. In the short time he'd known her, she had collected a motley assortment of strays. He among them. And Sam. He couldn't argue that Ashley was tenderhearted, but he disagreed with Sam when it came to her ability to strike hard, and fast, when the time called for it.

"Listen, Sam, Ashley's brother is hunting for these cats, too. Whether we like it or not, Ashley's going into that compound as a hunter. I can promise you that if anyone threatens Peter, she'll wipe them out without batting one of her long, dark eyelashes."

Sam considered. "You may be right. That's a womanly

emotion, protecting those she loves. Yep, you may be right."

"Here, grab some of this," Brak said, shoving the equipment toward Sam. "We need to stash it in the blue van parked down the street."

"What's this?" Sam peered into the brown wrappings, feeling the gun before he unwrapped it enough to see. "Now, that's a doozy of a gun," he said. "Automatic?"

"Yes." Brak didn't want to discuss the matter. When he went into San Antonio Safari, he was going in armed to the teeth. "Don't worry, Sam. I know how to use it."

"You one of those foreign terrorists?"

Brak couldn't help but laugh. "Actually, I'm a pacifist. Let's just say in my checkered past I was taught paramilitary training. And I was an able student."

Sam nodded. "I'll bet you were," he said softly. "I wouldn't want to get in your way when you're headed down a path."

"I wouldn't want you to. Now, let's get this stuff in the van before Ashley comes out here and starts looking for us."

ASHLEY CAME OUT of the bathroom, her skin glowing from the scrubbing. She stopped when she saw Brak coming in the back door. One hand went instinctively to the bathrobe that had opened slightly. Her skin came alive whenever he looked at her. Even her lungs reacted funny. She was short of breath.

Brak stopped just inside the door, his gaze moving from her wet hair down to the beads of moisture that glistened on the vee of exposed chest.

"I thought I heard you and Sam outside," she said. "I was coming in to put on a pot of coffee. Peter should be here any time. And I want to run up to the police station and see if John Keifer has discovered anything new." She talked to cover her awkwardness, since talking at least forestalled the power of the chemistry they shared. Still standing in the kitchen, their gazes locked in silent acknowledgment of the desire that sizzled between them.

"Sam went down the street. He remembered a newsstand and decided he wanted a paper."

Ashley's brow furrowed. "That's at least two miles away."

"He said the walk would do him good." Brak closed the distance between them. "Sam can be an irritation, but he does have an acute sense of timing. He knew I wanted to be alone with you."

The intensity of Brak's gaze only heightened her desire. Her hand went self-consciously to her face. "I feel two pounds lighter," she said. "That makeup was like a mud pack."

"You looked very glamorous, but I prefer the more natural look. Like you are now."

"Always the diplomat," she replied, the breathless sound of her voice surprising her.

"I've been many things, but never a diplomat. Ashley, we have to talk. We need to be alone."

Her blood thrummed, heating her body in what she recognized as the first stage of deadly desire. She wanted to be alone with Brak. Very much. She wanted nothing more than to feel his arms close around her, pulling her against him. He had the ability to make everything fade except his touch, his nearness. But there was something else behind his request to be with her. She could see it in his eyes, a need to share something. Ashley weighed the conflicting needs. She had to get dressed and get to the police station if she wanted to use the computer while John was still on duty. Her resolve faltering, she decided to put the choice to Brak. "If I want to run a check on the Ortega brothers, I have to go. Now."

Brak did not actually move, but he allowed a distance between them. At last he nodded. "When this is over, before you...maybe you could go to Oslo with me to deliver the cats."

"Oslo?" Ashley had never considered that he would leave the country. Truth told, she hadn't thought much about Brak's past. She'd conveniently put aside the details of his being wanted for questioning. Against all of her training, she'd almost forgotten he was a man wanted by the law.

"I have to take the cats home. You understand that?"

She heard the slight hesitation in his voice. In their agreement, he'd never mentioned going home to Oslo. Though he'd asked for time to be with her, he'd failed to negotiate an overseas trip.

The sudden weight of the future felt like a ton of bricks dropping on her shoulders, and mingled with it was a sense of disappointment. "We can't talk about this now." Her hand clutched at her robe, drawing it tight to her throat as if a chill wind had suddenly blown over her. "I have to get dressed." She retreated halfway down the hallway. "I'll leave it to you to explain Sam to Peter."

PUSHING BRAK COMPLETELY from her thoughts had proved as irritating and futile as trying to work the computer. Ashley searched the keyboard, hunting in vain for the symbol that would make the computer print out the information she'd finally managed to retrieve on the screen. It was a small success that gave her a tiny bit of satisfaction. Sam was a pain in the butt and a nonstop insult to women, but he was also deadly accurate in his information about the Ortega brothers.

She felt someone behind her and whirled to find John Keifer bending down. His hand closed over the small gizmo that rested on the pad beside the computer.

"You can do it from the keyboard, but the mouse is faster. Haven't you gotten your computer working yet?"

"Yes and no." Ashley was hooked up, but she hardly

ever turned it on. Besides, the programs she needed were available only at the PD.

"Let me help," John offered.

Ashley watched as John maneuvered the mouse, making a pointing finger jump across the screen. It went straight to the symbol for print, and with a click the machine beside the computer began to whir and spit out pages.

"Thanks, John. Once again, you've helped me out."

"My pleasure. I'm just glad we could find what you wanted. You having trouble down on the border with those Ortegas?"

"Not exactly along the border." She wanted to tell him about Crystal Creek. By all rights, she should tell him. But she hesitated. Too many cooks could spoil the soup. And one of the police officers would certainly recognize Brak.

"You look a little tired. Want some coffee?" John asked.

"Sure. Coffee sounds like exactly what I need."

She lifted the printed material from the tray and followed him back to the lounge area, where a giant, stainless steel urn was kept in constant use.

"I thought you'd want to know that Len Lovett—you met him here the last time—anyway, Len said they'd found a defunct company listed as Crystal Creek. Down by the border."

"Yeah?" Ashley felt like a real heel. John and his friend had been generous with information, and she'd repaid them by sneaking around behind their backs.

"We sent a couple of guys out there today, but the place was abandoned. The town was abandoned. There was an old office, but nothing relating to a bottled water company was on file. But it's sort of strange. The old guy who owns the place, Sam Horton, was gone. Disappeared without a trace."

"Too bad. Another dead end." Ashley looked down at

the rap sheet on Waymon Ortega. There was nothing she could say or do. Too much was at stake.

"What's your interest in those guys?"

"The younger brother, Johnny. His name came up during a conversation today. I'm just following a hunch."

"Gut. That's what makes a good cop," John said, smiling at her. "You've got a good reputation for following your instincts. I heard from Adam Salter that you saved his skin. Woman's intuition. He was telling us about an old army vehicle that you two pulled over. He said your gut told you it wasn't illegals in the back."

"No, it was illegal weapons." Ashley remembered the case. She'd been unable to stop her partner from rushing the truck. She'd saved his life. "When all was said and done, I had a lucky day."

"No, you had a gut instinct. Adam had a lucky day."

John's easy compliment only succeeded in making Ashley feel lower than a worm. Still, she met his smile with one of her own as she took the cup of coffee he offered her.

"Do you think that Brunston-Lofthammer guy was involved in the theft of those large cats? At the time, I really believed he cared about those animals," John said.

The question caught Ashley flat-footed. She sipped her coffee, then blew into the cup before she answered. "What would make you think he was involved in stealing his own property?"

John shrugged. "Some of the reports we're getting on him are strange."

"In what regard?"

"He's lived all over Europe."

She heard the evasiveness in John's voice and decided the best way to play it was cool. "Most of the countries in Europe could *fit* into Texas," she answered.

"True enough. But he's *known* in all those countries. There wasn't a single place I called... It was like his name was coded or something. I was immediately transferred to the head guy. I just found that sort of odd. I got the impression our Norwegian cat trainer is very well known on the Continent."

"Known?" Ashley had a bad feeling. If her gut instinct was kicking in now, it was a little late.

"Yeah."

"Are you saying he's wanted?"

John spooned another measure of sugar into his coffee, stirring it for a good fifteen seconds. "I probably shouldn't be telling you this, but..." He looked directly into her eyes. "I think you're more heavily involved in this than I want to know. Somehow, you're connected to those cats. And if you're involved with the cats, this information might prove useful to you."

Ashley couldn't lie. Not to a man who'd so generously offered her a blanket pardon without even asking her sin. "Thanks, John. This is really important to me. In a lot of ways I can't explain right now."

He nodded. "Lofthammer, which, by the way, is only one of his aliases, has a curious habit of disappearing. Or he did. He's worked in Paris, London, Prague, Berlin, even for a period in Rome and Madrid."

"Worked as what?"

"That's just it. Some high-powered business. A family business."

Ashley felt as if she had gotten a second wind. "So? A lot of businesses have employees in the major European cities."

John lifted another spoon of sugar, but instead of putting it in his coffee, he returned it to the bowl. "Most businessmen aren't identified by police in every country they've worked in. We faxed a recent picture of him around. The response was pretty amazing. In fact, we're still getting inquiries about him from half a dozen law enforcement agencies overseas."

"And what are they asking?"

"That's the strange part. They're more or less polite questions. What's he involved in? Will he be returning to Europe? That type of thing."

"He isn't wanted?"

John shook his head. "That's the part I like the least. It's just one of those crazy hunches, but I got the feeling that they did want him. But not for questioning. I think they want to kill him. I get the feeling he knows too much."

Chapter Eleven

Pork tenderloin. Pork tenderloin. With, perhaps, a bit of Jezebel sauce. Peter, of course, won't touch it, but I'll eat his share. What's important is that Blond Bruiser is listening to me. Ah, he's going through the refrigerator. He's getting out the meat, eyeing it with speculation. Ah, yes. Now he's going through Ashley's collection of cookbooks. I can rest. The menu is decided.

He is extremely attuned to my thoughts, but I can't be certain if he knows he is, or if he's merely responding. I wonder...

Drat! I can't figure out a test that would show, without a doubt, how intense the connection between us is. Not as strong as with Ayla, but he's had years to develop the link with her. The only thing I can do is trust that he'll listen to me when the time comes. I can usually manage to get Peter to do what I want, but it takes so much more effort. With Brak, the response time is much shorter. That could prove to be invaluable when we go into the compound. At least now I know Blond Bruiser will help me. My ride is assured.

Uh-oh, here comes Cowpoke Sam. Somehow I get the impression he's not a big animal lover. Oh, well, another convert to make. A few nuzzles, purrs and a little sandpaper tongue and he'll swoon to my will.

SAM TAPPED LIGHTLY on the kitchen door before he entered. He took a minute to survey the sight of Brak, cookbooks scattered on the counter, pouring over recipes.

"What in thunderation are you doing?" he asked.

At his incredulous tone, Brak glanced up. "Making dinner." Somewhere in the back of Brak's mind had been an idyllic setting—candlelight on the small patio table, Ashley sitting across from him, a few hours of quiet. Sam had shattered that fantasy into a million bits.

"Where's the woman?"

"Ashley went to check out the Ortega brothers."

Sam hesitated, then took the plunge. "Don't you think you've got the roles reversed? Men do the investigating, women do the cooking."

Brak's smile was amused. "By whose code book?" He would have liked nothing more than to accompany Ashley, but he couldn't possibly show his face in the police department. After the initial burst of enthusiasm in pursuing him, it seemed that the focus of the law officers had turned to other more violent criminals. That's exactly the way he wanted to keep it.

"Hell, that's the way it's always been. That's the way it's supposed to be." Sam stared at the tenderloin. "That's a good hunk of meat. You'll probably ruin it."

"Care to lay any money on that statement?"

"You mean a bet?" Sam's eyes brightened.

"That's exactly what I mean. I'll bet you twenty dollars I can prepare a meal that will make you beg for mercy."

"You're on!" Sam reached toward his back pocket and stopped. "Except I don't have twenty dollars," he admitted. "Whoever took the truck also took the cash I had."

"Not to worry. You can owe me."

"And if I win, I'll be twenty dollars richer."

"You can put that out of your head."

"What're you cooking?" Sam stepped closer to inspect the cut of meat.

"I had this strange compulsion to cook pork tenderloin. And Ashley happened to have one in the refrigerator. It was almost as if fate..." Brak stopped in midsentence. His gaze swung to Familiar, who wore a superior but innocent look. Had it been fate—or a cat's desire?

"What's that cat doing sitting on a stool!" Sam started forward, his arm out to push Familiar to the floor.

Brak caught him by the shirtsleeve. "Hold on there, cowboy. That cat may be our secret weapon."

"Meow!" Familiar jumped to the floor and began to do figure eights around Sam's legs.

"Four-legged critters belong in the yard! Whoever heard of a cat in the house? Put him in the barn where the rats are."

"Hold on, Sam," Brak said, tugging at his sleeve. "Familiar is a very unusual cat." He eyed the black feline. His ability to communicate with Ayla and the other large cats had come unexpectedly. He'd never thought that he might share that unique ability with a domestic cat. Especially not one that might be able to manipulate him. It was an extraordinary thought.

"Yeah, he's black and he's about to trip me."

Brak's laughter was deep and rich, completely covering his thoughts. "Old-timer, you have a lot to learn."

"I know animals belong outside. Why, he was eyeing that pork like it was his supper, ordered up just for him."

Brak bent down and scooped Familiar into his arms. He gazed into the cat's golden eyes, studying him for the moment. Still holding the cat, he turned to Sam, a wicked smile on his face. "Familiar thinks you need a bath."

"A what?"

"A bath," Brak repeated in a sterner tone. "As in soap, water and about thirty minutes' soaking."

"I had a bath just—" his face fell "—I guess it was a day or so ago."

"And leave your clothes outside the door. I'll find you something to wear and put those in the wash."

"You don't mean you wash clothes, too!"

Brak turned Familiar so he could look at Sam. "I have a multitude of talents. Familiar and I are modern creatures. We do whatever is necessary. Something you're going to learn. And right this minute, a bath is necessary."

Sam scratched his head as he stared at Familiar. "That cat is putting a hex on me. I don't know what's going on, but even a bath is preferable to standing around here and watching the two of you. You act like you're having a conversation with that fur ball."

He huffed down the hall, not even bothering to acknowledge Brak's chuckle.

As Brak bent to put Familiar on the floor, he lifted the cat's face. For a long moment they stared at each other. "We'll save Ayla. I promise. And whatever it takes, I won't allow Ashley to be injured." He stood and washed his hands before he turned to prepare the meal.

From down the hallway there was the sound of running water and an off-key rendition of what sounded like a wounded animal singing "Satin sheets to lie on."

The pork was browning in the oven and the lettuce for the salad washed and torn when the front door opened. Brak knew instantly it wasn't Ashley. He heard Peter's heavy tread. Sam, newly cleaned and slightly subdued, was sitting at the counter. Brak briefly explained Sam's presence and the story of the Ortega boys, then turned the conversation to the animals. "Any news?"

Peter nodded. "I got some aerials. The compound is a lot bigger than I thought. And better guarded. It's going to be tougher than I imagined," he admitted.

"How many people?" Brak's instant concern was for Ashley. He considered telling Peter about her plan to get inside the compound but held back, waiting for more details.

Peter selected a bottle of wine for dinner as he continued to talk. "There were twelve that I saw."

"Twelve?" Brak's concern was immediate. "You can't go in there alone. Even if you have an Uzi. You're going to have to let me go in—"

"I can manage it." Peter's tone was stubborn. "Some of them will be out on patrol. Some guarding the perimeter and checking the fencing and security systems."

"Right, so that leaves about six for you to deal with." Brak pulled out the roast. "This isn't about closing the SAS down. It's about protecting your sister and saving those animals. You need me to go in with you. Six is too many." This time Peter wouldn't be able to argue with him. He knew Ashley would be in there, and he had no intention of seeing her pitted against such odds.

"I need you and Ashley to stay in the van and do the sound work."

Brak caught Sam's attention and held his finger up to his lips, warning him to remain silent. "Don't be stubborn, Peter. You need a SWAT team. I'm very good with weapons. Very good. I've had training in the use of assault weapons."

"And I'm a helluva shot." Sam finished putting the plates on the table. "Give me a good rifle and I can shoot the rattles off a snake at three hundred yards. Twelve to one aren't good odds, Dr. Curry. Not even if you're Wyatt Earp."

Brak had a mental picture of Ashley pinned down by gunfire. It was simply too dangerous. "Let us help you, Peter." If only he could convince Peter to let him accompany him, then Ashley wouldn't have to go in. She could remain in the van.

"There isn't anything you can do. I got a clear view of the compound. I'm not certain that Ayla's there, but I saw cages. There were several lions, three tigers, cheetahs, baboons, wolves, four bears and the smaller bobcats, lynxes and, pitifully enough, penned buffalo, elk, zebra and rams."

"Tell me about the security." Brak's tone was deadly.

"High fences, high-voltage electricity. Very tight. One entrance that I could see. The compound is about five miles, mostly a square. At least, that's the best we could estimate from the air. Herd animals are corraled in the northwest. The cats all seem to be in the center, under the heaviest security. There's a clump of woods, a place where the trees are thick, and I couldn't see what was there. Most of it is open. I'd say they take the caged animals into the wooded section for the kills."

Brak laid out the compound in his head as Peter talked. A plan was already beginning to formulate, one that would circumvent Ashley's. "What about the plane?" he asked. "Did it stir up any attention?"

"A lot of sky divers fly over, and we didn't seem to draw the guard's interest until we made our third pass." Peter broke off. That's when he'd seen several men pull out camouflage tarps and begin to cover the cages.

"And what happened then?" Brak pressed.

Peter shrugged. "We headed home. I had enough photos and I didn't want to panic the hunters. I know where they are now. I want to put them out of business, not spend another six months finding their new location."

"I'd like to put them out of business. Permanently." Brak's tone and gestures conveyed a ruthless power.

Peter put aside the wine and went to the liquor cabinet to bring out a bottle of bourbon. "I'm not much of a man to throw my days away, but I recognize the need for a drink." He poured three neat shots and passed them around. "You guys can't go in with me, but let's drink to success. Brak, I know those cats mean a lot to you. I've thought about it, and I accept what you say."

"Cats, smats! I want my truck." Sam accepted the bourbon. He was about to clink his glass when he let out a yowl and jumped up and down on one leg.

Peter nudged Familiar away from the cowboy's feet. "Familiar takes it personally when you belittle felines." He glanced at Sam.

"Well, let me tell you something. Back when I was in my prime...yeow!" Sam jumped back from the counter. Right behind him, Familiar jumped forward, claws extended.

"Call him off! Call that black devil off of me!"

"Apologize, and he'll stop."

Sam danced around the kitchen. "Apologize to a cat? Yeow! He's biting my shins!"

"I'd say I'm sorry." Brak held out his drink.

"Dang it to hell and back. I'm sorry, you razor-tipped fleabag."

Familiar stopped and fixed Sam with a golden glare. His tail twitched three times.

"Fleabag is not acceptable, especially not from someone who has to be told to bathe," Brak said conversationally as he sipped his drink. "I'd change that apology to something like, 'I sincerely beg your forgiveness, you brilliant and handsome creature.'"

Peter gave Brak a hard stare. "You and Familiar seem to be on very intimate terms."

Brak pinched off a piece of pork and offered it to Familiar. "We've come to an understanding." Brak looked at Sam. "Apologize, or Familiar will start at your toes and work up to your ears."

Sam picked up his drink and downed the whole shot. "I'm sorry, your nibs. That'll have to do. Apologizing ain't part of the cowboy life."

ASHLEY CHECKED THE CLOCK in the coffee room. It was six-fifteen. Peter would be home by now, and Brak would be waiting for her. She could picture him, leaning against the counter with one hip. It was a delicious feeling, knowing he would be there. And she had news.

She stood and tossed her empty cup into the trash. "Thanks again, John. I seem to spend a lot of time thanking you for your help."

"My pleasure." He opened the door and she led the way into the corridor.

Ashley felt his fingers grasp her elbow and she turned to face him.

"If you need a friend to talk to, you can count on me. I know how to keep my mouth shut."

"That's terribly kind of you...."

"I know you're up to something, Ashley. I'm not asking questions because it must be something that could impact your job. I remember when you got in such trouble about that little girl. Even though you saved her life, when you brought her home with you, you broke the law and nearly lost your job."

"That's true. And it broke my heart to give her back."

"I'm not prying. I want you to know, if I can help, I will."

Ashley nodded. "There are things I wish I could tell you, John. Trust me. You're better off not knowing. If I told you, it would put you in the same position I'm in—caught between duty and justice." Though she spoke the truth, she didn't regret her choices. As tough as her position was, all she had to do was think of Brak, waiting for her to return, and she knew she'd chosen correctly. That was not to say she didn't have doubts. There were plenty. Despite the doubts, a trust had begun to grow between them.

"I don't really understand. All I'm saying is I'll help you as much as I can without asking any questions. That's the best friend I know how to be."

Ashley put her hand on his shoulder. "I couldn't ask for a better friend."

"I wanted more than friendship, but I can tell you're not

interested. We can still be friends, though. Sometimes, friends are even more important."

Ashley leaned forward and kissed John's cheek. "You are the best."

The squad room door opened and Len Lovett stepped into the corridor. His face lit up at the sight of John. "I just got the craziest report from San Antonio General."

"Shooting, stabbing, poison, what?"

"Clawing." Len looked from one to the other with an expression of satisfaction.

"Clawing?" Ashley didn't get it.

"Yeah, this tough guy is torn from one end to the other. He came in begging for a priest and cursing in Spanish about a panther."

"San Antonio General?" At Lovett's nod, Ashley continued. "Where was he picked up?"

"That's what was odd. He was dumped at the emergency room. When I say dumped, I mean dumped. A car wheeled up beside the ambulances, the door opened, and this guy was pushed out of the car. Then the car took off, tires screaming."

"Tag number?" Ashley asked.

"The orderlies out there were smoking cigarettes. They were so startled no one got the tag. I mean, this guy was soaked in blood. In fact, they thought he was almost dead."

"Is he going to live?"

Lovett shrugged. They've got him in OR, doing the needle-and-thread thing. I talked to the OR nurse, and she said he was shredded and lost a lot of blood. From what I could tell, he had the place turned upside down. He was yelling something about a devil cat that had gotten after him. The nurse said he was half wild, gibbering about a panther that had laid in wait for him for revenge." The cop shook his head. "He was weirded out."

"Did you actually talk to him?" Ashley asked, hoping for a casual tone.

"I looked at him. When he saw my uniform, he quit talking. Then they took him in to be stitched up. From what I could tell he was a long way from being dead. He was bloody but very much alive."

Ashley held out the photo of Johnny Ortega that had come over the wire. "Is this the man?"

"Well, I'll be damned," Lovett said, examining the photo. "That looks like him."

Ashley lowered her arm. "Johnny Ortega. I'm looking for him myself."

"On what charges?" Lovett was pulling a notepad out of his pocket.

"No charges. Not yet. But I'm more interested in his brother, Waymon. I think they were both involved in stealing the large cats."

"Pretty good guess, since he was torn to shreds by something big and mean and with claws."

"Did he say anything specific about where the cats might be?"

"Not from what the nurse could translate. He was off on that tear about how the cat was getting revenge. Naturally the medical staff was more concerned with stitching him together than listening to his half-baked stories." Len shrugged. "As soon as he's pieced back together, we'll get a location. Now I suppose our biggest worry is that one of those wild animals is free and roaming around San Antonio somewhere."

"Right. That's my concern, too. Thanks for your help, Len." Ashley shook his hand. She gave John a hug. "And thank you, too. One day..." She didn't finish. She turned and jogged out of the station house and sprinted the rest of the way to her car. She had to get home and talk to Brak. One of the cats was free—and in more danger than ever before.

Chapter Twelve

As soon as she was away from the station house Ashley pulled the cellular phone from her glove box and called the hospital emergency room. Johnny Ortega was in the emergency room, and would be for quite some time. The animal that attacked him had done a thorough job without inflicting mortal damage.

The nurse assured Ashley that the accident victim would be kept under observation for several hours. Ashley replaced the phone and aimed the car toward home. She was starting to reconsider. Should she tell Brak about the attack or not? It was obvious a wild cat had escaped, and Brak would assume it was one of his. The animal faced certain death. The SAS could not allow the wild creature to roam, possibly escaping the compound confines. Based on what Ashley knew of the type of people involved in SAS, they would not be setting up humane traps. They would track and kill the animal and be done with it. Brak was no fool. As soon as he knew an animal had escaped, he'd know the ultimate fate—unless someone intervened.

And that someone would no doubt be Brak.

It took twenty minutes to drive home, and she pulled into the driveway to a house that was well lit and welcoming. Laughter floated out the open windows to her as she walked around the house toward the patio. At the edge of the bricks, she halted beside a mass of dense four-o'clocks and looked toward the house. Brak, Peter and Sam stood in a semicircle, glasses lifted in the air.

"To successful hunting," Brak said.

They toasted and swallowed the amber liquor.

Watching their faces from the shadows, Ashley was shot through with sadness and fear. Once she stepped forward and gave her news, the night would be changed. The attack on Johnny Ortega would speed up the schedule. Would speed up Brak's departure and bring closer the danger that confronted all of them. One of them would have to get into the compound immediately in order to save the cat. Looking at Brak, she saw so clearly the qualities that drew her to him. Nothing would stop him from trying. She knew it as surely as she knew her name.

As the men laughed over some softly spoken joke, Familiar jumped to the table and stared directly at her. Ashley figured the cat could sense her, but none of the humans could. Very slowly Brak turned, following the direction of Familiar's gaze. His chin lifted a fraction as if he listened with extra sensitivity. His blue gaze moved slowly over the yard and finally stopped directly on her.

Ashley found that she held her breath as she watched him. For one extraordinary second it was as if she were hidden in a deep jungle and some exotic and untamable wild creature had happened into a clearing. When Brak's gaze found her in the darkness and the dense foliage of the shrub, a thrill coursed through her. Primitive. Savage. Completely sensual. They responded to each other without words or even looks. Her heart felt as if it would burst through her chest while her muscles felt liquid.

"Ashley," he called into the darkness. "Come join us."

His voice broke the spell, and with strict concentration she stepped away from the sweet-scented protection of the four-o'clocks and paused at the edge of the light thrown by the patio lanterns.

"How did you know I was there?" It was uncanny. Brak had *known* she was there.

"I just knew." Brak's tone held wonder. "I felt you." He touched his chest. "Here."

"Dinner's almost ready," Peter said as he took Sam's arm. "We'll take care of things inside."

Before Ashley could say a word, Peter picked up Familiar and hustled Sam into the house. She was left alone with Brak. When she met his gaze she felt the arc of awareness again, almost electric, almost a sensual touch. She inhaled sharply.

Brak closed the distance between them, pulling Ashley against him and holding her. "I've never had that experience before. Never felt that completely...in touch with a person. I felt you before I could see you, and I knew it was you. Without a doubt." His hands roved over her back, caressing and arousing.

Ashley reached up and captured his face between her hands. The slight stubble of his beard tingled her palms. The news she had to tell him was not good. Yet it would have to be told. But not at that moment. She could allow herself, and him, a small tidbit of time. When he'd looked out into the darkness and called her name, she'd felt something primitive. She'd seen it in him and she'd felt it in herself. One creature knowing another, recognizing something between them that went beyond the boundaries of civilized thought and socialized behavior. No words could express what she felt. She pulled his face down and stood on tiptoe to initiate the kiss that said what she did not know how to express with words.

Ashley gave herself to the kiss. She surrendered thought and control, allowing the passion she'd so carefully governed to rage through her. There were doubts about Brak, about the future. But there was no room for them now. There was only the moment, the feel of Brak's hard body pressed into hers, the pounding of the blood that seemed shared between them and the soft darkness of the night.

ASHLEY SURFACED from the kisses as if she'd been long underwater, swimming in a world that was exotic and wonderful and filled only with pleasure and need. Brak's ragged breath was in her ear, but beyond that was the silence of the evening. She had no idea how long she and Brak had been outside. She only knew that she would have given almost anything to continue the evening without the news she had to give Brak.

"Why are you so sad?"

Brak's question drew the shadow of a smile. "We should go inside. I need to talk with you and Peter."

Brak's fingers closed on her arm, and once again Ashley felt the rush of passion. Whatever it was between them, it was powerful. If only... If only the cats were safe and Brak wasn't wanted for questioning. If only Peter weren't getting ready to put himself in danger. If only people weren't cruel and greedy. She fell into step beside Brak, taking comfort from the brush of his hip against hers as they entered the house.

Ashley stopped in the doorway as she took in the table set with wineglasses and candles burning. A small bouquet of fresh flowers was set in the center of the linen tablecloth.

Sam appeared in the kitchen, coming from the hallway. He yelled into the den. "Come on, Peter. Let's eat. Everything's ready and the two lovebirds are in now." He turned his full attention to Ashley. "I couldn't really cook, so I went down the street and stole the flowers for you," he said. "Some ole lady got really pissed, too. Acted like the dang things were gold. I told her they were just gonna die sticking in the ground and at least you'd enjoy them."

Ashley joined the laughter. "They're lovely, Sam. I hope that old lady didn't follow you back here and find out where I live."

"She was chasing after me, but I gave her the slip. I've been trying to tell this stubborn brother of yours that I'm a dang good shot and a pretty good tracker, but he won't listen to a word I say."

"Peter has always had selective hearing," Ashley responded. "It smells wonderful." She took the chair that Brak held for her. It was going to be hard to sit through a meal. Her appetite was completely gone, but she helped herself to the food and tried to keep her gaze off Brak, who ate as if he tasted nothing and watched her.

When the plates had been cleared, Ashley could delay no longer. She checked her watch and saw that it was nearing ten. Time to go to the hospital. Time to make Johnny Ortega talk.

"Are you expecting a deadline?" Brak asked. "You keep looking at your watch."

"Johnny Ortega was attacked by a big cat this evening. He was brought into San-An General and dumped out of a car. He should be able to talk soon."

"One of the cats has escaped." Brak's face was a mask of coldness. "Which one? Was it one of mine?"

Ashley shook her head. "I don't know. We'll have to question him."

"It doesn't matter. One of those animals is loose. Out there somewhere in a land that is alien to her. Afraid. Alone." He stood up and faced Peter. "I have to go, and you have to tell me where this place is. There's no more time for games. They're hunting her now. She doesn't have a chance."

Sam snorted. "Don't go rushing off half cocked. You better take some protection, from that critter and from the other Ortega boy. Johnny's bad but Waymon's pure vicious."

Brak rounded on Ashley. "Why didn't you tell me sooner?" he demanded. "All of this time... She could be dead."

Ashley didn't comment on Brak's use of the feminine pronoun. He'd assumed it was one of his cats as she'd known he would. She'd also known Brak would take it hard, but she hadn't expected him to bolt up. "We have to talk to Ortega first. I didn't say anything before because he was in the emergency room getting sewn up. We can drive over and see if he'll talk." She had to keep Brak calm. "The more facts we have, the better our chances. Surely you can see that. Think, Brak, we don't even know where the compound is precisely."

Brak's blue gaze swiveled to Peter. "Yes we do." He waited.

Peter stood also. "The compound is this side of Kerrville. I know exactly where it is. I flew over it today and took some photos."

"Can we get those photographs?" Brak asked. A vein in his neck pulsed with tension.

"I'll check." Peter tossed his napkin down as he hurried to the phone in the kitchen. "Sam, want to take a ride with me to see if the photos are finished?"

"Sure thing." Sam glanced at Ashley and Brak. "Looks like they need to do a little talking, and something tells me I don't want to hear it." He strolled out the back door to wait for Peter to join him.

"What are you going to do?" Ashley asked. She'd never felt more helpless in her life, or more afraid. Brak was going into the compound. No matter what the risk. Just as she'd feared.

"I don't have a choice," he answered, unwilling to meet her gaze. "They're hunting the cat, and I'll hunt them. If I'm quick enough, and my aim is good enough, I'll get them before they get the cat."

"It might not be one of yours." She tried for reason.

He shook his head. "It doesn't matter. This one might not be mine. But the next one will be. Or the next. It ends now, Ashley. Now. And if these men demand it, it will end with their death.''

Ashley grasped his hand. ''You can't do that, Brak. It doesn't matter that what you want to do is right. It's still murder in the eyes of the law. This isn't stealing jewels. This is murder.'' Her hands slid up to grasp the heavy muscles of his arms. ''You can't do this. I know you can't. Give Peter and me some time and we'll come up with a better plan. There has to be another way. Talk to Ortega first.''

Brak listened to the panic in her voice more than to her words. She was afraid for him. Afraid of what might happen to him and afraid of what he would do to the SAS men. He was responsible for her fear and it tore at him. He fought back the fury that had taken hold of him and forced himself to think. Rushing into the compound might be the worst thing. For him and the animals there.

Ashley saw the dawn of reason in his eyes, and she took a deep breath of relief that came out as a trembly sigh. ''We can come up with a plan,'' she repeated. She rubbed her hands up and down his arms.

Brak's eyes intensified. ''If I can get into the compound, maybe I can communicate with the cat.''

It was the most frightening thing he could have said. ''This is an animal that's fighting for survival. This may not be one of your cats. It could be another. Or even if it is one of yours, there's no telling how frightened it is.'' Ashley couldn't help the fear in her voice.

''Whatever else you believe, Ashley, you have to know that those cats would not hurt me. That's what I've tried to tell Peter. I could be an asset. What I share with those creatures is unique. Special. Of all people, you should understand this.''

Ashley chose to deliberately ignore his softly spoken reminder of the moments that had passed between them not an hour before. ''You can't go rushing in there. The compound is enormous. First of all, it's dangerous. Second, you could waste precious time."

"Let's talk with this Ortega and then take a look at the photographs." Brak turned to the hallway. "Peter? Are the aerials ready?"

Peter entered the den, looking first at Ashley then Brak. "Penny said she's processing the film now. She realized how important it was so she decided to work late. She can't get prints, but she can get a contact sheet."

"That will be fine," Brak said. He clenched and unclenched his hands at his side. "How long?"

"Sam and I will ride over and get them. Maybe an hour."

"Why don't we go to the hospital and try to get Johnny to talk?" Ashley suggested. She knew she had to keep Brak busy. Johnny Ortega was a good place to start. "It should take us an hour or so. By then, Peter can have the contact sheets arranged so we can study them."

Brak's nod was curt. "Let's all get going."

"Right." Peter picked up his keys and waved as he stepped into the night.

"I don't trust those two," Sam said loudly enough for his words to drift back into the house. "Both of them think with the wrong muscle, their hearts instead of their heads."

"I don't think the brain is classified as a muscle," Peter said.

"Since when?"

ASHLEY PULLED INTO the emergency room parking lot, betting that Johnny Ortega, insuranceless and without identification or funds, would be parked somewhere along the halls of the overflowing emergency room. Since she wasn't questioning him in an official capacity, she could only hope she and Brak would stumble upon him and find a nook or closet where they might interview him alone.

They entered the emergency waiting room and were assaulted by the motion and noise of what appeared to be a human anthill in a moment of dire crisis. It seemed as if everyone in the room was up, moving, talking or crying.

"I'll check at the desk," she said, motioning Brak to a position against the wall where wheelchairs and stretchers could pass by him—and where he could look for Johnny. She'd shown him the photos she'd gotten from John Keifer. "Wait here," she cautioned him after a survey of the room showed her a question or two would certainly hasten their quest.

She approached the desk and held out her identification. After examining Ashley's badge, a harried nurse consulted a chart, then explained where the cat-claw victim had been taken.

"Thanks," Ashley told her.

Leaving the desk, Ashley motioned Brak to join her. "He's around here somewhere. When we find him, you do the bad-cop routine where you make him think you're going to break his neck."

"That would be my pleasure," Brak assured her.

Fifteen minutes later, Ashley found Johnny Ortega's stretcher in a hallway, complete with a unit of blood and glucose running into the prone occupant. The young man lying as still as death looked to be about twenty-three. As she stared at him, his eyes blinked open.

Ashley watched fear cloud his eyes, then slowly fade as he took in his surroundings.

"I'm in a hospital?"

"That's right."

"Are you a nurse?"

"No." Ashley showed her badge, knowing that in his weakened condition Johnny wouldn't be able to discern what branch of law enforcement she worked for, and it would be to her advantage. Johnny closed his eyes, and she called to him.

"I know you were attacked by a wild cat. I need some details."

"It was a bobcat, man," Johnny said, refusing to open his eyes. "A big bobcat. I think I must have shot him."

Ashley felt Brak's muscular body press against her, nudging her out of the way as he reached into the bed and grasped Johnny Ortega by the hospital gown.

"You *think* you shot the cat?" Brak said through clenched teeth as he clutched Ortega's shirt. "You think you shot her?"

"Hey, man, let me go." Johnny was frightened. His eyes, heavy-lidded with fatigue, were wide open and darting from Ashley to Brak.

"Brak." Ashley put her hand on his forearm, pushing down so that he released Johnny. "You can't do that out here in the hall," she said, looking left and right. "We can't abuse the suspect. At least not in public. Let's wheel him over into that storage room." She began pushing the wheeled stretcher.

"Hey, man, leave me alone," Johnny said. "I got my rights. I know about my rights."

"You've got the right to tell us what we want to know or I'm going to make that cat look like a stuffed toy," Brak warned him.

"I'll report you. I'll have your badge," Johnny said, looking left and right.

"Dead men don't carry tales," Brak said, putting a hand over Johnny's mouth to stifle any further protest.

Ashley exchanged a glance with Brak and almost couldn't hide her grin. She'd never allow harm to come to Ortega. But he didn't have to know that. For the most part she didn't agree with strong-arm tactics, but time was running out. And Brak didn't have any such compunctions. As they closed the door of the storage closet she and Brak had passed only a few moments before, Brak released Ortega.

"Now, Johnny, we know you were at San Antonio Safari

near Kerrville, and we also know that one of the cats has escaped.'' Brak's statements were rewarded with a look of panic from Johnny Ortega. ''We want to know which cat, where the others are being held, and if the escaped cat is injured.''

Johnny swallowed. ''I'm sick, man. I'm gonna be sick all over the place.''

Brak's hand was swift as he grasped Johnny's hair. ''It will be the last thing you do. Now, answer my questions and then you can be sick to your heart's content.''

''I don't know, man. Those cats seemed okay, until we got them to the compound. That was some trip and they were crying....''

''You stole these animals from a hotel in San Antonio, right?''

''Yeah, man, it was some cool plan. I never dreamed an animal could be worth that kind of money.'' Johnny's memory softened his face. ''I was gonna be rich, man.''

''What happened?'' Ashley pressed, aware that sooner or later someone would enter the supply closet and their chance of talking with Johnny would be over. Brak, too, was growing angrier by the second.

''Those cats went crazy. Once we unloaded the cages and had a look at what we'd gotten, it was like the fact that we were looking at them made them insane. Especially that black bitch. She'd stick that paw out and snatch at us, try to pull us right up against the cage where she could get us good. We were gonna teach her a lesson.''

Ashley wanted to put her hand over Johnny's mouth. She saw the effect his words had on Brak, and she knew a split second of panic. Johnny Ortega was playing with fire and he was too stupid to know it. ''Get on with it,'' she said, trying to avoid the details of any brutality. ''How did the cat escape?''

''Some maniac comes flying over in a plane. He's too close, coming in too low and making another pass. It got

Charles upset. He's the guy that runs the place, and he said the cats had to be moved." He shrugged. "Somehow, in moving the cages deeper into the trees, one of the hinges got damaged and the cat pushed it open and got out. Instead of running, she came right at us. She got me bad, man. She really hurt me."

Johnny started to moan softly, and Ashley saw Brak's hand reaching into the bed. "Brak!" Ashley stopped him before he could take physical action against Johnny. "We need more answers. Don't!" She shook Johnny's shoulder. "Who is Charles?"

"Charles Lawton. He started the hunt. Leased the property from a cousin of his who went bankrupt or something in the cattle business."

"Which cat escaped?" Brak asked again.

"The black one. The youngest, I think. Anyway, the one that was the maddest."

"Ayla," Brak whispered under his breath. He looked at Ashley. "I knew it. She's out there, lost. We have to find her."

"You find her, you put a bullet in her brain," Johnny said. "She tried to kill me."

Brak could no longer contain his fury. His large hand clasped around Johnny's throat. "I should squeeze the breath our of your miserable carcass right now," he said, tightening his fingers until Johnny's eyes bulged.

"Brak." Ashley brought her hand down in a karate chop across Brak's forearm, but it didn't phase the big blonde. "Brak!" She struck at him again. The explosive fury she'd sensed in Brak had come to the surface. She had to stop him. "Brak, let go! You can't choke him here. He's injured. Unarmed. What you're doing isn't any better than what they do to those helpless animals."

At last her words seemed to penetrate and Brak unclenched his fingers.

His gaze lifted from Ortega and connected with Ashley.

The shock of it was like a physical slap. She looked into the face of a ruthless stranger. She'd asked him to play the "bad cop," but this was no acting session.

"Don't worry," he said, his voice cold and controlled. "Of the men I've had to kill, none were helpless." He stepped back from the bed.

Johnny flopped weakly on the bed, his breath rasping into his bruised throat. "You crazy bastard, I'll get you...."

Brak's smile was hungry. "Any time, any day, any place. You come on. Nothing would give me greater pleasure."

Ashley forced her body forward, stepping between Brak and Johnny Ortega. "How many men work the compound?" She wanted to get the information she needed, and she wanted to clear out. Once she finished with Ortega, there were things she had to ask Brak.

Johnny's face twisted. "I'm not telling you anything else. That crazy fool tried to choke me. You two better get out of here before I get a nurse and press charges for police brutality." He rubbed his throat but his bravado had returned.

"Brak isn't an officer," Ashley said, her voice soft and casual. "And I'm not police. And the more I think about it, you'd be less trouble dead." She nodded to Brak. "Go ahead. I'll finish him." She didn't dare leave Brak alone with him.

"Wait!" Johnny reached for the sleeve of her shirt and clutched it. "Don't kill me."

"Why not? If you're dead, you can't make any trouble for us with the cops," Ashley said, smiling. She focused only on the job before her. Brak had stepped against the wall, and though she was acutely aware of him, she ignored him.

"I was only kidding about the cops, man. I wasn't gonna call no cops. Cops make me nervous. And I thought I'd tell you there are twelve people at the compound. Charles lives out there, with my brother Waymon and their girls. Then there are the day workers, the hunt leaders, those of us who take care of the animals.'' He looked from one to the other. ''Twelve, but they aren't all there all the time.''

''How are they armed?'' Brak's question was hard.

''They have some serious firepower. Man, they got big guns. I told them they should have brought that nosy plane down. Hell, none of this woulda happened if they'd listened to me.'' His voice was filled with hurt by the end of his statement.

''What type of guns?'' Brak insisted.

''M-16s, some of those safari rifle things that will bring down an elephant, everyone has a nine millimeter, in case an animal gets out of control—'' Johnny hesitated ''—maybe some bigger stuff. Charles didn't let the day workers inside the offices.''

''What type of water supply system?''

Johnny gave him a curious look. ''A well.''

''What about electricity? Do the fences run off generators?''

''Yeah, man, they got electricity *and* emergency generators by the office. They even got air. We had to live out in hundred-degree weather, but Charles and Waymon and the top dogs got to stay in the air. That didn't sit well with the rest of us.''

''I'm not interested in your whining. Is Charles gone often?'' Brak asked in a pleasant voice that did nothing to hide the ruthlessness beneath it.

''Yeah, man. I mean, no. I mean he's gone some. He has another business.''

''And what would that be?''

''He's, uh, into exotic animal renderings.''

''Ugh,'' Ashley said. ''Like rhino horns, that kind of thing.''

''Yeah, for those people who think powdered tiger tooth will make them more macho.'' He smirked. ''There's lots of money in it.''

Brak finally drew closer to the bed. The white-hot fury was gone, replaced by determination. "How does Mr. Lawton market his goods?"

"What do you mean?" Johnny's furrowed brow was a clear indication he didn't understand.

"Does he have a store on the compound?" Ashley interpreted.

"Hell, no, he mails them out. People order from a catalog. Charles has a building where he makes the stuff, then he mails it out. No one is allowed on the compound."

"Damn!" Brak turned away.

The sound of someone talking outside the storage room door made Ashley clutch Brak's sleeve. "We have to get out of here."

"Yeah, man, you'd better scram. They find out you got a patient in here terrorizing him, they're gonna be after you."

"If they find out anything about this, I'll be back." Brak walked to the side of the bed and leaned down so that his face was only inches from Johnny's. "I promise you, you don't want me to come looking for you. Now, you take my advice. You heal, and you find some other means of employment. You clear out of this part of the country, and if anyone asks, you stick to your story about a wild bobcat. If I ever hear of you working with people who slaughter helpless animals, I will hunt you down, and what I do to you would make cannibals look like good neighbors. Do you understand?"

Ashley stood transfixed. Brak's face had lost every shred of civility. The threat he made to Johnny was cold, ruthless, that of a wild animal engaged in survival. Capable of anything...

"Of the men I've had to kill..." The phrase was branded in her mind. She'd known he was a thief, but not a killer.

Johnny reached toward Ashley, dragging her out of the

terror of her own thoughts. "Don't let him come after me," he begged.

"Don't give him a reason to," Ashley said matter-of-factly. "Don't give either of us a reason to regret letting you live." She turned away before Brak could see the harsh doubts that had entered her mind.

Chapter Thirteen

The humanoids have scattered like leaves in the wind. I'm sure they'll dredge up something useful. As usual, though, the creative thinking is up to me. It's very strange, but I was debating between another taste of that delicious pork tenderloin and a nap when I had this surge of mental acuity. Not a hunch, and not a nudge. Not even an insight. More like a flash.

In my many years as a private investigator, I've never experienced such a thing. It was as if someone had torn a page out of a magazine and thrust it before my eyes. Such sharp detail. So clear. In my mind's eye I saw a tiny vial. Glass, cylindrical, filled with a dark brown powder. A hand is reaching for the vial. A man's hand. The skin is sun-roughened, and the nails clean, manicured, even. The hand touches the vial with great care, as if it contained some very rare substance. Something with the power to kill or cure.

I have no idea where this image came from, but as a world-class detective, I've learned to trust my instincts. And all the bells and whistles in my brain are going off.

What could a vial have to do with our case? Poison? I can't seem to make that angle work at all. Medicine? Perhaps some sedative they're using on the wild animals?

The trouble with a flash is that it doesn't come with in-

structions. This flash, in particular, is even more troubling. Since it feels as if it were implanted in my brain from an external source. In the past, I've occasionally been able to trigger a reaction in one of the lower life-forms, such as dogs and humans. But I've never had one sent to me. I'm not so sure I like the idea that my thought processes are being invaded. Unless, of course, it comes from Ayla. And I know beyond a shadow of a doubt that if one of those cats got loose, it's Ayla.

I can't think about that now. I have to concentrate on a small vial filled with some dark powder. There's no other clue in the picture. I can't see the location or even the room. Maybe a little walk around would stimulate my brain. Now's the perfect opportunity to scope out the rest of the house.

Ashley has made a point of leaving the door to her private boudoir shut tight as a clam. It's that nasty compulsion of hers to avoid a bit of cat fluff. Too bad for her Cowpoke Sam isn't so fastidious. I now have access to the inner sanctum, and I must say our little sister has a taste for the sumptuous. The younger Curry may act like a cop, but she sleeps like something from the heyday of Hollywood.

The bed hangings are an exceptionally nice touch. I wonder where she found that golden shade of material. Very gossamer, as if spun by fairies. I'd say that bed would be the perfect place for a late-morning nap. Just enough sunlight, filtered through that golden fabric, to give a kitty the sweetest of dreams.

The faux fur by the side of the bed is perfect for bare tootsies. Looks like sheepskin, feels like sheepskin, washes like the acrylic that it is. So nice to see what's being done with fake fur these days. And no living creature has to sacrifice its skin.

Speaking of skin, not to be too gruesome, but I wonder what happens to the rest of those wild animals after the hunter has taken the trophy head? I can't imagine that those cunning killers would miss an opportunity to capitalize on furs, hides and other medicinal supplies.

I saw a television show on hokey cures. Eleanor is obsessed with making sure that Jordan watches educational shows. Some of them are a real snooze, but there are some terrific ones. Wolves in the wild, the Civil War, an amazing accomplishment for the race of bipeds. On the other hand, how that purple dinosaur can be considered anything but a trigger for mass dementia, I'll never understand. I mean, really. He sings, he shuffles, he never changes facial expressions. But little Jordan worships him. I wouldn't dare tell The Dame, but I do believe Barney *was the first word Jordan uttered. She will watch him for hours on end, clapping, dancing, singing, as if she'd been programmed by a cult.*

If, and that's a mighty big if, some genius had to create a fantasy figure for the toddler set, why couldn't they have worked with a truly admirable specimen? Such as a cat. Preferably a handsome black cat. That would be something a kid could truly enjoy and aspire to. Think of it this way—if dinosaurs are so smart, how come they're extinct? Cats, on the other hand, are survivors. I might even go so far as to point out that we thrive.

Back to that show on exotic cures. The program made the lovely Eleanor furious. It seems a peculiar human trait that when some species, whether it's reptilian or fuzzy, comes close to near extinction, Neanderthals begin to believe that eating it will invest them with youth and virility. Some of the potions humans were paying huge prices for were completely ridiculous. Concoctions of hooves, horns and powdered privates...oh, my!

I think I've just had another big flash. Vials of nasty-looking powdered substances. High prices. There's a connection here. I know it.

And look what's tucked away in this cozy little windowed nook in Ashley's room—a computer. Ashley's personal PC.

I'd forgotten she had one because she's always running down to the station to get someone to help her hook up to the "crime network." I wonder what I might find about wild animals and their uses.

Let's see. Here's the switch. There's the menu screen. How sweet, she hasn't got her mouse hooked up. That's fine with me. To be truthful, the keyboard is easier for me. What code word would Ashley use. How about Acurry? *That was too easy. I'll have to recommend a harder access word for her in the future. Any amateur hacker could sneak in here.*

Now all I have to do is hit that button, and this one, and there's the Web. Hang on, we're going to travel at high speeds now, all the way to exotic cures.

PETER'S CAR WAS at the house. Brak felt a surge of adrenaline. They were back with the photos. Now, with the information he and Ashley had pulled from Johnny Ortega, they could begin to make plans.

He glanced at Ashley as she pulled into the driveway and killed the car's engine. The lights of the dash made her seem too pale, too remote, almost as if she was hewn from the pale driftwood that sometimes washed in from the North Sea. For a moment he felt as distant from Ashley as he did from his homeland. As she unbuckled the seat belt he reached across and touched her hand.

"Ashley?" She'd been strangely quiet on the trip back from the hospital. Johnny Ortega had given them plenty to think about.

"Let's see what Peter's learned." She slid from his light grasp without even looking at him.

Brak held the door for her but she brushed by him.

"Maybe the photos will give us some ideas," she said as they stepped into the den. Peter's glum expression halted them both.

"The pictures didn't turn out?" Brak asked.

"They did. It's just that Eleanor forwarded a call to me. It was on the answering machine when we got back." Peter's jaw tightened and his hands formed fists at his side. "Not surprisingly, my hunt has been canceled. They said not to call back. There's been 'an emergency.' They'll be back in touch with me." He slapped the wall lightly but with enough force to make a resounding thud. "My whole plan is shot. I tried to call SAS, but no one is answering the phone."

Brak looked at Ashley, ready to tell Peter of the backup plan she'd initiated with the local gun dealer. For the first time since leaving the hospital, Ashley made eye contact with him. Her expression was veiled, but she shook her head slightly, then dropped her gaze. He could easily read her cue, and he didn't mention that she was set for a hunt. Besides, if SAS wouldn't let Peter in, they certainly wouldn't allow a woman on the premises when a wild animal was loose. At least he could hope that was true.

"Is Familiar with you?" Peter asked. "I haven't seen him since we ate dinner."

"No. He has to be in the house," Brak answered, moving down the hallway toward Ashley's room. He opened the door, which was not completely closed, and saw the multihued flash of a computer screen.

"Why, that little monster," Ashley said, breathless with exasperation. "He's somehow managed to turn on my PC."

Brak's hand stopped her. "Wait," he said.

Even as he spoke, Familiar slapped a button on the keyboard and the small printer began to whir.

Brak walked forward and lifted the sheet from the printer. For a moment he read, then his jaw relaxed and a smile transformed his face. "I think this is living proof that great minds think alike," he said, looking over the page at Ashley, Peter and Sam. "I don't know how that cat thought of this. We must be on the same wavelength." Brak gave the feline a questioning look. Familiar returned the stare, blinking once, as if to concede.

"What's he done this time?" Peter asked.

Brak handed the printed material to Peter. "At the hospital, Ashley and I discovered that the owner of SAS is also involved with exotic animal ingredients for fake health cures." He nodded at Peter's disgusted expression. "I know, but it may be my route into the compound. Familiar has discovered the catalog for the company, and there are several items that involve thousands of dollars. If I pose as an international buyer—" he couldn't hold back the hope in his voice "—I have my ticket inside."

"Not so fast," Peter said, easing the sheet from Brak's hand. "I think it would be best for me to go in. Brak, you're forgetting that you're still a liability. What if they recognize you as the owner of the cats? They could kill them all. And you, as well."

Brak recognized the truth in Peter's words, but he immediately rejected it. "I've been known to master more than one disguise. I have a background that suits me for this type of work."

"And you have a face that no one would ever forget," Ashley reminded him. "What exactly is your background?"

The question stopped everyone. Brak felt the attention turn to him. He shrugged. "With some hair dye, some scissors, I can change my appearance."

"But not your accent," Peter pointed out. "You might get inside, but it could cost the cats their lives. Are you willing to risk that?"

"Damn!" Brak clenched his jaw.

"Why don't we just go in with guns blazing?" Sam asked from his post by the doorway. "Seems to me a little firepower would do more good for those boys than trying to trick 'em."

"I'd like nothing better than to blow them to pieces,"

Brak said. "Unfortunately, if we rush them, they'll kill the animals."

"Going in as a medicine buyer is a great idea, Brak." Peter put his hand on the man's shoulder. "It's one I can use. And I can promise you I'll do everything in my power to save all of the animals there."

"But you're one man, and there are at least twelve people on that compound." The indisputable facts only intensified Brak's frustration. "You can't manage it alone."

Peter found a tablet and a pen. "Ortega told you twelve?" At Brak's and Ashley's nods, he continued writing. "It's tricky, and I'm going to have to change my plan, but...let's study those maps and see what we can come up with."

Brak bent down to scoop Familiar into his arms. "You're one intelligent cat," he whispered into Familiar's ear. "One very smart feline."

"Meow." Familiar licked his cheek.

Brak nuzzled the cat's head with his chin. He lifted his gaze to Ashley and saw once again that strange look that swiftly passed when she became aware of his scrutiny. He registered a new distance from her. "Ashley?" This was something they had to confront.

"Excuse me a moment." Ashley sidestepped the men and went over to the computer.

"Look at this, Brak. I don't know how that cat managed to get this information," Peter said, following his sister. "Familiar's gotten onto the Internet. He's always hanging around the computer at home when Eleanor or I use it, but I never dreamed he was really paying attention."

"That danged critter is possessed," Sam said, lingering in the doorway and giving Familiar a squint-eyed look. "It's against the laws of nature."

Brak sighed. "Not hardly, Sam. Cats are very bright. They just normally don't display their intelligence in ways that humans consider smart. They don't like to be measured."

"Yeah, right. They're shy geniuses."

"In a manner of speaking."

"Familiar *is* exceptional," Peter agreed. "Now, let's study those photos."

"Go ahead and get started. I'll be there in a minute and put on some coffee. I'm going to unhook from the Internet. No telling where Familiar might decide to roam next." She busied herself at the screen. "Peter, I suggest you get one of those locking devices for your computer at home. We wouldn't want Familiar caught up in some information highway high jinks."

The three men, Familiar still in Brak's arms, headed for the den to scatter out the photos as Ashley turned off the computer and pulled the plug from the wall. When she was alone in her room she softly closed the door and leaned against it. The tears were silent, and after a moment she brushed them away and forced a look of composure on her face. Opening the door, she returned to the den.

THE PHOTOS SPREAD on the floor of the den were a blur of browns and greens. At first glance, Ashley felt as if she were looking at badly focused nothingness. As she knelt with the others and began to examine them, though, she saw where Peter had done an exceptionally thorough job.

"How many times did you go over that compound?" she asked, remembering what Johnny Ortega had said. Peter, most likely, had spurred the decision to move the cats deeper into the wooded area.

"Three times. We had to quit, because even though Penny was doing some stunts and trying to make it look as if we were larking around, I could see ground movement. I think they got suspicious."

"I think you got lucky," Ashley said. "According to Ortega, they could have blown you out of the sky."

"They have a lot of weapons?" Peter's question showed all of his concerns.

"More than they'll need to stop us." Ashley was suddenly overwhelmed with anxiety. "There's no way we're going to get in there and take those men—and women—prisoner." Not if Brak is armed, she almost added. She felt him staring at her and once again busied herself shifting photos around. He knew something was wrong with her. He was too acutely attuned to her emotions and feelings not to know. Before she confronted him, she had to think it through.

"Women are on that compound?" Sam asked. "What kind of woman would live in a place like that?"

"Stupid women," Ashley answered. "Nonetheless, they're there, and we need to remember it."

"Great," Peter said. "One more complication."

"Okay." Brak took control of the conversation, turning it from defeat to action. "Here's the road in. It looks as if there's only one. That works to our advantage. Peter, if you go in, then someone can take the sound van to this road and pick them off as they come out."

"Ashley?" Peter looked at her.

She drew a breath. Now was the time to confess her own skewered plans. "I've met a local contact for SAS."

"What?" Peter and Sam said in unison.

"You are the foolishest woman," Sam grumped. "I've never met a female so hell-bent on getting herself shot up."

"I wasn't going to let you go in alone. So I made a contact. I've paid money down." She'd somehow managed to block that little detail from her memory. Her savings and every penny Brak had in the States.

"You can forget that plan." Peter was adamant.

"No, listen. The people at SAS would never suspect some bimbo who's trying to out-trophy her husband, and that's the way I played it. I've made arrangements to get inside. Brak could man the sound equipment with Sam."

It still wasn't enough manpower, but it was the best she could think of. "Peter, if they buy into your medicinal-seller story and you get inside, you could insist on seeing the animals, sort of a quality check. I'll be there. We could coordinate our rush." She had a burst of inspiration. "Then use the sound equipment to notify Sam and Brak to contact the authorities. They could come barreling in. We'd have the element of surprise—"

"And what about Ayla?" Brak interrupted. "If I could get inside, I know I could communicate with her. You remember how she responds to me. You've seen it. *I* could convince her to remain calm, to let us capture her. I'm the only one who has a chance of saving her."

"Ayla listened to you under optimum circumstances," Peter reminded him. "That was before she was tormented and frightened by humans. You can't count on that link still being there. Not with Ayla, and not with the other cats."

"She'll listen. All of them will." Brak dared anyone to contradict him. "If I can get to the cages, I'll let the others free. They can help us round up the thugs who run that place."

Ashley saw the stubbornness on Brak's face and knew it was foolish to argue the point with him.

"Think about what you're saying, Brak. If any of those animals should kill a human, they'll have to be destroyed." Peter spoke with great compassion but a voice of iron.

"Over my dead body," Brak answered.

Ashley grasped the back of the sofa as if she'd been struck a blow. The tension spiked through the room and was broken only when Familiar went to Brak and gently bit his shin.

"Easy, boy," Brak said, managing to convey regret in his tone of voice. He looked around the room, lingering on Ashley, who would not meet his gaze. "I'm sorry," he said. "That outburst was irresponsible. Of course I wouldn't free the cats."

Peter looked down at the photos, giving Brak a moment to recover from his anger. "Here's the main compound. The cages are somewhere in these oaks."

"How far from the entrance?" Sam asked.

"Maybe three miles," Peter estimated.

"Then, we have to have a vehicle of some type. Or horses," Sam said. He, too, kept his attention focused on the photos. "With a panther loose, I don't suppose horses are such a good idea. Mighty spooky when they smell a big predator around. Likely break my scrawny old neck, and I've lived too long and come too far to end my days upside down on the dirt, neck broken and some African jungle cat gnawing on my backside."

Sam took a breath. "Why, I remember back when I was a sprout, there were dangerous wildcats all over the Texas range. A friend of mine even told me he seen a saber-toothed tiger. Ole Christian was something of an exaggerator, though, so I never really believed him about the saber-tooth. Never you mind, though, because there were plenty of fearsome wild beasts roaming the Texas range, and when they couldn't hornswoggle a heifer, they were content to chomp down on a tough old cowboy. Why..."

For once Ashley was relieved that Sam had focused the conversation on himself. Ever since Brak's outburst in the hospital, she'd been tormented by doubts. His loyalty to the animals was unquestionable. Maybe even noble. He felt responsible for their safety and care, which was only right. But how far would he go? There was a fine line that couldn't be crossed between justice and revenge, between enforcing the law and persecuting a community, between loyalty and fanaticism. Watching Brak with Johnny Ortega, she'd seen his raw fury, his capacity to push to the limit—and possibly beyond.

She'd pushed that line once, when she'd pulled Maria

out of a hell-hole existence in a Mexican border town. She'd technically kidnapped the little girl. She'd been on the edge of forging citizenship papers, but she hadn't been able to force herself into an illegal act. Not even to save the child.

What was Brak truly capable of? She knew so little about him. What she did know wasn't comforting. A man wanted for questioning in a major jewelry heist. A man who admitted killing other men. A man she hadn't pushed for answers to the questions that were now eating away at her. A man who had unnerved her with his fury—and his passion.

"Ashley," Peter said, waving his hands to get their attention. "Think about this. Sam and I have a plan."

Before he could speak, Familiar sauntered into the center of the photos. With a delicate paw he nudged aside several pictures, revealing one that had been on the bottom.

Everyone leaned forward for a closer look.

"What's so special about this one?" Sam asked. "That cat's trying to pretend to be smarter than us."

"Wait a minute." Brak picked up the photo. "Ayla!" He exclaimed softly. He held the photo down for the others to see. "Look just beside that black Jeep. A shadow that doesn't exactly match the vehicle."

"It's the cat!" Ashley said, seeing it first. "She's stretched out there as if she were taking a nap in the shade."

Brak bent closer to the picture. "Thank God she's not injured. She looks perfectly fine." He hesitated. "But she's not napping." He turned to Peter. "Look closer. See the way she holds her head? She's watching. Completely relaxed, but watching. Something, or someone, has her attention."

"She looks like she's about to go to sleep to me," Sam interjected.

"Trust me, Sam, she's nowhere close to sleep. She's stalking."

"She's right up close to the main buildings," Peter said, unable to completely hide the worry in his voice.

Brak sat back on his heels. He looked around the room until he had everyone's attention. "I know you've given me good reason not to go into the compound. I've listened. Now I'm telling you that I'm going in. Ayla is uninjured and so far no human has been mortally wounded. Johnny Ortega won't be around to press charges against Ayla. At this moment, nothing I care about has been irretrievably lost." He let his gaze fall on Ashley. "I'm going in. Tonight."

Ashley finally locked gazes with Brak. For several seconds, they stared at each other. Finally Ashley broke the silence. "I have one question, Brak. What if she's reverted back? If she is wild and she goes after you, or Peter, or even one of the SAS men, are you going to be able to do the responsible thing?"

Brak's face was expressionless. "Ayla won't hurt me." He took a calming breath. "You've put your trust in me about my past, Ashley. Now you have to trust me about my cats. Ayla will not harm me. And I won't allow her to harm anyone else."

"I hope you're telling the truth." Ashley pointed across the room. "Peter's life may hang on your actions."

"Doubt is a treacherous emotion," Brak answered. "If you don't eradicate it, it'll eat you alive." He looked down at the photos. "Now all I have to do is figure out how to get past the perimeter. They'll be out there hunting Ayla. I'm sure the border of the compound will be closely guarded."

Peter spoke first. "Sam, do you think you can learn the sound equipment?"

"I never believed it when they said you couldn't teach

an old dog new tricks. If that cat can run a computer, I'll be damned if I can't spin a tape recorder."

"Good." Peter turned to Brak and gave him an assessing look. "I'll make the necessary arrangements with the SAS and I'll take you in as my assistant. We'll come up with some type of disguise. But you have to promise to do exactly what I tell you."

"No." Ashley stood up. "I don't like this." She had no intention of putting her brother's life in the hands of a man she didn't completely trust.

"Could I have a word with you alone?" Brak motioned her toward the patio.

Chapter Fourteen

So, Johnny Ortega was talking about animal ingredients just about the time I had my flash. I know that biped brains work in a series of visuals and symbols, sort of like sophisticated cave drawings, if you will, so it must have been Blond Bruiser who sent me the flash about the medicine vial. I've been able to "send" messages to him. This is an interesting development. The two of us will make a real team, although I have no intention of strapping a big sheet onto my back and jumping out of an airplane. Cats may always land on their feet, but in this instance I have two more legs than Blond Bruiser to break. And I prefer not to ruffle my kitty fur in the wind. No, I'll find a method of ground travel. That old cowboy won't be hard to fool at all.

I'm a bit worried about our dashing animal tamer jumping into that compound in the middle of the night, just as worried as I am, on occasion, by the mental connection we seem to share. Ayla might not injure him, but the humanoids running that place will shoot first and ask questions later. Also, I'm not sure that Ayla will give him the greeting he expects. From what I've overheard, she's been abused and terrorized. Not exactly the milk of human kindness showered on her head. That has a way of affecting a kitty. I remember back when that evil scientist had me in his clutches. He acted as if I didn't feel any pain simply because I was a cat. I could have done damage to him without any qualms. Ayla might be in the same position.

I know this handful of humans well enough to know that common sense won't prevail. Their course of action is set, and the wheels are turning. Right now, Blond Bruiser isn't thinking about danger. Neither is Peter's little sister. Blond Bruiser appears to be dragging her out onto the patio for a few moments of privacy. There's a definite knot in this relationship. Miss Law and Order is acting like she's going to her doom, and BB is almost carrying her out the door. Dr. Dolittle is giving them a speculative look. Cowpoke Sam is doing his best to pretend he doesn't know what's going on. Funny how humans react to the magic of attraction. Cowpoke Sam is embarrassed, and Peter is wondering what his role as older brother requires of him.

I know the answer to that—nothing. Whatever is going on between Ashley and Blond Bruiser needs no interference from Peter. If the lovebirds need help, I'll take care of it.

Cats are far more complex in their range of emotions, but we are more direct in our actions. Take me and Clotilde, that gorgeous calico kitty. When we first saw each other, we knew. She was an upscale kitty and I was a garbagemonger at the time, but we knew we couldn't thwart destiny. And my alley cat pals knew it, too. One look at Clotilde, and they grudgingly accepted that I'd been lassoed and culled from the herd. How's that for Texas lingo? I'm afraid Cowpoke Sam is rubbing off on me. Anyway, I'd better get a few breaths of fresh air, too. Just to keep an ear on what Blond Bruiser and Ashley may be plotting.

"NOW THAT YOU'VE GOT ME out here, what is it that must be said?" Ashley slipped from Brak's light grasp and stepped to the edge of the patio.

"I want to know what's wrong. Your feelings for me have changed."

Ashley turned to face him, the light from the patio catching in her angry brown eyes. "That's pretty direct for a man with a secret past who admits, in a moment of fury, to having killed men."

Brak stood perfectly still. "I see."

"What exactly do you see?" Ashley felt the doubt and worry and fear rise up in her. "Do you see that I put my trust in you? You said there was an explanation for this jewel business, and I trusted you. I took you at your word. I let you into my home and I let you into my life." The more she talked, the angrier she became. Brak's complete lack of expression only infuriated her more. "My brother's life could be in your hands when he goes into that compound tomorrow. It's finally occurred to me that I don't really know a damn thing about you except that your touch is like a drug." She found that she was near tears. "I want some answers and I want them now."

Brak's eyes narrowed but he made no other movement. "Your life, too, will be in danger," he finally said. "Don't think that I haven't considered this. I can only hope that the guards at the gate do their job properly and detain you."

The absolute calm in his tone was like a jolt of electricity. Ashley stepped across the patio intent on doing physical damage to him.

"Easy," he said, catching her shoulders before she could swing. "I owe you some answers and I'll give you what I can."

"I want the truth," she said. She tried to twist free of his hands, but he only tightened his grip.

"Give me a chance," he said. "It's complicated. There are things I can't reveal." He took a breath. "Let me ask you a question first. In your work as a law officer have you ever had to use your gun?"

The question startled Ashley, but the answer was there, always right at the back of her mind. "Once." She didn't like to think about it, and she certainly didn't like to talk about it.

"You shot someone?"

"Yes." She twisted away, but he held her.

"To keep someone from breaking the law?"

"No, dammit! To keep someone from shooting my partner," she said, her anger growing with each syllable. "This is none of your business, Brak. This is just a means of avoiding what you don't want to tell me. I'm not the one who stood up in a hospital and bragged about shooting men. I realized then that I didn't have a clue as to who you were and that you were capable of anything." She was panting when she'd finished, and she found herself confronting the calm of a man patiently waiting.

"So you used your weapon to protect your partner?" he asked.

"I am not going to answer another of your questions." She jerked. "Let me go before I..."

"This is between us, Ashley. We can finish it now, or I'll go if that's what you want. One or the other. We talk or I'll leave. I know enough to get into the compound, and I can find Ayla. Together we'll do the best we can to save the others, and ourselves."

His tone told her that he meant business.

"Now, tell me what happened with your partner."

This was a memory she never liked to relive. "We stopped a truck that an informant had told us was transporting illegal aliens." She remembered the day clearly. She shrugged. "They were gunrunners. When we pulled them over, one of them grabbed my partner and held a gun to his head." She remembered the fear on Adam's face, the realization that he was going to die. "The gunrunners were wild, crazy, capable of anything." She met Brak's gaze. "I shot the one holding Adam, then I wounded the other one." As the last word was spoken, her anger evaporated. "I acted without thought. My training kicked in, and I did what I had to do."

Brak gently eased his arms around her. "I know," he said softly. "I do know. The men that I killed had kidnapped my brother. By the time I got there, it was too late, though. He was dead, but I didn't know it. It's a complicated story—one that involves the past and an obligation my family had to honor."

"I'm sorry, Brák." She meant it. "I'm so sorry." Beneath his shirt she could hear his heart thudding. "When you said you'd killed..."

"I know." He kissed the top of her head. "I was so angry. I wanted to kill Ortega, but I wouldn't have."

"I looked at you and I had this terrible thought that you were capable of anything. That I'd put so much trust in you and I didn't really know you at all."

"I guess the thing that I've learned is that given the right circumstances, we're all capable of anything." Brak lifted her face so that he could see her. "Even great love. I do love you, Ashley."

"Brak, I was so afraid that I'd given my heart to someone who would only break it." She shook her head, half smiling. "It was a little late to worry about your character since I'd already fallen for you."

"A little late," he agreed, kissing her forehead. "But not too late." He drew her closer. "I only wish we'd discovered each other under other circumstances."

Brak's arms around her felt right. Perfect, in fact. Nothing had ever felt more right.

"Ashley?"

They both looked up to find Peter standing in the patio door.

"Sam and I are going to the sound van to check out the equipment." He looked at his watch. "We, uh, we'll be back early in the morning."

Still tucked against Brak, she gave her brother a half-bashful smile. "Thanks, Peter."

"Do you think Sam will have any trouble with the equipment?" Brak asked.

"For all of his grumbling, Sam's a smart old coot. He'll catch on right away. And we need him."

"I know. We need all the help we can muster," Ashley said.

"You two try to get some rest." Peter closed the door, then killed the outside lights so that Brak and Ashley were alone, wrapped in the privacy of the night.

Ashley watched her brother leave and felt Brak's arms tighten around her.

"Why don't they drive the van here, to the house?" Brak asked.

"I think it's my brother's way of leaving us alone for a little while." Emotion swelled in her chest once again. It seemed whenever she put her heart on the line, fate stepped in to endanger the person she loved. First Maria. Now Brak. In both cases there wasn't a single thing she could do to protect either of them.

"How about a glass of wine?"

"We've got a rough day ahead of us tomorrow. I don't think alcohol is such a good idea."

"One glass." He led her into the house and poured them both a glass of merlot. Standing at the kitchen counter, he cradled her so that she leaned against him, his arms crossing lightly over her chest. Bending low, he spoke softly in her ear. "There's so many things I need to tell you. So many things I want to say."

"I have more questions." She thought about his past, the jewels, his brother's death. It all seemed less important, since the future was so uncertain. "I'll get my answers when this is all over."

"Should anything happen to me, promise that you'll contact my brother, Erik. He'll answer your questions. And he'll take care of everything else.''

''Brak, please don't...'' She turned to face him, unashamed of the tears that eased down her face.

Brak used his thumb to brush them away. ''You've put so much trust in me.'' His smile was rueful. ''I never understood how important trust was until I began working with the cats. I learned that trust is the only thing that truly matters. Have you ever wondered why you trusted me? Right at first, I mean.''

''I've asked myself that question.'' Ashley put her untouched glass on the counter and placed both hands on his chest. ''Now I feel your heart beating beneath my palm. For some crazy reason, that's enough.''

''When I first saw you, I knew you would be the one. I have to be honest and tell you that I didn't anticipate falling in love with you. But I knew you would believe me. Your heart would understand.''

''I understand here—'' she touched her chest ''—but when I think about things, I get frightened. At first Peter thought you were a con man.'' She felt his arms tighten around her, drawing her against the solid comfort of his chest. ''I was so very drawn to you, yet I wasn't sure, especially when I learned you were wanted for questioning in all the major cities of Europe.''

''But you didn't turn me away.'' He bent and kissed her cheek, his lips trailing lightly across her skin, tasting the saltiness of her tears. ''When you let me into your home on a pledge that I would turn myself in, you reminded me of some wild creature taking the first step toward trust.''

Ashley felt the tide of emotion that threatened to overwhelm her with the bittersweet sadness of knowing that sometime in the past several days she'd given her heart to this man. Given it without any holding back. Not a shred of wisdom or common sense protected her. ''Brak, promise me that you'll come back to me," she said, trying to hold herself together.

"I promise you that I'll do everything in my power. And you must stay safe, too."

"Brak..." She buried her face against the cotton of his shirt. She felt his fingers lift her face, and she opened her eyes to find his clear blue gaze willing strength into her.

"We can spend the next few hours in tears and sorrow, or we can spend them in joy and pleasure."

His hand slipped beneath her hair, stroking her emotionally charged body. Everywhere his fingers touched, Ashley felt a tingle of need and longing. She lifted her lips to his, wanting only to claim him for the moment, to hold him as close as possible for the short time they had left.

Instead of safety, his lips ignited other emotions, other needs. She couldn't stop herself from melting against him, molding herself to his body. His lips held hers, claiming her and devouring her until she could no longer tell for certain which heartbeat she felt, his or hers. He was there, in her blood, pounding through her racing heart.

She forced herself back from him. Without a word she took his hand and led him down the hallway to her room. Once inside, she closed the door and locked it.

There was no talk, no need for words as they undressed each other, their clothes falling to the floor in a careless heap. Skin to skin, Ashley knew the meaning of how a heart could be branded. No matter what happened in the future, Brak had left his mark on her. He had claimed her heart while yielding his own.

As his hands moved over her body, she cast aside thought and gave herself to sensation, to the man who had tamed her heart.

DRESSED IN BLACK JEANS and a turtleneck, Brak stood beside Ashley's bed. The golden glow of the lamp passed through the gossamer material that draped the four-poster bed, making her look like an enchanted princess. "Sleep," he whispered, pulling the sheet over her silken shoulder. Leaving her was the hardest thing he'd ever done. The thing that in all of his deeds would be the hardest to explain to her. And the most necessary.

He had to get into the compound first. As soon as he knew Ayla was uninjured and on the prowl, he knew he had to find her—before she found whoever she was looking for. In the photos Peter had taken, she'd been nothing more than a small black spot, a shadow. But he knew her, and he recognized her behavior. She was hunting with a skill she'd never shown before. Her life had never been in danger until now, and Ayla had resorted to all of her predatory wiles to survive.

Brak could not risk losing Ashley or Peter in the compound. He had to get in before them, and he had thought of a way. There was a possibility that Ashley would never forgive him. He'd come close to losing her trust already. By leaving, he risked another breach of her faith. One that might be irreparable. But he'd rather have her alive and angry at him than trusting and dead. Or guilty because something tragic had happened to Peter. Brak was all too familiar with guilt.

He hovered over the bed for another moment, tempted to risk a light brush of his lips across her perfect skin. Without touching her, he eased away, the lamp still burning the way it had when she'd finally fallen asleep.

He picked up the notepad and pen she'd used earlier, and began to write.

> I had to get to Ayla before she could hurt anyone. Follow the plan—and stay safely at the gate. I'll look out for Peter.
>
> Love, Brak.

He propped the note where she would be sure to find it.

It was two o'clock, and in spite of the clouds, the moon shined a pale white sliver in the darkness as he left the house, his arms loaded with weapons. He started down the street on foot, then glanced at the sky and felt a boost of his spirits. It was cloudy. That would work in his favor.

When he was five blocks away, he spotted a car parked along the curb. It took him less than thirty seconds to work the lock and another twenty to get it started. Lucky for him Peter had left the envelope with Penny King's address on the coffee table. Peter had not said a lot about the young pilot, but from what he did say, Brak hoped he could count on her as an ally. If she wasn't willing to pilot the plane so he could take the jump, he didn't know how else he could get inside the compound.

When he was on the outskirts of San Antonio, Brak placed the call to the young pilot, who answered in a groggy voice. As soon as she heard who he was and what he wanted, she snapped awake. Within a matter of minutes, the arrangements were made and Brak was headed toward the airfield to meet her. Penny had asked only pertinent questions, proving as Peter had said that she was no dummy. Most important, she had offered the assistance of her brother and several of his friends.

"Before you turn them down, know that the men I'm talking about are former marines. You might need some help, and what SAS has been doing is abominable to them," she'd said. "It never hurts to have backup."

When he arrived at the small airstrip, Penny was ready.

"I've got five guys who want to help. What should I tell them?"

Brak decided he liked the spunky young woman. "As soon as you get back, call Peter. He'll tell them what to do."

"Does Dr. Curtain, I mean Curry, know you're about to jump blind into a compound filled with thugs and wild animals?" Penny looked him over as if she might report him.

"No, and you aren't going to tell him until it's an accomplished fact. Some of those animals are mine. They're my responsibility."

Penny nodded. "Let's go, then. I want to get back and make some calls. You seem to know what you're doing."

THE NIGHT WHIRRED like a black void outside the door of the plane. Brak had coordinated the jump time with Penny, and now all he had to do was keep an eye on the watch he'd borrowed from the pilot.

As the appointed time arrived, he moved to the door, feeling the pull of the air. At the exact minute, he leapt into the night, feeling the rush of atmosphere and gravity propel his body toward earth. With just enough time to clear the airplane, he pulled his chute and felt the reassuring tug of the folds opening and catching the air. After the initial jolt, his descent became smooth and easy. The black silk parachute was undetectable in the night sky, and Brak hit the ground, rolled and gathered up the material, restuffing it in the pack and hurrying toward what seemed to be trees in the distance.

He was in. Now he had to concentrate on finding Ayla.

A soft rustling to his right made him halt. It was too noisy to be Ayla, but it might be one of the SAS men. The gun in his hand gave him some sense of security, but he didn't want to kill anyone. And he didn't want to shoot. Gunfire would draw all the others to him, and he wanted to find Ayla. Once he found the panther, the smartest tactic would be to hide until Peter arrived and Ashley began her frontal assault. But could he really find the panther, locate the other cages and stay hidden long enough?

The hair at his nape bristled as he heard the soft shuffling sound again. There were all types of animals in the compound, none as dangerous as the men, but plenty that could kill him. He'd given Ashley his word that he would take care, and he intended to follow through. For a brief second he allowed himself the luxury of recalling the hours they'd shared together. *Intense* did not begin to describe them. He'd never known such pleasure, such passion, such...the noise came again and he halted, ears straining. When the body burst out of the brush, speeding past him, he was ready. The gazelle was terrified, and Brak held perfectly still. Imported herd animals. More fodder for the guns of the hunters.

He eased into the trees and put aside his anger, focusing his energy on Ayla. He called to her, using his mind to send the message that he was near. If she responded, all the better. He didn't have long.

From the photos Peter had taken, he determined that he was in the belt of trees that ran through the center of the compound. It was the logical place for Ayla to go, which meant the hunters might be there also. But he was counting on the fact that the SAS men were basically cowards. They wouldn't go into the woods at night, chasing a healthy panther who had retained her claws and teeth.

Ayla. He projected his thoughts to her, sending her an image of where he was. *Ayla.*

It seemed that hours ticked away, but he knew it was only minutes. Nothing in the woods moved. The leaves shivered in a gentle breeze, but Brak listened closely. Was it the wind, or someone, or something?

Ayla. He thought of her as a young cub, rambling over his house, playing with him with an unexpected gentleness for an animal that, even at a few months old, could have killed him. *Ayla.*

He felt her before he saw her. She was waiting beneath the overhanging limbs of a tree. He could sense her heart beating rapidly. He could feel her newfound distrust for him because he was human; it was warring with her memories of the past.

Ayla. He waited, thinking only of her, feeling the panic fight with the need for the haven he'd once offered. *Ayla.* He thought only of her name.

The big cat eased forward slowly, tail flicking, alert to any betrayal he might offer. Brak stood, wondering if a sudden movement in the woods by another animal might trigger her to jump and maul him. His life, his future, came down to one issue—trust. After the abuse she'd received, after what she could only view as abandonment by him, would Ayla be able to remember the bond they had once shared and respond to him?

He felt her nose against his palm, but he made no effort to touch her. She had to come to him. All the way. Without any encouragement. When he felt her body against his leg, the sheer weight of her nearly knocking him down, he finally exhaled the breath he'd been holding. His hand found the place beneath her left ear where she loved to be scratched. Her response was a lick of his other hand with a tongue so rough it felt as if she were punishing him.

"Ayla," he whispered, kneeling down and running his hands over her body. She was painfully thin, and he could tell by the way her skin pulled and didn't retract that she was also dehydrated. Too afraid to go for water, which told him instantly where the hunters had set up their kill zones. At water. All animals, even those smart enough to know it was a death trap, would eventually have to go there. It would be a shooting gallery with little risk to those with the guns.

Until now.

Brak pulled the panther to him and held her. "We have a chance," he told her. "Together, we have a chance. But we have to be smarter than they are. And you have to trust me."

Ayla nuzzled against him, pushing her massive head roughly against his chest. Brak ran his hands over her a second time, making certain she hadn't been wounded.

When he was as sure as he could be in the darkness that she wasn't injured, he picked up his weapons and together they moved deeper into the woods. Hunting with his feet, he found a depression in the ground and knelt to make sure it was in solid rocks. He poured the contents of his canteen into the depression and listened with satisfaction to the sounds of Ayla drinking.

One problem solved. And that's how they would take it, one problem at a time. Now they would find a place to rest.

Later, when dawn began to seep over the eastern horizon, Brak eased away from a tree trunk and stretched, careful not to disturb the cat, who slept with her head in his lap. He could tell by the rhythmic movement of her chest that she was exhausted. She probably hadn't slept since she'd been taken. The other cats would be in similar condition. A surge of sudden fury made Brak tense, and Ayla awoke, so keenly aware of his emotions that she growled before she even sensed danger.

"Easy," he said, stroking her sleek hide. "Time to get busy."

He'd come up with an idea. Bold. Perhaps slightly crazy, but the best he could think of. If he and Ayla could get into the area where the primary buildings were clustered, that would be the one place no one would look for her. While they were there, they could also go through a few files. It might be interesting to Peter and the Friends of Animals to discover who the clients of the SAS were. Though no legal action could be taken against the patrons of canned hunts, there were other methods. Brak grinned. If he got out of this scrape, he might even consider volunteering as an FOA agent—one who paid a visit on "hunters."

ASHLEY STRETCHED and blinked, reaching out automatically for Brak. She had no desire to wake him, just a longing to run her hands over his skin, to make a small contact that would reassure her that this night had not been a dream.

To her surprise, the bed was empty, the sheets cool. She opened her eyes and blinked against the unexpected light spilling from the lamp beside the bed. They'd left it on...she remembered. Even at the thought she felt a slight flush. Once they'd begun to make love, they lost all shyness. The memory of his body, sculpted by the lamplight, was something she'd never forget.

But where was he? And who was scratching at the bedroom door? She sat up, pulling the sheet over her as the sound of gentle scratching came again.

"Brak?" She spoke his name softly. Where could he have gone? Easing out of the bed, she pulled the sheet with her and used it as a toga.

Her gaze fell on the note propped beside the lamp, and her heart plunged. She knew before she read it that he was gone. He'd gone into the compound. "No," she whispered, dropping the pad back on the bedside table. "No." He'd gone in alone, without any help.

Every inch of her body suffered the loss of him. Never, in all of her life, had she experienced anything like she'd felt with Brak. They had joined together with a perfection that seemed as if it had been created in a fantasy. But it had been real. Brak had felt it, too. And he had told her it was because their hearts beat in rhythm. Smiling down at her, he had said their bodies moved with a single heartbeat.

And she had thought she would die of happiness.

Now he was gone.

Her first impulse was to go after him, but she quickly realized it was impossible. She didn't even know how he planned to get inside the compound. He had gone to bed with her and then sneaked away in the middle of the night, knowing how it would hurt her.

The bitter emotion that was taking root in her heart was

betrayal. She recognized it and knew the anger that came with it. Brak had tricked her.

He'd deceived her.

Even as she thought it, she remembered their conversation of only a few hours earlier. He'd cautioned her against doubt. Doubt and distrust—of him. Still holding the sheet to her chest, she struggled against her negative emotions. She'd given herself to this man, body and soul. Could she afford to doubt him? Yes, he'd left her, but why? Because he was trying to keep her safe. Her and Peter. And the animals.

If he abandoned his cats to their fate simply to prevent hurting her, their love would begin on the suffering of innocent creatures. Not the foundation she wanted. Not one he could ever live with.

The soft scratching at the door came again, this time followed by an insistent meow. Slowly she got up and opened it. Familiar stood there, staring up at her, something golden winking in his mouth.

"Come on in," she said to the cat. If she and Brak had any future together, it would include felines. Many a good bit larger than Familiar. It was time she learned something of the nature of cats.

As Familiar jumped into the bed, the wink of gold caught her attention again.

"Familiar?" She went to him, puzzled by the way he sat, the gold chain dangling from his mouth. "What is that?" she asked, reaching over to pick up the shimmering chain. As soon as she touched it, Familiar let it go. A pendant swung on the chain, glinting in the lamplight.

"What in the world?" Ashley examined the strange-looking emblem. It looked something like a Celtic cross, with two dolphins leaping out of foaming waves jumping the crossbars of the cross. The gold was finely crafted, and the detail well done. She held the metal and knew that it was Brak's. She turned to Familiar. "The question is, did he give you this, or did you take it?"

"Meow. Meow."

"I take it you pilfered it."

"Meow."

Ashley clutched the emblem in her hand. "I can't believe I'm standing in my bedroom having a conversation with a cat. I know I'm losing my mind, as well as my heart."

"Meow." Familiar blinked twice and offered his chin for a scratch.

Ashley sat down beside the cat. "So Brak is gone and this is probably his lucky piece." Ashley opened her palm and looked at it again. It wasn't just a piece of jewelry. To her knowledge, Brak had never worn any jewelry. Now that she thought about it, not even a watch. And he'd not been wearing the chain. So why did he carry it?

The cat curled against her side, purring softly. She absently stroked him as she stared at the golden emblem. Brak wasn't the kind of man who wore jewelry. He was, essentially, a man who needed no adornment.

She traced her fingers through Familiar's fur, drawing a strange comfort from the purring black cat. Slowly, she eased down in the bed beside Familiar and waited for the final hours of the night to fade beneath the first rays of the sun.

Chapter Fifteen

Ashely cupped her hands around the hot coffee and let the steam rise to her face. For a moment, she closed her eyes and Brak seemed so near she expected to feel his touch on her back. The sensation was quickly followed by an ache and then fear for his safety.

When the phone rang, she started, spilling the hot liquid all over. She picked up the receiver, surprised by the young female voice. The woman launched into details of Brak's parachute jump into the compound and ended with the fact that five brawny men were available, awaiting directions.

Ashley assimilated the new facts on a surge of hope. With more men, the odds would be better for them. Then she remembered that Brak was in the compound alone. And additional manpower might only make matters worse for him.

"Have them wait half a mile from the gate," Ashley told Penny. "And thanks. Do you know if Brak landed safely?"

"Too dark to tell."

"What time did he go in?"

"Two-thirty, three. He knew what he was doing. I wouldn't worry about that one," Penny said. "I'll see you shortly."

Ashley replaced the phone. It was amazing how people

rallied to help endangered animals. Truly amazing. Penny. Her brother and his friends. Sam. Even herself.

She sipped the coffee and tried to keep her thoughts from spinning in an endless circle. Brak was in the compound. Had been for hours. There was no way to check up on him, no way to know if he'd made the jump safely or if he was injured—a leg or arm broken—waiting for help. Or maybe he'd been captured. Or shot. Or both captured and shot. The possibilities were endless and the outcome always the same, cause for worry.

She forced her eyes open and looked out through the patio door. Dawn was breaking over San Antonio. The few moments of curling with Familiar on the bed had given her a sense of peace. It was as if the cat had transmitted hope to her. And confidence that Brak was a man with honed skills and high intelligence. But with the dawn had come reality—he was one against many.

"Ashley, are you okay?"

Peter had entered the house and the kitchen, and she'd been so absorbed in her own thoughts that she'd failed to hear him. "I'm fine. Brak skipped out and caught a ride with your young pilot. He parachuted into the compound several hours ago."

She felt her brother's hand on her shoulder, gentle but firm support. "I knew he was going to try something. I can't blame him, Ashley. I hope you don't. There was little else he could do."

Peter's words didn't help, but they did confirm what she'd been thinking. "I know. It's just that I'm worried sick."

"Brak's going to be okay. Somehow, we're going to pull this off. Without injury to anyone."

"Not even the bad guys?" She tried for a lighthearted note and gave Peter a smile. "I think I'm just exhausted. I don't mind telling you this has been an emotional roller coaster."

"I've given it some thought, and I believe Brak is a good man at heart. I don't know the circumstances of his past, but I was wrong about his attachment to those cats. They are a part of Brak. It's hard to admit, but I'm a little jealous. Even Familiar seems to have some connection with him that I can't fathom. And I thought I was the one with a talent for communicating with animals."

"Have a cup of coffee and sit a minute," Ashley said, smiling as her brother complied. "I don't know what it is about Brak and those cats, but I accept it." One corner of her mouth quirked in a smile. "I don't think I have a choice. Brak and his charges are together. A package deal."

"Maybe that's not bad. A man who can win the trust of a wild creature is surely something special."

"What about the jewels?" Because Peter had not said a word about them, Ashley wondered what direction his thinking had taken.

Peter gave a shrug, imitating the one Ashley had earlier given him. "I put my faith in the fact that there's a good story behind those accusations. I'm perfectly willing to wait and see."

Ashley gave her brother the first real smile of the morning. Some people weren't capable of changing their opinion of a person. Peter wasn't like that. He'd seen things in Brak's character that had given him reason to like and respect the animal tamer. She sighed, looking over her shoulder. The house was too quiet. "Where's Sam?"

"Down the street practicing with the sound equipment. He's caught on fast, and he's determined to do this right. He's a real character, though. I considered using some of the duct tape I had in the toolbox on his mouth."

"Thank goodness he isn't involved in the stealth side of this operation. I don't think he could help but talk if he was caught by the enemy." Ashley grinned. "We could use him to torture *our* captives. He can talk to them."

They shared a laugh together, and finally Ashley

broached the subject they could no longer avoid. "Wha
are we going to do? By parachuting into the compound
Brak has radically changed all of our plans. We were se
to go for Saturday. If we're going to help him, we have tc
do it today."

"I've been thinking." Peter picked up Ashley's hand anc
gave it a squeeze. "I know the SAS holds the hunts or
Saturday, but if I can get in on the pretext of buying medicinal products, it would be a big help if you could create
a distraction at the main gate."

Ashley's eyes widened. "I think I know exactly what tc
do." She stood up. "I'll go see old Zeke and tell him I
have to do my hunt today. He'll freak out when he realizes
I'm going there without him. He'll call to warn them, anc
I can put on a big show at the gate."

"Perfect." Peter grinned. "With any luck, they'll senc
several guards up to the gate just to quiet you down. That'l
clear the way for me and Brak to look for the cats."

"It's a plan," Ashley agreed. "And Sam will be coming
in the sound van with the reinforcements." She rose. "I'c
better get after Zeke. The sooner we get started, the quicker
we can help Brak."

"You be careful." Peter took in her outfit, checking ou
the worn cowboy boots that came to her knees, the sage-
colored jeans and the sand-colored long-sleeved shirt she'c
chosen. "You look the part."

"Work clothes," she said. "When we have a hunt along
the border." She patted beneath her left arm, feeling the
weapon she'd strapped on. She would carry a hunting rifle
but she wanted her pistol, too. At close range, it migh
prove invaluable. "What are you going to do?"

"Put on my most expensive slacks and safari jacket, improve my Boston accent, and set about buying exotic medicines for the northeastern market at prices these guys won'
be able to ignore. Naturally, I'll want to see their supplies
and processing facilities to make sure the products I'm buy

ing are genuine and pure. Sam will handle the sound equipment and the volunteers. You'll be at the front gate, and you said Penny has arranged to meet us about a half mile from the main gate."

"Remember to give specific directions into the mike." She couldn't help being worried.

"Will do. And don't you dare come in unless I give the word."

Ashley looked down at her boots.

"Is that clear? You could endanger both Brak and me if you rush in there."

"Okay," she agreed.

"Are you sure you can get Zeke to call the compound?"

"I believe you can count on me for that." She put the coffee cup down and stood. "I'll be on my way."

"It's still early." Peter rose also, stuffing his hands in the pockets of his jeans. "I'm ready to get going, too."

"Please be careful, Peter. Eleanor would never forgive me if I let anything happen to you." Ashley took the two steps to her brother and hugged him. "There's a little part of me that keeps saying none of this is really happening."

"It shouldn't be. It wouldn't be if we had proper laws."

"That's what you and the FOA are working on so hard to change. And it will change. It's just a slow process." She kissed his cheek. "We'll all be back here for an early dinner." She gave him her best smile before she walked through the house and out the front door. It was only when she reached her car and got inside that she leaned against the steering wheel and bit her lip to keep from crying.

PETER LOOKS DASHING in his safari attire. The cane lends the perfect professorial attitude, and a bit of the British fop, which translates into a very phony personae—just the type who would be selling dried tiger parts as a libido booster. That theory goes back to the old "you are what you eat" concept. If that were the case, Americans would look more like greasy burgers and fries than humans. An entertaining thought, at best. It's amazing to me that folks won't consider that clogged arteries and fifty pounds of extra weight around their middle might tend to make the old libido a little tired. Nope, they want to sprinkle a magic powder on their greasy cheeseburger and knock ten years off their life.

As a fully grown cat, I tend to eat foods that are, shall we say, on the high caloric end. Salmon in cream sauce, prawns in butter sauce, you get the picture. But with the superior feline metabolism, I don't have to worry about such things. There's also the fact that felines run, jump, climb, roll and rock. My personal theory, and you heard it here first, is that felines expend a greater amount of energy for brain function than any other species. It only goes to show—our brains are superior, therefore they require more fuel to function. That is how we eat so well, sleep so long and retain our handsome physique. Maybe I shouldn't say this out loud or some maniac will determine that eating cat brains will make him smarter! Jeez, that's a scary thought.

Anyway, Peter is gone and Cowpoke Sam is hauling supplies out to the van. So far he's taken bedding, water, foodstuffs, hey, hey, a man after my own heart, and now he's looking around to see what he's missed. This is my chance. Peter warned me sternly to stay in the house and behave. He should know me better than that after all these years. But before I go, I need to tend to a few little errands that everyone else has overlooked.

I've been listening to the talk about manpower at the SAS compound. The odds aren't exactly in our favor, not even with the ex-marines that female pilot has lined up for fall-back forces. So, I have a little plan up my sleeve. It's risky. But I think it'll work.

Let me get a few of those photos that Peter and Blond Bruiser marked up. If I'm not mistaken, they labeled some of the buildings. And there's Penny's business card that gives her name and number, and, finally, there's John Keifer's telephone number and name from the pad beside Ashley's phone. All I have to do is leave this stuff on the front steps—after Cowpoke Sam heads out. There he goes. Now, let me drop my bundle and dash back inside to knock the telephone receiver off the hook and dial 911.

Time to scram. Sam's almost ready to roll, and I've got to get in that van before he closes the door.

"Yee-ooowww!"

That got his attention, and he's rolling down the window to speak to me. One fancy, flying kitty leap and I'm in his lap. Ah, mission accomplished.

"DANG YOU, CAT, PETER will skin me alive if I take you along."

Sam managed to get his hands on the black cat, but when he tried to lift Familiar from the seat, the cat dug in with all four paws. Sam tugged and Familiar stuck like a burr.

"You sharp-clawed hunk of ornery fur." Sam released the cat and glared at him.

Familiar gave back an unblinking golden stare.

"You better get out of this van. There's no telling what's going to happen today, and I can't be worried about you." Sam opened the door and pointed to the ground. "Scat, cat! Before I get a bat."

My word, the old fool thinks he's a rapper. Well, he's the crusty sort, but he's no match for me. I happen to know he's on a deadline and he has to put this vehicle in motion soon, or he'll be behind schedule and in a mess.

Sam made one final attempt to wrest Familiar from the upholstery. When the cat held firm, he slammed the door, rolled up the window and started the van. "Peter will be on me like white on rice, and it's your fault. But I'm not waiting any longer. If you get out on the compound, they'll make kitty stew out of you, and I'll bet Peter will be the only one crying." Sam kept up a constant grumble as he headed out of San Antonio and west toward the town of Kerrville.

BRAK WAITED UNTIL the sun was fully above the horizon. At last he could see the terrain in which he'd landed. He bent to touch Ayla's head, telling her to wait, to be patient. As she gazed across the distance, her tail flicked rapidly. She sensed a human approaching. Someone she didn't like. Her senses were so much keener than his own, though he'd trained and sharpened his. Using the bond he'd shared with Ayla, he tried to sense what she did, but the events of the past few days seemed to have eroded the closeness they'd once shared. Ayla, like so many other creatures, had shut down her ability to make contact with the human race. Well, Brak had no time to waste on bitter thoughts of what was lost. He had to concentrate on what could be gained—Ayla's life, as well as his, Peter's, and that of the other animals on the compound. Perhaps, with time, Ayla would learn to trust him fully again.

"Let's go, girl," he whispered. Together, they moved across the open yard and stopped in the long shadow cast by the building Peter and Brak had targeted as headquarters. It would be the perfect place to hide Ayla. And maybe to find her some food. Once the cat was safely taken care of, Brak had some scores to settle. Hopefully before Peter and Ashley arrived and put themselves in danger.

As he skirted the outside of the building, he could find no sign of life inside. No vehicles, no sounds or movements. So far, the building appeared empty.

The door was locked, and Brak held back a curse as he kicked it open. The heavy wood, set solidly in adobe walls, didn't want to give. But three good kicks and he was inside, Ayla slipping through the door as if she were more spirit than three-hundred-pound cat. Moving stealthily, she paced down the hallway, pausing before a closed door.

"A little rat?" Brak asked her, kicking the door with such force that it was blasted from its hinges.

"Don't hurt me. Please, don't hurt me." A woman cowered in the corner. Her long blond hair was tousled and her mascara slightly smeared. She took one long look at Ayla, shrieked and fell into a faint.

There wasn't time to waste. Brak jerked the cords from the blinds at the window and with rapid motions bound her arms and legs. One woman accounted for, one to go.

He motioned the cat into the room. "Watch her, Ayla." He'd discovered long ago that the cats were more inclined to obey if they had something to occupy themselves with. He considered gagging the woman, then decided against it. Ayla would take care of it.

The panther settled back on her haunches, eyes glittering.

Chapter Sixteen

Peter waved at the guards at the compound gate. It was much as he expected. High-voltage electric fencing. Enough to keep all but the most determined range creatures inside. And to deter all but the most determined invaders. Charles Lawton had gone to great expense. Obviously, he intended to make SAS a retirement plan. Peter finally braked when one guard pulled out what looked like a bazooka. The SAS workforce was well equipped. The men looked fit and well trained. This was going to be a challenge. As he looked over the area, he accepted the fact that though Brak had gone in against his wishes, he would be the ace in the hole. The thought of success was swiftly followed by an assessment of the cost—at the top of the list was his sister's heart. Ashley was head over heels in love with the animal tamer. As a guard leaned down to speak to Peter, he put aside his speculations and focused on the task at hand.

"Buddy, you better have a good excuse for cruising in here like that." The lean man with close-cropped hair held a gun at Peter's head as he spoke.

"I'm Dr. Craig Peterson, renowned healer and I'm here to see Charles Lawton. Very private, very important, very lucrative business. I'm a buyer for a major...medicinal distributor with a large order to fill."

The guard punched his radio and spoke briefly, the crackling voice coming back so that Peter could hear his approval to proceed.

"We have a wildcat loose on the premises. Remain in your car until someone appears to walk you inside."

"Oh, how exciting," Peter said in a Boston accent. "This will surely be something to convey to my associates over cocktails when next we meet."

The guard gave him a disgusted look and waved him on. Peter drove down the road, taking in as much detail as he could and talking into the wireless microphone he wore so that Sam could relay the information. The SAS had sophisticated radio contact, presumably throughout the compound. That would prove to be a problem. And the men were trained and fit, not a bunch of bubbas with high-powered guns. Both facts were against the success of their mission.

As instructed, Peter waited in the Land Rover he'd rented until another heavily armed man came to escort him to the door.

"Seen anything of the escaped animal?" Peter asked.

"My men will find her." The man kept his attention trained on the horizon, his gaze shifting to anything that moved.

Peter nodded grimly, though he felt a surge of hope. Brak had not been discovered. While the guard at the gate might not have been aware of Brak or his capture, this man was a leader. He would surely have known. "Pesky animals. If only they'd understand that they're on this planet to serve our needs," Peter said, clucking his tongue in what he knew to be an annoying fashion.

"Inside," the guard barked, clearly conveying that he didn't have time for affected fops.

Peter sauntered into a brown adobe building, the smallest of several in a hard-packed area. After the brilliance of the morning sun, the shadowy interior was a cool surprise.

"Your visit is rather inconvenient." A tall, elegantly dressed man stepped out of the shadows. He wore riding breeches, a tweed coat with patches on the elbows, and the black, stovepipe boots of a horseman.

Peter took in the man who could be none other than Charles Lawton. "Dressed for the hunt, are we?" Peter couldn't resist.

"My men will kill her. Then we can get on with business as usual. This...untimely delay is costing me money." He pointed toward two leather chairs that were separated by a small table. A silver coffee service was already in place on the table with two china cups.

"How elegant," Peter cooed. "I had to rush out without breakfast, I'm afraid. The coffee will be wonderful. This trip has upset my schedule, too. It seems my former supplier has left me in rather a bad place. I've orders to fill and nothing to fill them with."

"My office manager, Elise, should be here." Charles gave an annoyed glance out the window. "She knows how I despise lateness," he muttered.

"After a cup of coffee, I'd love to see your stockroom. The handling of the ingredients is so important in my medicines. Some disreputable dealers have been known to substitute such interesting things as tree bark, powdered pecan shells, that sort of thing. You can understand why I insisted on seeing your operation for myself. After all, my reputation rests on the quality of my medicinal ingredients."

"Of course." Charles could barely grit out the words as he poured coffee.

Peter lowered his face to hide his smile. He'd adopted the perfect disguise—one that would grate on Charles Lawton's nerves like fingernails on a chalkboard.

"Is this milk or cream?" Peter asked, examining the silver cream pitcher as if it might contain snake venom. "The butterfat in cream is a wonderful stimulant to the, ah, pancreas. I don't know if you're aware of the fact that daily stimulation of the pancreas can do wonderful things for your lower colon.'' Peter sniffed the cream. ''I suppose this will do. So many people are reluctant to discuss the colon. But those of us in the field of medicine find it a fascinating subject. If you have any difficulties with yours, I'd love to help.'' He looked with arched brows at Charles.

''No, thank you,'' Charles said stiffly. ''Really, Doctor, let's get on with the tour. I have a busy morning.''

''May I finish my coffee?'' Peter asked in a sour voice. ''I fear I've displeased you. I do find that those with irritable bowel syndrome are often annoyed by a discussion of it. I can recommend some medicines that would improve your nature.''

''My nature is not up for discussion.'' Charles stood. ''If you want the ingredients, I suggest that you come with me.''

''Ah, that faint color beneath your skin. Perhaps your arteries could stand a good flushing. I find that just a pinch of dried toad combined with about a quarter-teaspoon of dried earthworm is very good for cleansing the arteries.'' Peter daintily sipped his coffee. ''This is delicious. What type of bean do you use?''

Just as Charles reached the point of complete exasperation, Peter heard the crackle of a radio in the adjoining room. In a moment, a worried man of Spanish descent came into the room. Black jeans were tucked into cowboy boots, exaggerating the man's swagger.

''Charles, there's a woman at the gate demanding entrance. She says you have her *de niro.*'' He slipped into Spanish.

''I'm going to kill Zeke,'' Charles said sharply. ''Everyone has done nothing but bungle things for the past week.'' He glared at Peter. ''I'm going to have to ask you to leave. Perhaps we can take care of your business tomorrow. Today is simply not possible.''

''But I've come such a long way....'' Peter held the cup

halfway to his mouth. "I don't think that would be wise, Mr. Lawton. In a briefcase in my car is well over three hundred thousand dollars, cash. I need those ingredients, and I want them today. If you turn me away, I won't be buying from you in the future."

The Spanish man stepped forward, hand extended. "I'll be glad to show the doctor our supply room. I am Waymon Ortega. It's a pleasure to have such a distinguished man of medicine here. I think you'll be pleased with our setup. The ingredients we sell are very pure. They come from our own supply of animals and are processed here under strict supervision. And, of course, you can hunt, as well. Those who deal with our imported goods can never be assured of such high quality."

"This isn't exactly a business regulated by the FDA," Peter pointed out archly. "I have nothing but your word on this matter." He gave Charles Lawton a cold look. "Perhaps I should reconsider my order. I've never before been treated like an intrusion."

"Forgive my partner," Waymon said smoothly. "He is agitated. There is this potential female client..." He gave a one-shouldered shrug that implied volumes before he glared at Charles.

"Yes, do forgive me," Charles muttered. "Waymon, if you'll see to the good doctor, I'll take care of the problem at the gate."

"Take two of the men with you," Waymon said. "Make sure our visitor leaves promptly. Return her deposit, promise her we'll make the necessary restitution. We do not allow any of our customers to feel disenchanted with us." He smiled at Peter.

"Right." Charles narrowed his eyes.

Peter started to detain Charles but let him go. If it was Ashley, he could only hope she'd leave here unscathed. Apparently Waymon Ortega was the brains behind the business. At least he was acting the part.

Giving Waymon a wide smile, Peter followed him out into the morning. "Any signs of that dreadful beast that escaped?" he asked, pretending to control a shudder.

"Not yet. She'll have to come out for water. And soon." Waymon didn't pause as he walked rapidly toward the largest of the buildings.

"This panther has great heart. Perhaps I might be interested in various ingredients...."

In the shadow of the large sand-colored building, Waymon turned to Peter. "How did you know it was a panther?" His dark eyes held suspicion and concern.

"Mr. Lawton mentioned it, or perhaps one of the guards. Is there a problem?" Peter feigned surprise.

"Maybe. Maybe not." Waymon stepped closer to Peter. "I'd like to see your money before we proceed any further."

"I'd like to see the supplies first."

Waymon turned to call out, but Peter was quicker. With deadly accuracy he delivered a blow to the man's neck, crumpling him like a sack of stone.

"Excellent," he muttered to himself. "Now I've got to do something with the body." He checked the doorway of the building where he stood, but the metal door was securely locked. Half dragging, half carrying, he moved the unconscious Waymon to the next building. To his surprise, the door had already been knocked from its hinges. He froze, listening for anything inside. When he heard nothing, he dragged Waymon in and closed the door.

Cautiously, he walked down the hall, stopped by the sight of a long black tail flicking out of a doorway. "Ayla," he whispered, not daring to move. The sight of the unrestrained cat scared him, but it also gave his heart a boost. Somehow, she'd managed to survive.

The cat's head appeared. She made no move to come closer.

"Easy, girl," Peter said. It was too late to run. If the cat wanted him, she'd have him. Still, he didn't want to do anything to trigger her.

The irony of leaving Waymon in the building with the very animal he intended to destroy struck Peter with a force that made him laugh out loud. From a nearby desk he jerked a telephone cord and used it to bind Waymon's feet and hands. He pulled the handkerchief from his pocket for a gag and set it in place with mailing tape he found in a drawer.

Easing down the hallway, he looked into the office where Ayla had been and met the frightened eyes of a pretty blonde.

"Thank goodness you've come," she said, craning her neck to search for the cat. "Kill that black bitch and get me out of here."

"Wrong side," Peter said. "If I hear a peep out of you, I'll let Ayla have you for a chew toy. Now, sit quietly and behave." He grinned at her and gave a thumbs-up sign before he left Ayla to watch both prisoners.

Just outside the doorway, he punched his shoulder where a small black radio was pinned. "Waymon is out cold. Ayla is safe and in one of the main buildings. I haven't seen Brak, but I'm going out now to look for him." He couldn't help the elation in his voice. By his count, two SAS members were down and several more were three miles away at the gate with Ashley. Things were working out better than he'd anticipated.

ASHLEY AIMED THE CAR at the gate and revved the engine. "I'm getting my money," she told the guard. "You shoot me and my husband will be all over you. He'll have your heads hanging from his wall. You don't know who you're messing with."

The guards looked around for guidance, clearly uncomfortable with the turn of events.

In the distance, a plume of dust announced the arrival of

Charles Lawton. "Here's the boss," one told her. "You can take your problem up with him."

Ashley got out of the car. The rifle was on the seat under her jacket, her pistol in the holster at her arm. There were two guards at the gate, and three men in the approaching car. Five. That left seven people for Brak and Peter to handle. She touched the microphone pinned to the strap of her bra.

"Cowboy, this is cowgirl. Send in the marines. We've got five, count them, five men, four definitely armed and one possible." As she walked toward the gate, a tall man dressed as if he were going for an English hunt approached.

"Are you the man who took my money and canceled my hunt?" she asked angrily. "Here in Texas, we've got a word for people like you, and it's not pretty."

"I'm sure we can work this out," Charles said, sweat beading on his forehead. "I've brought your money. A full refund." He extended an envelope.

"A refund's not good enough. I want a cat. A black panther. I've already made arrangements to redecorate my house around this trophy, and I intend to have it." She allowed herself a quick survey of the gently rolling terrain. Brak was in there somewhere. Had he survived the jump without injury? Had he found his cats? Even at the possibility that he was hurt or in danger she felt a rush of adrenaline. There was no time for emotion. She had to concentrate on doing her job. She stepped forward and pointed a finger at the nattily dressed man. "I want my cat or you're going to have trouble you never dreamed about."

"That isn't possible." Charles looked beyond Ashley. "What in the world?"

Ashley turned to see a dark blue van headed her way. She suppressed her grin. The cavalry had just arrived.

BRAK SECURED THE TWO MEN he'd overpowered to a tree, making sure that the knots would hold them for a good, long time.

"That cat is loose," one of the men said as Brak prepared a gag. "You can't leave us here. She'll kill us."

"That would be a pity." Brak's tone implied the exact opposite.

"We're like bait!" The man grew hysterical.

"Exactly. How does it feel?" Brak asked angrily. "What's it like to be confined and hunted? To watch as the hunter comes upon you and to know that you have no defenses, no weapons, that you're going to be slaughtered." Brak jammed the gag in the man's mouth. "Think about it as you wait for the panther to come for you. I saw her about half a mile from here. She looked hungry. And thirsty. It seems she couldn't get to water."

The wild fear in the man's eyes gave Brak a brutal satisfaction as he walked away. Ayla was nowhere near, and he would never have left the guards there as victims of attack, but they didn't have to know that. It would do them good to wear the shoe on the other foot for several hours. Perhaps it might improve their greedy natures.

He'd canvassed the area around the main buildings. What he'd come across was a list of client names, which he'd taken for Peter. The FOA might find the list interesting, especially when it came to a campaign of writing letters to local newspapers. Public sentiment, when awakened, could be a tremendous weapon.

He'd also found books for the SAS's accounts. The business was incredibly lucrative. The figures made Brak ill. What he hadn't found was a map showing the locations of the animals. By searching, he'd discovered elephants and rhinos nearby. Three lonely buffalo were hemmed in by pens constructed of railroad ties. The sight sickened Brak. But the cats were his priority. Before he left Texas, all of the animals would have a chance, but the cats came first. He was drawing closer to them. He could sense them more easily. The bond he and Ayla shared had always been the strongest, but he could connect with the others. Now he felt them, shared their outrage and fear at being caged and tormented. The two guards he'd captured had finally told him the location of the big cats.

Brak slipped through the woods, intent on stealth and speed. Ahead of him he saw a sudden movement. The dark-haired young woman who darted from behind a tree surprised him. She didn't appear to be carrying a weapon, and she seemed intent on fleeing. Brak watched her scurry away and chose to let her go. She wasn't worth the effort.

"HOWDY, MISTER." Sam got out of the van. "It seems I've gotten myself lost. I've been driving around here for the better part of an hour, and this is the first sign of humanity I've run across." He squinted past the electric wire. "What kind of place is this? Mental institution?"

"Beat it, old man," the guard said.

"Who're you calling old?" Sam bristled. He glanced over at Ashley and gave her a wink.

"This is private property, sir," Charles said, stepping forward. "Go back the way you came, and at the first intersection, take a left. Go two miles, take another left. If you follow that road, you'll eventually find your way back to the interstate."

"My radiator's running hot. Could I get some water here?"

"No." Charles waved him on. "There's a little grocery store down the road. They have water."

"You don't understand, I need it now," Sam said, scratching his head. "That needle's showing in the red, and I won't get a hundred yards from here if I don't get some water."

Charles looked at the guard, who nodded. "Fine," he said. "Do you have a container?"

"Let me get it." Sam went to the van and walked back with a plastic jug.

As he approached, Ashley eyed the jug. Something wasn't right. Something was... The jug arched over her head toward the building where several of the guards were lounging. Their hair-trigger reactions kicked in and they dove into the dirt just before the building exploded.

"Heh! Heh!" Sam said, grabbing Ashley and pulling her out of the way of a piece of wall that blew over them. He covered her body with his to protect her from the blast fragments. "Guess the perimeter is breached," he said as he rolled off her.

Before Ashley could react, several men jumped out of the back of the van. Automatic weapons at the ready, they began rounding up the guards.

Even as she brushed the dirt off her face, Ashley looked up. Charles Lawton's car was leaving a trail of dust as it headed back toward the compound.

"Quick! Lawton's escaping!" She pointed at the car as she got to her feet and ran to join the ex-marines Penny had rounded up. The gate was wide open, and she was headed into the compound where she would find Brak. Peter was okay. He'd radioed several times. But Brak was ominously silent. "I'm going after him," she called.

"Wait for me," Sam called as he joined her.

In the front seat beside Sam, Ashley gave him a searching look. "Where did the explosives come from?"

"Oh, a cowboy is never without resources." He drove like a bat out of hell.

"Explosives? A lariat or horse or six-gun, maybe. Not explosives."

"In the good old days, we learned a lot of tricks when dealing with desperadoes. One of the best ones is to walk up with something powerful and deadly. Takes the starch out of your opponent when he sees his building blown up."

Ashley shook her head. "I swear, Sam. Half of me wants to lock you up and the other half wants to kiss you."

"I'd be obliged if you didn't act on either one," Sam said, a deep blush climbing up his face. "I don't think Familiar would approve."

"Familiar?"

"Meow."

Ashley whirled around in her seat. "What in heaven's name is that cat doing here?"

"He insisted," Sam said. "In case you haven't noticed, once this cat has his mind made up, there's no stopping him."

"Trust me, I've noticed." Ashley picked up the cat and held him on her lap. She could feel his entire body vibrating with a purr. "You'd better stay safe, Familiar. As much as Brak loves his cats, I think he's fond of you. And Peter and I would be heartbroken if anything happened to you."

Familiar turned to her, blinking twice.

"I'll take that for a yes." Ashley pointed out the front window. "There's Lawton's car. If he's alone, we shouldn't have a problem. He doesn't seem like the physical type."

"Even if he is, I'll take care of him." Sam pulled a lariat from behind his seat.

"Where did you get all of this gear?"

"There's plenty of shopping to be had between here and San Antonio."

As Sam whipped in front of Charles's empty car, Ashley jumped out, pistol at her side. So far, everything had gone better than she'd ever hoped. At least five of the SAS men had been apprehended at the gate. Peter had radioed Sam that Waymon Ortega was tied up, Lawton was on the run, and discounting the two women, that left three men for Brak and Peter to take care of. The odds had turned considerably in the favor of the pro-animal forces.

"Lawton, come on out with your hands up," Ashley called out.

There was no sign of life.

"I'm giving you to three, then we're coming in and we'll use whatever force is necessary. We don't want to harm anyone, but we will if we have to."

"Who are you?" Lawton called out. "What do you want?"

"We want those cats you stole, and we want to put you behind bars for the rest of your natural life," Sam answered.

"Sam!" Ashley was ready to gag him.

"Well, he asked."

"You don't have to answer."

From the building, Lawton spoke again. "What stolen animals?"

Ashley put her hand on Sam's mouth. There was the ring of honest confusion in Lawton's voice. "Come out and we'll talk. Maybe we know things you don't."

"I've broken no laws." Lawton's voice sounded closer. "This is a legitimate business. There's no law against hunting these animals."

"I'm not so sure about that, but come out and we'll discuss it."

"Okay, I'm coming out." The front door opened a crack. Charles Lawton poked his head out, both hands extended in front of him. "I'm unarmed. Ever since Waymon brought in those new animals, everything has turned upside down. I should have known there was more to his story than appeared. He said he'd bought them from some freaky rock star who didn't want them any longer. They looked healthy and well-cared-for. They weren't afraid of humans. I should have known." Charles stepped out of the building.

"Come on over to the van and put your hands on the hood," Sam directed. "Once we make sure you aren't packing steel, we'll talk."

"I assure you, I'm innocent," Charles said. "Whatever has gone wrong, Waymon Ortega and that little—" The crack of a rifle came just as Charles's eyes widened. His hands dropped to clutch his chest, where a bright red splotch had appeared. Slowly he crumpled to the ground.

"Duck!" Ashley directed Sam. Too late, she saw the old cowboy spin as the rifle cracked again. Sam hit the ground with a loud whoof as the air was expelled from his lungs.

"Dang it all to hell and back! I've been winged!" Sam called out. He began the torturous crawl to the van as Ashley ran out and helped him to safety. "Where the hell did that shot come from?"

Ashley wanted the answer to that herself. Peering out from behind the van, she tried to find the shooter. There was no movement anywhere. She'd been so intent on capturing Lawton that she hadn't paid proper attention. It was a classic ambush, except that Lawton was dead. One of his own men had killed him.

"I wonder who decided to send Lawton to the great beyond? I never..." Sam stopped talking, eyes widening. Ashley felt the prickle of dread whisper along her neck as she turned toward the barrel of the deadly revolver aimed at her head.

"You have made a serious mistake, *señorita,*" the woman said, her dark eyes flashing fury. "You and your *amigos* are going to pay. Where's Waymon? Answer me! Now!" She pulled back the hammer on the gun.

Ashley didn't have to be told that the angry woman standing over her was Waymon Ortega's girlfriend. Her sleeveless shirt revealed muscled arms and a portion of a tattoo, the bluish black ink indicating that it had been done in prison.

The woman noticed Ashley's focus. "San Quentin," she said proudly. "I did time for a gang-related murder. Ever heard of the Pistoleros?"

Ashley knew the gang, composed solely of females, and with one of the worst reputations in the nation for violence.

"I've heard of them."

"I'm Angel Martiz."

Ashley felt fear touch her heart. Angel Martiz had a reputation for brutal violence and unnecessary cruelty. Her rap sheet made Waymon Ortega look like a choirboy.

"Do you know why Charles is dead?" Angel asked.

Ashley shook her head.

"He was stupid and he talked too much." She shifted the gun to Sam. "Old man, I should kill you now. Give me one tiny reason to pull this trigger, and I will. As for you—" she tapped the barrel of her gun against Ashley's skull "—you're my ticket out of here, just as soon as we find Waymon. Do one single thing to provoke me, and I will shoot you. I won't kill you. Not at first, but I will start with your hand. Then your arm. Then a foot. You understand what I'm telling you?"

Ashley nodded. "Let the old man go."

"Okay."

Angel whipped her gun down with a force that made Ashley gasp. The butt impacted Sam's skull with a dull crack. The old man dropped into the dirt.

"He won't bother us," Angel said, pushing Ashley forward. "We have to find Waymon. I suggest you show me the way or I'll kill you."

Chapter Seventeen

Brak knelt beside the young lion's cage, his gaze roving over every inch of her. "Kiki," he whispered. To his satisfaction she inched closer. "Good girl," he said softly. "Good girl."

Kiki was the last of the cats, and they all seemed to be physically undamaged. So far. As soon as the SAS was shut down, he'd...

A shot rang out, then another. Brak checked the direction of the gunfire and began to run. Moving with deadly speed he raced through the trees and headed toward the sounds of the fight, his heart pounding. He'd urged Ashley to stay at the gate. Peter had, too. The plan was arranged so that she faced minimal danger. But he knew Ashley, and he knew she wasn't one to hang on to the fringes of a battle. She was as courageous as she was beautiful.

He made the last row of trees and halted, surveying the main building where the navy blue sound van was now parked. His blood surged when he saw two bodies lying on the ground. With a curse he recognized one as Sam. The other was unidentifiable, but at least it wasn't Ashley. Movement at the corner of a building caught his attention. The sun struck Ashley's hair, and the relief that followed was sweet—and short-lived. Ashley walked stiffly around the corner of the building, the sun also reflecting from the barrel of the gun that was held only inches from her head. To Brak's chagrin, he saw that Ashley was followed by the woman he'd allowed to escape through the woods. Looking at her in the bright sunlight, he knew her for what she was. Bad news.

The sound of a stick snapping behind him made him whirl around.

"Easy," Peter whispered, moving up beside him. "I heard gunshots."

"Sam's down." Brak turned back to the scene. "He's not moving. Neither is the other guy."

"The other one's Lawton," Peter said. "What's the situation?"

"They've got Ashley." Brak swallowed. "But not for long," he vowed.

"Ashley's smart, and she's highly trained." Peter's brave words were spoken too quickly to hide his fear. "Where is she?"

"Headed toward the office building." Brak turned to Peter. "And Ayla."

"I know. Ortega's in there. Tied and gagged. Are there any other guards?"

"Back in the woods. Tied to a tree. Two of them. There may be a couple more, but I haven't seen them."

"Good work," Peter said.

"Not good enough. If they harm a hair on Ashley's head..." He left the statement unfinished.

As they watched, they caught a brief glimpse of Ashley and the dark-haired woman between two buildings. The gun barrel remained only inches from Ashley's head. When Brak raised his rifle, he felt Peter's hand on his arm.

"Don't even try. She could pull that trigger by reflex."

Brak's rifle dropped down. "Look," he said, directing Peter's attention to Sam's prone body.

Beside Sam was a small black cat, busy nudging and licking the old cowboy's face. Sam began to stir.

"That darn cat!" Peter said. "But Sam's alive. I've got to get over to him. He'll need medical attention."

"I'll take care of Ashley," Brak said. "I have an idea."

Relief swept through Peter's voice. "Be careful, Brak, please. What's your plan?"

"Ayla's in that building. If I can... She would be a surprise. It might give me a second or two to make sure that Ashley is out of the way of any gunfire. It's the best plan I can think of."

Both men knew the risks. Their eyes met in agreement.

"Good luck," Peter said. "Kiss my sister once for me when she's safe." He inched away from Brak and began working his way toward Sam.

Moving in the opposite direction, Brak began to chart a course to the office building. The plan he'd come up with was full of dangers, and there was no way he could accomplish it without putting Ashley right in the middle. He had to act fast, before Waymon Ortega was freed from his bonds.

Ayla was physically unharmed, but not mentally. There had been a time when she would have been able to understand extremely complex requests. Now he wasn't so sure.

A long stretch of open ground remained between him and the first building. There was no way to tell if one of the SAS men was hiding in ambush nearby—and no choice but to run for it. Staying as close to the ground as he could, he sprinted. When he gained the cover of the building, he peered around the corner, then drew back instantly. Ashley and her captor were only a few yards away.

The woman's tone was ugly. "You'd better find the right building this time, or you'll be sorry."

Brak's hand tensed on the handgun he carried in lieu of the rifle he'd left in the woods. Ashley's voice was calm, easy, and Brak thanked God that she was a highly trained law officer. She was doing everything right.

"I told you, I don't have any idea where Waymon Ortega

is,'' Ashley said. ''I'm here for a hunt. If you'll take that gun out of my hair, I'll be more than glad to help you find the man you're looking for.''

''Shut up! Just keep moving.''

Brak chanced a peek and saw they were headed for the office building. Ortega was there. And Ayla.

Brak took a breath and cleared his mind of everything except the memory of the building's layout. *Ayla, leap.* He pictured the cat flying through the door, knocking the dark-haired woman into the dirt.

Gun extended, he eased to the corner again. Ashley was at the front door, the woman right behind her, gun pressed into Ashley's back.

''Get in there!'' the woman ordered.

Before Ashley could touch the door, it flew open and a huge black beast roared past her into the air.

Brak saw the pistol lift from Ashley's back to take aim at the panther. Before the woman could squeeze off a shot, Brak fired. The woman screamed as the bullet struck the pistol and sent it careering into the dirt. In the next second, Ayla was on the woman. The weight of the cat knocked Angel to the dirt. Cat and woman went down in a tangle as Ashley scrambled for the gun.

Calling on every ounce of speed he possessed, Brak started forward. There was no clear shot of the woman. Ayla and Ashley were in the way. Even as he ran he saw the dark-haired woman break free of Ayla, viciously kick Ashley and clutch the gun.

''Drop it!'' Brak yelled.

Angel rolled once and came up, gun whipping from Brak to Ayla.

''Run, Ayla!'' Ashley yelled as she rolled to cover beside the building. At her command the panther bounded away just as Angel fired.

''Put down that gun,'' Brak called, squeezing off a shot that kicked dirt right beside Angel's foot.

Angel turned the gun at him. With her face drawn into a snarl, she fired. The click of the hammer on an empty chamber seemed to echo over the compound.

"Damn you!" Angel yelled. "Damn you!" She threw the gun at Brak as he ran toward her. Turning to the right, she started to run.

Ashley was right behind her.

"Ashley!" Brak was so glad to see her alive and uninjured that he pulled her into his arms. "You're okay," he said, hands moving over her as if he didn't believe what he saw. "You were supposed to stay at the gate. You..."

"She's getting away!" Ashley pointed toward the fleeing Angel Martiz. "She's..."

"She won't get far." Brak smothered her protests with a kiss.

In the distance was the wobbling wail of sirens.

PETER RUSHED TO SAM'S side, immediately probing the shoulder wound. The injury wasn't serious, but the old man had lost a lot of blood. Ripping off his shirt, Peter quickly made a compress bandage and began to apply pressure to stop the bleeding. Even as he worked, Sam began to talk.

"I'm too mean to die," Sam said, groaning. "My head feels like I was kicked by a mule."

Peter checked the gash in his head. "Pistol butt, I'd guess. Now, stay still. The bleeding's slowed, but if you move around, it'll start again."

"I don't feel too spry, anyway. Maybe I'll just take a rest right here." Sam let his head settle back on the ground.

"I've got to check on Lawton," Peter said, but even from a distance of twelve feet, he suspected the other man was dead. He moved over to him. The bullet had gone clean through his heart. He was turning back when he saw Familiar flying around a corner. At first he didn't believe his eyes. The black cat skidded to a halt beside the van. Before Peter could move, a sleek black panther appeared.

Peter froze, his hand going involuntarily to his gun.

"Meow!" Familiar cried, rushing to Peter and jumping on his leg, claws extended.

"Damn it, Familiar!" Peter tried to shake the black feline off.

Familiar turned loose and ran to the van, crying at the door. Ayla stood quietly watching. For a moment, Peter wasn't certain, then he moved to the van and opened the door. Familiar and Ayla hopped inside. With a sigh of relief, Peter reached down to scratch Familiar's head. "Good work, old buddy."

The sound of two gunshots echoed off the adobe walls of the cluster of buildings.

"Who's shooting now?" Sam asked.

Peter went back to Sam, checking the wound once more. "Stay very still. I hate to leave you, but Ashley or Brak could be hurt."

"Go on!" Sam motioned him away with his good hand. "Get out there and kick some ass. I can't believe that now it's time for the showdown, I've got a flesh wound."

The rolling wail of a siren drew Peter's attention. He had no idea who'd called for help, but whoever it was, he wanted to shake his hand. In the distance, Peter could see vehicles approaching. Several of them. To his surprise, they appeared to be from the San Antonio police. Mixed in with them was the welcome sight of an ambulance and an old green truck that could belong to no one except Penny Wise King, photographer and pilot extraordinaire.

Gripping his gun, Peter turned as a young Spanish woman, dark hair streaming behind her back, came flying around the corner of the building. The woman didn't bother to stop. She jumped into the open door of the van. The keys were in the ignition where Sam had left them. The van roared to life. Gravel slung from beneath the wheels as it headed directly into the path of the oncoming police.

"Familiar!" Peter came up with his gun aimed at the van.

"Don't worry. That woman won't ever be smart enough to outfox that cat." Sam was sitting up watching.

Almost before he'd finished speaking, the van swerved erratically on the road.

To Peter and Sam, it looked as if two people were fighting for control of the steering wheel. As the van careered, panda units surrounded it, steadily closing in.

"This is the San Antonio police. Come out with your hands up!" a familiar voice called out over a megaphone.

The door of the van burst open, and Angel Martiz ran screaming, hands over her head.

"Help! Help!" One arm dripped blood and her face had been badly scratched.

Just as the police surrounded her, a small black cat popped out of the van, every hair fluffed and his back arched in anger.

"La gato diablo!" Angel cried. *"La gato diablo!"*

John Keifer walked toward Angel. "Hands in the air." He searched her, removed a pistol, then cuffed her hands behind her back. "Take her and read her her rights," he told the other officers as he started toward Peter.

"I can't tell you how good it is to see you," Peter said. The young officer looked slightly worried but determined to prove himself professional.

"I don't exactly know what I'm doing here, and I wasn't certain what that cryptic message Ashley left for me meant, but I can see I made the right decision." He gave Peter a worried look. "Did your black cat hurt that woman's arm?"

Peter grinned. "Let's just say that Familiar was acting with provocation."

"You can second that." Sam had regained his feet, though he wasn't steady. "That woman tried to kill me. And she did kill that other fella."

John Keifer's gaze went to the body of Charles Lawton. "Who is he?"

"He was the head of San Antonio Safari," Peter said. "I think we've recovered the large cats that were stolen from the San Antonio Towers."

"Ashley's here?"

"She's here." Peter realized that if Keifer saw Brak, he would have no choice but to arrest him.

Sam started toward them. "We've got to find out about Ashley and—"

"Easy, Sam." Peter grabbed the cowboy's arm. "Help me, John, he's about to collapse."

"Take your hands off me, I'm not about to faint." Sam struggled.

"Give me some help," Peter whispered in his ear. "For Ashley."

Sam clapped a hand over his heart. "I think my ticker's going. I feel..." He spiraled around. "Like I'm going to pitch face down in the dirt."

John hurried up and grabbed Sam's arm. "Let's get him to the ambulance."

Sam let loose of Peter and clutched at John with both hands. "Don't let me fall," he said.

ASHLEY GAVE HERSELF to Brak's embrace. Her frustration at him for sneaking away was nothing compared to the relief she felt at seeing him safe.

When she finally broke the kiss, she stared into his eyes. He was a stubborn man. As stubborn as she was herself. It was something they would both have to work on. And she didn't care, just as long as they had time to work on it. "Peter? The cats?"

"Fine." His hands tightened on her. "I was so afraid you would get hurt."

"I've had a little anxiety myself."

The sirens were growing closer, and Ashley looked beyond Brak in the direction Angel had fled. "You'd better find a place to hide out. Someone's called the cops."

"Remember Waymon Ortega's in the office building with a woman." His hand caressed her cheek. "Ashley, whatever happens, know that I love you."

"Brak?" Something in his voice pierced her heart. She reached out for him, but he was already moving away.

PETER ROUNDED THE CORNER, almost colliding with Brak. "You'd better hightail it out of here," Peter said. "Someone called the cops. If they see you..."

"I know." Brak's voice was grim. "Ashley's fine. She's collecting Waymon Ortega."

Peter slapped him on the back. "Good work. We got all of them. Listen, find a place to hide until this blows over, and I'll take care of everything."

"My cats..."

"I give you my word. They'll be fine."

"And Ashley? I didn't get a chance to tell her goodbye."

Peter's face registered his disappointment. "You never meant to take a few days, and then turn yourself in, did you."

"I can't, Peter. Trust me. It's something I can't do. If I could, I would. But there's more at stake here than it appears."

"My sister's heart is at stake."

Brak heard the anger in Peter's voice. "Ashley is lucky to have a brother like you. Tell her this isn't the end of it. Send my cats to Norway. To my brother, Erik. She knows the address."

Before Peter could say another word, Brak was gone. The last thing left was his shadow, disappearing after him.

Chapter Eighteen

"I can't believe he left his cats," Ashley said, fighting the tears that had threatened for three days. She watched the last of the spacious cages being loaded into the cargo hold of the plane Peter had chartered to fly them home.

"I know." Peter held Familiar in his arms. He glanced at his sister. "I honestly didn't expect him to run out like he did."

"I guess you were right about him from the first." Ashley looked straight ahead, fighting the pain. "He was a con artist. A very handsome, charming con man. The only difference in this case was he needed my help to save his cats. I didn't have any jewelry worth stealing."

Peter put his arm around his sister's shoulders and gave her a squeeze. "We saved the cats, and SAS is out of business forever. There was even some talk that the property may be donated to the Friends of Animals for a preserve. At any rate, the Ortega boys will spend a while in prison, and Angel Martiz will be a very old woman before she's ever released. Funny that she turned out to be the driving force behind the canned hunt. I never suspected a woman would be involved in such a heartless business."

"She's a real piece of work, to quote Sam."

Peter grinned. "That Sam! He was happy. They found his truck in one of the warehouses."

"Before he'd even gotten out of there, he'd talked John into a job hauling the cats back to San Antonio." Ashley shook her head. "The man was bleeding, and he wouldn't get into the ambulance until he was assured he had a contract. Poor John. I was afraid he was going to pull money out of his pocket to seal the deal."

"I wouldn't feel too sorry for Officer Keifer. Did you see the way Penny was looking at him?"

"And him at her. I think there's romance in the air." Ashley spoke the words lightly, but she felt a knifing pain in the region of her heart.

"How *did* John know to show up at the compound?" Peter put the question to Ashley, but he was also asking it of himself.

"Meow!" Familiar put his paw on Peter's face.

"I should have known," Peter said, nodding. "Familiar. The telephone, 911, the materials left on the steps." Peter held the cat up so that he could look into his eyes. "So, another case of the interfering kitty."

"I'm sorry I ever doubted your stories about Familiar." Ashley reached over to scratch the black cat behind an ear. "I've learned a lot about animal intelligence. I won't be selling them short again."

"Does that mean we can make that trip to the animal shelter to pick out a suitable cat for you?"

Ashley forced a smile. "I suppose it's time for me to get my life back together. My vacation is over, and it's time for me to get back to my job." The idea of returning to work was the only thing she had left to hang on to after Brak's abrupt and unexplained departure.

Up until the very moment that they'd loaded the cats on the plane bound for Oslo, Ashley had believed that Brak would appear. She'd lived with the secret hope that he would simply walk into her home the way he had before.

Now she knew he was gone. He'd lied to her. There was

no reasonable explanation about his past. He'd been a thief, and in order to avoid being prosecuted, he'd run away.

He'd broken his promise to her—and her heart.

She felt her brother's worried gaze on her, and she looked up. "Did he say anything else?"

"Oh, Ashley." Peter hugged her tight. "He said he couldn't allow himself to be turned in. He said there was more to his past than appeared on the surface. He said he was sorry."

Pressed against the crisp cotton shirt Peter wore, Ashley got a grip on her emotions. She'd been played for a fool. There was no point in making it worse by crying on her brother's shoulder over a bad romantic choice—especially one he had so vehemently warned her against.

"If it makes you feel any better, Brak won me over, too," Peter said. "And no matter what, I still believe he cares about you." He looked at the lions and panthers, Ayla sitting so quietly in her cage. The plane that had been chartered was designed for living creatures. The animals would have air-conditioning, pressurized cabins and all the rest. Ashley had recovered the money Brak had left for a deposit for the hunt and used it to pay for the shipping expenses.

"If he cares so much for these animals, why isn't he here to make sure they're okay?" Beneath that question was another—why wasn't he there to make sure *she* was okay?

"He knew he could trust us." Peter put Familiar on the ground. "If you're going to say goodbye to your girlfriend, you'd better do so. They're about ready to leave."

Ashley watched as Familiar rushed into the plane, moving straight to Ayla's cage. Peter had attended to the care of all the SAS creatures. More than half had already been moved to zoos, others to private preserves where they would be cared for by professionals.

"It breaks my heart for Familiar." Ashley felt her eyes

fill as she watched the small black feline. Ayla rubbed against the bars, getting as close to Familiar as possible.

"He'll survive. Besides, he has a steady girl in Washington. And I'm sure Ayla will find another panther...." Peter let his sentence die.

"I'll be fine, Peter." Ashley lifted her head up and straightened her shoulders. "I promise. I'll be just fine."

"Come on, Familiar." Peter called the cat to him and scooped him up as they walked away. The plane door was shutting, and in another ten hours, the cats would be in Oslo in the careful hands of Erik. "Did you ask Erik anything about Brak?" Peter asked.

Ashley had spoken to Brak's older brother several times in the course of making the flight arrangements for the cats. "Yes and no. I hinted, and he responded by saying that he had lost touch with Brak for a number of years. He said Brak was a man of secrets, and that he'd never pried into his past."

"A man of secrets and disguises," Peter agreed.

"At least I didn't have to make the decision of whether to turn him in or not." Ashley gave her brother a grim smile. "I don't know that I could have. Maybe it's just as well things turned out as they did."

Peter held Familiar in one arm and put the other around his sister as they continued to walk across the tarmac. "Maybe it is. Things have a way of turning out."

ASHLEY SAT ON HER kitchen floor and pulled the plastic containers from the cabinet, beginning the tedious process of putting them in order. Peter was at the SAS compound finishing the job of shipping the remaining animals to new homes. She was due to go back to work in the morning. If she could only fill the final few hours of her vacation, she'd be back in a routine that she knew and loved. She'd be able to find new things to think about—and maybe Brak would be pushed to the back of her mind.

"Meow!"

She looked down the hall at the black cat. "Come on in, Familiar. I bought some shrimp for dinner tonight. Texas barbecue. Your favorite."

Ashley had grown extremely fond of the black cat. For the past few nights, he'd even curled up beside her in bed and slept. Though Ashley had remained sleepless, her heart and mind centered on Brak, it was amazing how much comfort she'd taken from the cat.

Soon, even Familiar would be gone. Back to Washington with Peter. But they had yet to pick out a kitten from the pound. That was the final chore Peter had set himself.

"Meow!" Familiar's voice was strident.

"What's going on?" Ashley stacked the plastic bowls and stood, brushing her slacks with her hands. "I never dreamed I would be desperate enough to clean cabinets to take my mind off something."

"Meow." Familiar went up to her, snagging her pant leg with a paw. He tugged her toward the hallway.

"What now?" She stepped over the plastic containers and followed the cat to her bedroom. As soon as she stepped through the doorway, she knew he'd been at the computer again. "I don't believe you." She went to the screen. Her E-mail message light was flashing.

"Okay," she said, bringing up the latest message.

"Ashley, call me at the main station. Urgent information. John Keifer."

She went into the kitchen and picked up the portable, dialing the number she'd memorized.

An assured male voice answered, "John Keifer."

"Congratulations, *detective,*" Ashley said. "I had an urgent E-mail."

"I found something on the pendant you left for me to examine."

"Pendant?"

"Yeah, the dolphins and the cross. It's pretty incredible. Where did you get that thing?"

Ashley looked at Familiar. She'd completely forgotten about the chain. Brak's chain. "I, uh, it's a long story."

"I'll bet." John spoke eagerly. "Someone's going to be looking for it. Someone you don't want to mess with."

"What are you talking about?" Ashley was intrigued by the hint of mystery in John's voice.

"It could be simply legend, but such pendants are worn by members of the EJC."

Ashley knew John had to be pulling her leg. "Oh, yes, the dreaded EJC."

John laughed. "Very funny. It's actually the European Justice Committee."

"Ah, how could I not have heard of that well-known organization?"

"Because it's top secret, and for many years it's been thought to be defunct. Most of its members were top officials of the Allied forces' war efforts during World War II. Hardly anyone knows about it."

Ashley paused. "You're not teasing me, are you?"

"Not at all. It was a select group of men who were determined to enforce codes of justice throughout Europe. Several of them were involved in the assassination attempt against Hitler. Others were in the Russian army, some in the U.S. forces. It was an international group. Very high-minded. When the courts failed, they stepped in. But as far as anyone knows, they've been out of business for decades. The pendant itself is a real work of art, and my initial investigation shows it to be authentic."

"Forgive me for asking, John, but how did the pendant come into your hands?" She knew before she finished speaking. Familiar was curled in the middle of the pillow on her bed, watching with interest.

"It was with all the stuff you left for me. Surely you intended for me to work on it, didn't you?"

Hearing the doubt in his voice, she immediately reassured him. "Of course. I know you've got a million other things to do. It's nice of you to take the time to do this for me."

"Well, I thought I was sort of dumb at first, but once I examined the design and fed the information into the computer, the results were remarkable. Did you know that only the top echelon of members received the pendant? It was used so they could identify one another. Some of the men would give it to their wives on a chain very similar to yours. The women, unaware of what the symbol meant, would wear it as jewelry. It was a remarkably smart way for the members to become aware of one another when they moved into strange cities."

Only one word stuck in Ashley's head. *Jewelry.*

John continued. "The design for the pendant was created by a very famous Norwegian sculptor and jewelry maker. Rolofson. Joseph B. Rolofson."

Ashley found a pen in the kitchen cabinet drawer and began writing as John talked. "Is this Rolofson still alive?"

"No, he died in 1972. He was very proud of his contribution to the EJC, though. That's about when the work of the EJC became public. In a speech, Rolofson said that of all his artistic work, he felt that his design for the pendant was his most important."

"Who could become a member?" Ashley asked.

"It was strictly for men." John waited for her acid remark. When she didn't rise to the bait, he asked her, "Are you okay?"

"I'm getting better by the minute. So who belonged to the EJC?"

"Young men, for the most part. All extremely intelligent, perfect physical specimens, those who were in, or could achieve, a position of power. It was a sort of spy group, but they didn't work for any single government. James Bonds without allegiance to England. They worked for world peace, justice, all of those noble things. It was a pretty unique organization, to be honest. There are times I wish something like it existed in the world today.'' John sighed. ''I guess issues are too complicated now, though.''

''Listen, John, thanks for your help. It always seems that when I fall down a hole, you help dig me out.''

''I'm going to teach Penny how to use the computer to check basic facts. She's had a few clients who ran up expensive photo and flight bills and then didn't pay her. She can check into their pasts and maybe save herself a little grief. If you want, you can come over and I'll show you, too. You've got a good computer at home, you just need to get over your fear of using it.''

''That sounds like something I need to do.''

''Should I hold on to that pendant for you?''

''I'll stop by and get it.'' Ashley started looking for her car keys. If her hunch was right, that pendant would be the one thing that would bring Brak back to her. At least long enough to collect it—and to answer a few questions.

''You never did tell me where you got it.''

''John, you wouldn't believe me if I told you.''

''Try me?'' he insisted.

''Remember Peter's cat?''

''How could anyone forget Familiar.''

''Well, Familiar appeared at my bedside with the pendant in his mouth. He'd found it somewhere.''

There was a pause. ''You're right. I don't believe that story.''

Ashley laughed out loud. ''I told you. And it's the complete and honest truth.''

''See you later, Ashley.''

''Thanks, John.'' She replaced the phone and turned to Familiar. ''You knew all along, didn't you.'' She bent and kissed him on one ear. ''You are one special cat. Very special. Now all I have to do is get the pendant and wait for Brak to come back for it.''

For a broad who didn't want cat hair in her sheets, Miss Law and Order has done a complete one-eighty. Ah, another human converted to the ways of the feline. In my days of being a private investigator, I wonder how many hearts and minds I've won to the feline cause.

This has been a very satisfying case. Peter is finishing up at Kerrville, and I'm about to conclude my work here at Ashley's. All I really have left to do is wait—and eat Texas barbecued shrimp.

I can't help thinking about Ayla. She was a magnificent creature. Even if she'd stayed here in the good ole U. S. of A., things wouldn't have worked out for us. I truly am dedicated to Clotilde. She is my heart of hearts. Ayla spoke to some savage part of my soul, some moment in prehistory when I might have been like her. Wild and noble and magnificent. Things that domesticated cats have traded for a life within society. The bipeds might not be smarter than us, but they are in control. Who would have thought that a prehensile thumb would have been the ticket to dominance. And they don't even have a tail for balance!

Don't get me wrong. I wouldn't trade Peter and Eleanor for anything in the world. Even that little tyrant Jordan has her moments of magic. But watching Ayla, I guess I had to realize what domesticated felines have given up. In her, I saw what might have been. I can only hope that Erik makes certain she is loved as she deserves. As Blond Bruiser would want her to be.

Ah, Blond Bruiser, the elusive animal tamer. I don't think I'll ever forget my first sight of him, standing on that stage with all of those cats beside him. Although my attention was on Ayla, he was impossible to miss.

Impossible to forget.

If Ashley is half the girl I think she is, she'll have the answers to all of her questions before this issue is put to rest. Now all I can do is wait and hope. And figure out a plan to delay Peter for another day, if necessary.

ASHLEY CLUTCHED the pendant in her hand as she drove to the library. She and John had admired the craftsmanship of the emblem, and then she'd left. If she was correct, it would be better if John didn't know the truth.

"I need to look up a famous sculptor. Joseph B. Rolofson. I'm interested in his family."

"There's a computer right over..."

"Would you mind helping?"

The library assistant sighed. "Right this way."

With a few clicks of the keys, the woman had several options on the screen, and she left Ashley with the periodicals and reference numbers for additional material. Ashley scrolled through the microfilmed newspapers and found what she was looking for in record time. The obituary of the famous sculptor. As she suspected, Marlay Rolofson Brunston was the sculptor's daughter.

Now the only question that remained was if Brak was a member of the EJC, or if he'd simply inherited the pendant from his grandfather, a family heirloom of sorts.

"Thanks a million," she said as she hurried out and headed home. She'd promised Familiar barbecued shrimp, and she also had an unexplainable desire to be in her own home as night began to fall over San Antonio.

Familiar greeted her at the door with a big kitty yawn and a friendly nip on the shin. As she started to work in the kitchen, Ashley felt an inexplicable tingle that seemed to move from her chest along her extremities, little tiny electric jolts. She practically hummed with energy.

She finished the shrimp and slid the pan into the oven. She was up to her elbows in the dishwater she'd just drawn when she froze. The most peculiar sensation of hands moving over her back made her jerk her hands out of the water and dry them off.

Deep inside her mind, she heard Brak's voice. *Let me explain.* She heard the words as clearly as if he'd spoken them in her ear. In fact, her ear tingled, as if his breath had gently touched her skin.

"Brak?" She went to the patio door and paused, looking out through the glass before she opened it. "Brak?"

Night was falling, and the sky was shaded from dark purple in the east to brilliant pink in the west. As beautiful as the sky was, the patio was empty. Ashley had not been aware how much she'd anticipated Brak until she felt the burning disappointment. Once again she'd deluded herself. She'd bought into another package of hocus-pocus and secret spy rings. Shoulders suddenly aching, she turned inside.

"Ashley?"

The tiny voice was that of a young child. Ashley whirled. The patio was empty. Very slowly, the shrubs parted and a young girl stepped out. She walked slowly, as if she were afraid. "Ashley? It's me, Maria."

Ashley couldn't believe her eyes. "Maria!" She ran toward her and scooped her into her arms. "What are you doing here? Where did you come from?"

"The man..." Maria turned back, but there was no one there. "He said I could come and live with you. He said to give you this." She reached into the tiny bag she carried and drew out a sheet of paper.

Ashley cradled the young girl in her arms and moved so that the light fell upon the documents. She scanned them, not believing what she read. Maria's mother had finally agreed to the adoption.

"Maria!" Ashley hugged her tightly, trying not to let the hot tears of joy slip from her eyes. "How did this happen? Do you want to live here?"

"Sí," Maria answered, hugging Ashley with her tiny arms. *"Sí."*

The leaves of the four-o'clocks shifted and rustled, and Brak stepped onto the patio.

"How did you find her?" Ashley asked, never relinquishing her hold on the child. "How did you ever talk her stepfather into letting her go?"

"He was reluctant. At first. But I made him see that Maria would be better off with you."

"And her mother?" Ashley felt a pang of guilt. Maria's mother was addicted to drugs. She'd never had the time or money to care for her daughter, but Maria was still her child.

"She's very sick. She asked only that you love her with all of your heart. She knows without her, Maria would have a terrible life."

"Thank you, Brak. Thank you."

Brak touched the little girl's hair, his hand gliding down the long, brown tresses. "She's a beauty. Just like you."

"I have something of yours." Maria still in her arms, Ashley managed to reach down her shirt and pull the pendant out. "Familiar stole it from your things."

Brak reached for it, relief evident on his face. "I was worried that I'd lost it."

"Naturally you wouldn't want to lose your grandfather's creation."

Brak's expression showed shock. "How did you know?"

"I did a little research. I know about the EJC. I know why you took those jewels from that woman in New York. It had something to do with that, didn't it?"

"I'm sworn to secrecy. I—"

"I *knew* there was a reason."

Brak enfolded Ashley in his arms. "I wanted to tell you," he said, "but I couldn't. I'm sworn to secrecy, but I will tell you that Cleo stole the pendant from my brother. Her actions resulted in his death. To minimize the importance of the EJC emblem, I took several other pieces of her jewelry. Very expensive pieces."

"So, the EJC is still in operation."

Brak kissed the top of her head. "You can ask me anything except that. Anything at all."

Ashley had never felt so happy in her life. Maria was in her arms and she was in Brak's. It was perfection. Total perfection. If she could hold this moment forever. But there were things she had to know. "Brak, would you have come back if I didn't have the pendant?"

Brak's grip tightened slightly. She felt the whisper of his words at her ear. "I didn't know you had it. I thought I'd lost it in the hotel when I had to run away."

"Oh, Brak!" Ashley kissed his chin and jaw and finally his lips. Snuggled between them, Maria giggled.

From inside the house came a cat yowl and a cry of surprise. "Hey! What's going on out here?" Peter stood in the doorway and flipped on the patio light. "Brak?"

"He came back." Ashley turned so that Peter could see who she held in her arms. "And he brought Maria!"

Peter came out the door and crossed the patio in three long strides. "Good work, Brak! Good work!" He held out his arms and the little girl looked beyond him to the doorway. *"Gato!"* She cried.

"Maria wants to meet Familiar." Peter took the little girl's hand and led her inside.

"Spanish, Peter," Ashley called after them, her heart so filled with joy that she thought she'd burst.

"Thank you, Brak. Thank you a million times. I don't know how you did it, but this time I'm not going to ask questions. I'll accept the gift of her." She kissed his cheek.

"I love you, Ashley," he said, his lips moving from her temple to her nose to her lips, where he teased her with light kisses.

More than anything, Ashley wanted to melt into his embrace, but there was one final, unresolved issue. "Why did you leave like you did?" She needed an answer. One that would put her heart to rest.

"I promised you that I would turn myself in. I couldn't do that, Ashley. Because of the committee. I couldn't tell you about it." He hugged her tighter. "Worse yet, I couldn't walk away from you, though I tried. So I decided to do something about Maria. If I couldn't be with you, I could at least do the one thing that I could for you."

"You weren't going to say anything, were you? You were going to deliver her and vanish again?"

"That was my intention. But we stood out here and I saw you at the sink. I knew I had to make a choice. A vow that I took long ago when my brother was killed. I never wanted to be part of the secrecy. Erik, my other brother, was right. We can accomplish justice in the open. My work with the EJC was finished long ago. Now I have a new vow I want to make. One for the future." He kissed her lightly. "Our future."

AH, ANOTHER LONE HOMBRE bites the dust. In this case, it's an instant family. Somehow I think Peter and I will be staying. The Dame and the little tyrant will be coming down from Washington for what looks like a celebration. Peter's on the phone calling Eleanor now. Another happy ending, engineered by moi. *I think I'll take a bow, then a few of those shrimps, then I think it's time to take a nap. I'm going to need all my strength to accept all of the praise that should be coming my way any minute now.*

couldn't walk away from you, though I tried. So I decided to do something about Marie. If I couldn't be with you, I could at least do the one thing that I could for you."

"You weren't going to say anything, were you. You were going to [illegible] her and vanish again?"

"That was the intention, but when I stood out here and saw you at the curb, I knew I had to make a choice. A vow that I took [illegible] of my brother was fulfilled. I never wanted to be part of the Agency. [illegible] my other brother was right. We can accomplish justice in the open. My work with the DEA was finished long ago. Now I have a new vow I want to make. One for the future." He kissed her lightly. "Our future."

[illegible] Peter and I [illegible] The house and the little ones will be coming down from Washington for [illegible] like a celebration. [illegible] Another [illegible] I think I'll [illegible] of those shrimps, then I think it's time to take a nap. I'm going to need all my strength to [illegible] But [illegible] that should be coming [illegible]

For a preview, turn the page....

He was drawing closer to them. He could sense them more